# The Drop of the Hammer

# The Drop of the Hammer

Mary De Gruttola

Copyright © 2021 Mary De Gruttola

All rights reserved.

ISBN: 9798545914333

# DEDICATION

This book is dedicated to
**Jehenne Anseau**
and all the other women who were accused, tortured, and burned at the stake during *The Burning Times*.

Jehenne Anseau did not leave Françoise's side during the whole period of her accusation and trial in *The Drop of the Hammer*
----- nor did she leave my side for a single second as I was writing.

# CONTENTS

|     | Preface | Page 1 |
|-----|---------|--------|
| 1   | 29th November 1599 | Page 7 |
| 2   | 29th November 1599 | Page 19 |
| 3   | 29th November 1599 | Page 35 |
| 4   | 29th November 1599<br>Almost dusk | Page 58 |
| 5   | 29th November 1599<br>Dusk | Page 67 |
| 6   | 30th November 1599<br>A little past midnight | Page 74 |
| 7   | 30th November 1599<br>A short while before dawn | Page 82 |
| 8   | 30th November 1599<br>Dawn | Page 86 |
| 9   | 30th November 1599<br>Early morning | Page 95 |
| 10  | 30th November 1599<br>Several hours later | Page 106 |
| 11  | 30th November 1599<br>Mid-afternoon | Page 115 |
| 12  | 13th December 1599<br>Evening | Page 124 |
| 13  | 13th December 1599<br>Evening | Page 132 |
| 14  | 26th January 1600<br>Late afternoon | Page 147 |
| 15  | 26th January 1600<br>Late Afternoon | Page 161 |
| 16  | 28th January 1600<br>La Boverie | Page 166 |
| 17  | 15th February 1600<br>Late morning | Page 180 |
| 18  | 15th February 1600<br>Late morning | Page 194 |
| 19  | 26th February 1600<br>Late at night | Page 213 |
| 20  | 27th February 1600<br>A little past midnight | Page 218 |

# The Drop of the Hammer

| | | |
|---|---|---|
| 21 | 29th February 1600<br>Early afternoon | Page 225 |
| 22 | 10th March 1600<br>Château of Franchimont | Page 233 |
| 23 | 10th March 1600<br>At the Château of Franchimont | Page 242 |
| 24 | 13th March 1600<br>Three days later | Page 258 |
| 25 | 14th March 1600<br>Witness One | Page 266 |
| 26 | 14th March 1600<br>Witness Two | Page 271 |
| 27 | 14th March 1600<br>Witness Three | Page 274 |
| 28 | 17th March 1600<br>The Sentencing | Page 277 |
| 29 | 26th March 1600<br>Evening | Page 280 |
| 30 | 2nd April 1600<br>A prison cell<br>Château of Franchimont | Page 290 |
| 31 | 2nd April 1600 | Page 309 |
| 32 | 2nd April 1600 | Page 325 |
| 33 | Official Message<br>Dated 4th May 1600 | Page 338 |
| 34 | Petition<br>Dated 4th May 1600 | Page 340 |
| 35 | 6th May 1600<br>Early afternoon | Page 342 |
| 36 | Document<br>Dated 7th May 1600 | Page 353 |
| 37 | 15th May 1600<br>Notice | Page 355 |
| 38 | 15th September 1600<br>Retrial   Day One | Page 358 |
| 39 | 15th September 1600 | Page 366 |
| 40 | 15th September 1600 | Page 372 |
| 41 | 15th September 1600<br>Remacle Le Rosy | Page 384 |
| 42 | 16th September 1600<br>Witness Two | Page 398 |
| 43 | 16th September 1600<br>Witnesses Three and Four | Page 405 |

| | | |
|---|---|---|
| 44 | 18th September 1600<br>Two days after the retrial | Page 418 |
| 45 | 5th June 1601<br>Liège | Page 420 |
| 46 | 5th June 1601<br>Françoise | Page 428 |
| 47 | 5th June 1601<br>Françoise and Roland | Page 434 |
| 48 | 5th June 1601 | Page 443 |
| | Annex | Page 445 |
| | About the Author | 465 |

# ACKNOWLEDGMENTS

I would particularly like to thank Christine Smolders Hurlet of Spa for all the help she gave me.

Without Christine there would not have been a *Drop of the Hammer.*

# PREFACE

The *Drop of the Hammer* is a fiction, but its roots are grounded in true events that took place in the village of Creppe in the late 1500s and early 1600s.

Creppe, located in the Ardennes of what is now Belgium, was at the time of the original events part of the Ban de Spa.

The Inquisition and *The Burning Times* arrived in the Ban de Spa on August 23$^{rd}$ 1581, when the Chatelain, Robert de Linden, in the presence of his two aldermen, Collard and Lambert, ordered an official inquiry into the problem of witches in the Ban de Spa.[1]

Armed with Kramer and Springer's *Malleus*

---

[1] Pierre Den Dooven **Sorcellerie dans le Ban de Spa**

*Maleficarum*, the authorities ushered in a reign of terror fed by: ignorance, fear and especially greed.

It is a fact that a large number of people living in Creppe at that time, as well as a good number of their animals (cattle and horses among others) seem to have been afflicted by a mysterious illness.

Even today, what is not understood creates fear. All we need to do is look at the Covid-19 pandemic, which is raging at the time of this writing, and the fear that is being created around it. . . .mostly by people who do not know what they are dealing with.

To be fair, De Linden's worries were not unfounded. Something was causing a 'mysterious illness' in the area and it was not something new. The only problem is that his ordered inquiry threw the spotlight onto a group of innocent people.

To understand this 'mysterious illness', it is necessary to know something about the geography of the area, and the type of work the people of Spa did. . . . long before and long after *The Burning Times* reached the Ban de Spa.

Belgium is an old mining country. For coal? Yes, for coal, but not only for coal. The Spa-Creppe area was especially known for its zinc and lead mining. In fact, its exploitation of zinc-lead deposits dates back to the Prehistoric times.

The name of this 'Mysterious illness' that seems to have haunted de Linder was/is none other than Lead Poisoning.[2]

It would be unfair to put all the blame of *The Burning Times* onto Lead. There was another reason why the witch trials took like wildfire and it was called self-interest.

The most incriminating fuel was 'greed', a common denominator in all the cases during *The Burning Times*. How easy it was to get rid of a bothersome wife, a hated neighbor, a way to speed up an inheritance, and anyone who for some reason or the other was just in the way. No one was asking witnesses to prove anything. All a witness had to do was

---

[2] National Institute for Occupational Safety and Health - www.cdc.gov "It does not matter if a person breathes-in, swallows, or absorbs lead particles, the health effects are the same; however, the body absorbs higher levels of lead when it is breathed-in. [...] Within our bodies, lead is absorbed and stored in our bones, blood, and tissues. It does not stay there permanently, rather it is stored there as a source of continual internal exposure. As we age, our bones demineralize and the internal exposures may increase as a result of larger releases of lead from the bone tissue. [...] Because these symptoms may occur slowly or may be caused by other things, lead poisoning can be easily overlooked. Exposure to high levels of lead may cause anemia, weakness, and kidney and brain damage. Very high lead exposure can cause death.

present to the court what they:

- thought
- could have seen
- would have seen
- might have hear
- and what the cousin of their friend's mother-in-law thought and the list goes on.

On February 3rd 1582, not six months after de Linden ordered the inquiry, various 'witnesses' accused Jehenne, the daughter of Henry Jehan Anseau of being a witch. The first witness was Father Leonard who accused her of not attending church and, last but not least, the fact that several members of her family were also witches. The second witness was Mathieu, son of Mathi of Creppe who claimed that she had made a child die simply by sitting and eating at the same table. These witnesses are only two of several who ran to the Sergeant-at-Arms to testify. They were successful. Jehenne was burned at the stake, being duly strangled beforehand at Jonkeu. According to Albin Body in his *Spa, Histoire et Bibliographie*, Jehenne was burned along with her three children.[3]

In 1610, two other women from Creppe were accused of being witches by a long parade of so-called witnesses who testified in court against them. The first was Catherine, the wife of Parmentier. The second was Françoise, the widow of Le Grand Henry.

The main witness to testify against Catherine was François Le Rosy (also called Remacle in other documents), from Creppe. He claimed she had used magic to not only kill his first wife, but also several of his farm animals.

Françoise was accused by Gilson Froidville of Spa of having been seen gathering mushrooms while another witness accused her of having given an apple to a little girl who died soon afterwards.

Catherine and Françoise were spared the horrors of Jonkeu, but not of the inquisition. Because both women were accused of homicide, their cases had to be tried by the Court of Justice of Spa and then presented to the Court of Justice of Liège before the sentencing could be carried out. Fortunately, the members of this court were more advanced than their colleagues in Spa and Creppe. They requested

---

[3] Albin Body **Spa, Histoire et Bibliographie**

additional information as they were not convinced that either one of these women was guilty.

Both Catherine and Françoise were acquitted, but had to pay the expenses.[4]

As I have already stated, the roots of *The Drop of the Hammer*, are grounded in what happened in Creppe so long ago. It tells the story of a young, rather naïve, widow from Creppe (also called Françoise) who, like the real Catherine and Françoise, is accused by a herder called Remacle Le Rosy de Creppe and who like the real Françoise becomes a strong woman, ready to fight for her life in a patriarchal society.

---

[4] P. Gendarme and J Lohest **Creppe, Sur la Voie du Temps Passé**

# CHAPTER 1
## 29th November 1599

On the road connecting Spa to Creppe, a young woman with soft brown eyes and an upturned nose, is walking home. Her name is Françoise Mathieu, but since the death of her husband, two years previously, people usually add 'the widow of Henry Hurlet de Creppe'. She is walking briskly in the snow with the steady stride of a person born and bred in the Ardennes. It will be good to get home after working long hours as a maid in the Nizet household in Spa.

The half-way point, an abandoned stable, often used as a shelter in bad weather, is in the field to her left. From the top of the rise in the road, where she is now, her eyes can make out part of the shelter, and the Iron Cross a little further off.[5]

Everything looks different under the cold white cover of snow, and it takes longer to get from one place to the other. Normally, she can cover the distance between Spa and the shelter in the time it takes to recite the Lord's Prayer slowly. Very slowly. Not today!

On a nice summer day, she is able to cover the distance between the cross and the Hurlet farm in three Our Fathers and two Hail Marys said at a normal speed. Well, summer is still far away and dreaming doesn't get you anywhere. Although the snow is pretty much hard packed in the middle of the road, here and there are hidden holes that are dangerously soft. They are traps in which a distracted walker can fall and easily sprain an ankle.

---

[5] The Iron Cross is still at a crossroad in 2020. It is a simple iron cross, the tips in the shape of a lance, thrust in the soil so long ago. Sometime before 1992, someone laid down a bed of local stones (parterre de pierres du pays) at the foot of the cross. Comité Culturelles de Spa, *Croix, Chapelles, Oratoires de la région de Spa*, 1992

. . . if not worse.

If Françoise can manage to get to the farm this evening in three times as much time as usual, she can consider herself lucky. The young woman has a trick of her own to help her make time go quicker in this weather. First, she thinks of Mam's hot soup, and then of the warm bread. Secondly, she imagines herself eating all this good food. It always works.

Better not let Father de Lazaar know this. For sure, he would give her a penance of two roseries in addition to going to confession.

She waves the thought of Father de Lazaar away with her hand, preferring to think about Mam's hot soup. She smiles at the thought of entering the farm house and being surrounded by that good smell.

It is snowing again.

The first flurries fall softly on last night's mostly hard packed snow. Within seconds, the air around Françoise begins to swirl with huge, wet, beautiful snowflakes.

She looks up to study the sky, takes a deep breath and enjoys the feeling of the cold crisp air inside of her lungs. It's not that Françoise dislikes the cold wind and the snow, after all they are both part of life here in the Ardennes. It's just she doesn't like walking in it. Well, to be fair, that's not quite true either. What she doesn't like is walking uphill in the snow.

A deep chuckle escapes from Françoise's throat as she
puts her hands out to catch the snowflakes falling silently around her. She imagines crystal butterflies fluttering about, caressing her hands and face as gently as a lover. The silence covers her, and fills her with awe.

As a little girl she thought God sent snow to clean the world. Every time it snowed, and it snows a lot in the Ardennes, Françoise would run out of the house, screaming to her grandmother, "Memère! Memère! Come quickly! God is cleaning!

Give me the broom! I want to help him!"

She smiles at the little girl she remembers being and the carefree days spent at her grandmother's. A gust of cold wind blows, she tightens her shawl around her shoulders and continues walking up the road.

Mam always says there are good things in everything. Sometimes you just have to try extra hard to find them. So, what could she find good about walking up hill in the snow? Ah! Yes, the sound.

She loves the way her feet make crunching noises in the snow. The left-right rhythm of her footsteps reminds her of a new song she heard at the Nizet's last night. Françoise starts to hum the first lines of the song, but it doesn't sound quite right. She tries again and then gives up.

Françoise reaches the bend in the road, wondering if yesterday's heavy snow fall has turned the gentle slope into a slider's paradise yet. She stops at the edge of the slope. Yes! Perfect! The perfect place to slide.

Mam is right. There are always good things in any situation. And sliding down the slope is certainly one of them.

The young woman looks around to check if anyone can see her, lifts her skirt, takes a few running steps, and slides along the short ice-packed slope. At the bottom of the slope, she tries to get up, and promptly falls back on her behind.

"Ohh, no," Françoise giggles, "This is not serious for a twenty-two-year-old widow. Not serous at all! I am acting like a silly thirteen-year-old girl."

The thought immediately dampens Françoise's joy. Her eyes begin to sting, and she presses her lips together to hold the tears back.

In spite of the tragedy that changed her life forever two winters ago, the white powdery snow continues to comfort Françoise.

With a sad, sigh she realizes, the little girl, who had wanted to help "God clean the world", was still deep in her. So deep.

A sense of shame overwhelms Françoise. Both Henry and their baby son, Paschal continue to live in her heart and soul every moment of the day and night. Poor Henry, how she misses him. [6] Her nights are always the same. She falls asleep easily, but then she wakes up in a cold sweat from the same recurring nightmare. Part of her knows and accepts their deaths. Another part of her insists that the epidemic, the suffering, the deaths, the pain she felt when she lost the two most important people in her life within two days of each other had to be a dream.

---

[6] I am writing *The Drop of the Hammer*, during Covid19, and like most of the rest of the world I am in "lock down". We tend to think that pandemics are new, but they are not. The only difference is that Spa and Creppe in the 1500s and 1600s adapted and lived with it, whereas we are shocked by it. In 1597, the year that Françoise's Henry and little boy die, and again in 1611 and 1631, Spa was greatly decimated by the Plague. According to the writer, Melchoir Crahay, the whole of the Liège area was infected by a type of dysentery, so contagious that it spread like wildfire. It was the plague and for a long time it was mistaken for dysentery. Foreigners, vagabonds and passing troops were blamed for the propagation of this terrifying sickness. Strict restrictions were put into place such as threatening vagabonds, and others, that if they did not leave the area within three days they would be arrested.

The dreams are always the same and are always so real. It's so hard when she has to come face-to-face with reality. People keep telling her that Henry and her baby Paschal have both died, but that "The pain gets easier as the time passes." It doesn't for Françoise, it just gets worse.

Not a night goes by that she doesn't feel Henry sleeping next to her. There is always that moment of the warmth of his body reaching hers through her nightgown. All the other women complain that their husbands' snoring keeps them awake. Françoise never could understand this. Henry's snoring used to put her to sleep. She knew he was there. All was well.

Sometimes, if she tries really hard, for just a few heartbeats, she can almost imagine the warmth of Henry's body against hers, and if she listens carefully, she can almost hear Paschal's cooing in his cradle. Yes, almost, but not quite.

Françoise feels her world collapsing around her. The weight of the truth crushes her. Hot, bitter tears stream down her cheeks. The nightmare never clears completely. Life never goes back to normal. Never.

With a last look of regret towards the slope, she tightens her shawl around her shoulders and walks towards the farm and then she stops.

Françoise shut her eyes tightly, and starts to tremble, hot tears brimming in her eyes and then spilling down her cheeks. A burning pain races through her head settling behind the eyes.

"Come on, Françoise," she says out loud, her hands balled into two tight fists, "Control yourself. Look around you. Slowly breathe in and out. In and out. In and out. Everything looks pretty in the snow. Concentrate on how pretty everything looks. See how lucky you are. You live in the loveliest place in the world. Think, Françoise, think."

After a few deep breaths, she opens her eyes and unclenches her fists. "Come on, Françoise", she whispers again to herself, "You're walking along your favorite road. Don't tell me you can still be sad with all this beauty around you."

Drained. Drained was the only word she could think of to describe the empty and lost feeling racing throughout her body.

Breathe in. Breathe out. In and out.

After a while, Françoise opens her eyes, and forces a smile on her face. That's better. A smile. True, it is a forced smile, but nevertheless a smile.

These attacks, as Françoise calls them, are happening more and more often. When they happen at home, she finds an excuse to leave the room so that her in-laws cannot not see her in this condition. It usually works, and when it doesn't work, there is always a good reason to explain it. The only way to get out of these 'attacks' is to concentrate on the things around her.

Sometimes, between the nightmares, the 'attacks', her work in Spa and helping out at the farm, she just wants to give up. She walks on scolding herself for her weaknesses, "So, Françoise, take a good look at the world around you. Get some calmness and balance back into your life. Some, no, not some, 'many' people are worse off than you. Besides, see how lucky you are. How good Mam and Jules have been to you. How much they love you. How many times they repeat that you are their daughter now."

And so, the young woman takes her own advice and focuses on her surroundings. On snowy winter days like this with temperature falling below freezing, the beauty of the row of trees on either side of the road create a magical world. A beautiful, pure crystal cathedral.

"Breathe in. Breathe out."

As calmness returns, Françoise, wraps her arms around her body, enjoying the warm hooded cloak and the shawl she wears to protect her from the cold. "Those trees don't need snow to look beautiful. They are beautiful all year long," she says out loud.

True, there are no cathedrals in Creppe[7] or in Spa and since Françoise has never gone further away than Spa and certainly has never traveled to Liège or Paris, she has no way to really know what a cathedral looks like. She is quite aware of this. "I know I have never seen one, but deep in my heart, I know this is what a cathedral looks like."

---

[7] Today, Creppe is a sleepy little town where nothing ever happens. It hasn't always been like that. Many of the original families have moved away, although some are still there. It was founded by Johan Hannon and basically all the people in Creppe were members of the same family, although they were divided into different branches: Hurlet, Henrard, Hanchoulle, de Creppe, Misson, Renier, Servais, Nicolet, Mathieu…

## CHAPTER 2
## 29ᵗʰ November 1599

About three months after Henry's death, Françoise decided to find work in Spa. Some of the other women in Creppe were already doing it. She knew she didn't have to. Mam and Jules were not asking her to go out to work, but it was for her own satisfaction. It felt good to be able to do so. After all, she was just the daughter-in-law. The Hurlets didn't have to continue taking care of her. Many women in her situation. . . .when the husband dies and there are no children. . . . are simply told to go back to their family. Thank you and goodbye.

For two weeks she went to Spa every day, knocking at the doors of the elegant, rich homes asking if they needed a maid. No! The answers were always the same.

Françoise remembers that period as if it were today.

One day, the Misson brothers tell her to try the Nizets, as they had heard they needed additional help. The next morning, she leaves Creppe early for Spa and goes straight to the Nizet house. She knocks on the front door. A stern, official looking man opens the door, looks at her from head to toe and says, "If you are looking for work, do not ever come to the front door. It is reserved for the gentlemen and ladies. Go to the back of the house, knock at the service door and ask for the cook." Without even having said a single word to him, he slams the door in her face.

The young woman does as she is told, walks around to the back of the house, knocks on the service door, and asks to see the cook. After so many negative answers and slammed doors, she is resigned to being turned away. So, when the young kitchen maid, who opens the door, says, "I suppose you are looking for a job," Françoise, surprised that she has even gotten this far, nods. The young girl flashes a big smile and points at a plump, no-nonsense looking woman surveying the kitchen staff with her hands on her hips. "That's Lambertine, the cook." And when Françoise doesn't move, the girl pushes her into the kitchen "Well, go and ask her." Françoise nods.

Françoise walks up to the cook, opens her mouth, but no words came out. "Are you looking for work?" the woman asks.

Françoise nods.

"Do you have a problem speaking?" asks the cook.

Françoise shakes her head.

The cook's face, suddenly, breaks out in a big smile, "Well that's a relief! I know I look stern and I expect everyone to give their best, but, Bon Dieu, I have never seen anyone as afraid of me as you are. Now, tell me your name."

That's how Françoise started working for the Nizet family in Spa. What she likes the most about working for the Nizets is the constant coming and going of people from outside Spa. Most of the guests at the Nizets come for the water cures.[8] They travel a lot and they are always talking about such interesting things and places. Of course, they don't come to the kitchen, but she can hear them talking as she helps serve the meals.

One day, she hears one of the guests, an elderly man with a pointed nose and a bald head, talking about a cathedral he had recently visited[9]. He describes it in such beautiful words that she stops serving and just looks at him. "Inebriating, my dear

---

[8] It may seem farfetched to the reader to hear that people went to Spa "for the waters" in the year 1600. The term 'Spa' in English comes from this Spa, the town in Belgium, and was known even back in Roman times when it was called Aquae Spadanae.

[9] In 1600, the majority of the people who come 'for the waters' are connected, in one way or the other, with the Church. They come for 'cures' mainly of water from the source called La Sauvenière. According to some archives, the source was also known as the Ecclesiastic Source. It is only after 1651, that it becomes fashionable for the upper class to come to Spa.

Catherine, simply inebriating. The Cathedral in Liège is quite beautiful, as is St. Gudule in Brussels, but when the Bishop of Paris invited me to visit Notre Dame, I was transported out of this world. Totally transported."

Madame Nizet scolds her. "Françoise, your job is to serve the guests, not to listen to the conversations."

"Yes, Madame."

"Oh, Catherine, don't scold her. You have no idea how rare it is for me to have such a pretty girl stop and look at me like that."

"Jacques, you are much too lenient with these people. Please excuse Françoise. She is from the Village of Creppe, up on the hill. You know how they are in Creppe.[10] However, she is a good worker, in

---

[10] Madame Nizet makes a thing about 'those people from Creppe.' It is quite clear that she, a member of the upper class, considers them 'below' her. The part of Spa where the 'curists' moved about was very small. It consisted of the Perron, the canopy covering the source, the church and the various lodgings. The "curists" did not go out of this very limited area (ALBIN BODY). Beyond, there was another poorer world, and beyond that was Creppe . . . .a world of itself.

addition to having a good command of the language. At least she understands what I say to her, which is more than what I can say of most of the others. She works mainly in the kitchen, but she sometimes helps me with the children. They love her."

Françoise is happy to hear the children love her, but doesn't quite understand the connection with 'coming from Creppe'.

Those important travelers who sometimes stop at the Nizet's for a few days or weeks bring magical scenes of color, inebriating height and light to Françoise's simple life.

'Inebriating' that's the word the guest had used to describe the cathedral in Paris. She says it out loud several times, not sure what it means but it sounds good.

A few days after being told off by Madame because she was listening to the conversation instead of serving, Françoise meets Jean Misson, the younger of the two Misson brothers, on her way back to Creppe. Although, Jean also works for the Nizets, they hardly ever see each other and when they do it is in passing and usually, they can only share a quick smile.

"Well, I hear you are appreciated in your new job", he says to Françoise with a big smile.

"How do you know that when I don't know it? In fact, I don't think I am very good. Madame Nizet had to scold me the other day. I was so embarrassed."

"Oh, you mean when you stopped serving to listen to the conversation?"

Françoise glares at Jean. "And how do you know that? And why are you laughing at me?"

"I am sorry. Very sorry. I am not really laughing at you, but sometime you can be so naïve."

"I am not naïve. How do you know I am appreciated?"

"Oh yes, you are naive."

"No, don't call me naive again", she insists, pouting.

"You are naive and now you are pouting. I like you, however, . . . .so, I think I will answer you," says

Jean, trying to hide his smile behind his hand. "First, you should know that all the serving people know each other and we all know what goes on everywhere. There are no secrets here in Spa and even fewer in the big houses where we work. Having said that, I will add that Madame Nizet is happy with your work and especially how you help her with the children."

Françoise's face breaks out into a huge smile, totally forgetting her recent anger with Jean. And Madame says that you. . . . hmm . . . .no, I don't think I will tell you."

"Is it bad?"

"No, it's very good."

"Then tell me!" Françoise insists, stamping her foot.

"Not if you start pouting again and stamping your foot like a little girl."

"No, I promise".

"Ok," answers Jean giving her an over-exasperated look "I will tell you the second reason. But if you start pouting again and stamping your foot,

I will stop."

"No, no, no. I promise. So now you tell me."

"Madame Nizet said in front of Lambertine that you had an in-born politeness mixed with a hungry need for knowledge which you find difficult to hide. And that you understood rather well."

"I am so happy to hear this. I love Madame Nizet. She is always good and kind to me."

One day going up the stairs to the nursery, Françoise sees Jean on the second-floor landing. He is standing behind a door listening to a conversation between Monsieur and Madame.

"What are you doing, Jean?" she hisses at him. Jean turns towards her, "Shhh!" he says putting a finger to his lips. Well, she knows what he is doing. He is eavesdropping. Françoise is so furious by what he is doing that she misses a step on the stairs. Her scream alerts everyone including Monsieur and Madame Nizet who come running out. Jean is quicker than they are. When they reach Françoise, they find Jean already helping the young woman up. "Ah,

Monsieur, it is lucky I was coming up the stairs when I heard Françoise scream. Otherwise, she would have had a really bad fall. Françoise, you need to be more careful." The young woman glares at him.

Madame Nizet starts fretting around the young woman, but Françoise assures her she is fine saying her scream was more from fright than pain. "Jean, help Françoise down to the kitchen. Cook will give her a hot tisane and check that she is ok," says Monsieur before he and his wife return to the room to resume their conversation.

Jean takes Françoise's arm and dutifully helps her down the stairs. Once out of earshot, she pulls her arm angrily away and gives him a mean look.

"You are going to go to hell, Jean, if you continue doing that and don't laugh at me."

"You are a silly little country girl".

"I am not a silly little country girl," she retorts in a fierce whisper. "And, at least if I am, I won't be the one going to hell. You are."

Jean sticks his tongue out at her and laughs.

"But I bet you'd still like to know what I heard, huh?"

"No, I don't want to hear what you heard. I'm not going to hell. It's not nice to listen behind doors. You'll have to go to confession. And then you'll have to spend a whole day doing Hail Marys and Our Fathers."

"They were talking about you," Jean says softly.

"What? They were talking about me?" asks Françoise, suddenly interested and forgetting her anger.

"Yeah. About you and the rest of us from Creppe."

"What did they say?"

"I thought you didn't want to hear."

"I don't, but…."

"But what? You do or you don't?"

"Ohh, Jean," she says with a shrug. "What did they say?"

"Well, Madame was talking about how polite you are and how nice you are. Then she said to Monsieur that all 'those women' from Creppe are like that. Then she said the Creppe men are rough, easily fired up and simple-minded."

"Simple-minded?" repeats Francoise.

"Let me tell you the rest," Jean continues. "On the other hand, she said, their women are generally gentle, want to please, although they are not too bright either."

"Gentle? Wanting to please? Not bright? You are making all of this up, Jean. It's not true. You just want to upset me."

"No, I am not. Ask Jules when you get home tonight. Everyone knows what the people of Spa think of us."

"What did Monsieur say?"

"Hmm, seems to me for a person who doesn't want to hear anything, you are very nosy."

"I don't care if I am nosy or not. Tell me what Monsieur said."

"Well, Monsieur Nizet tut-tutted his wife. He said he wasn't so certain the Creppe men were simple-minded, but agreed that we are rough, and flare up easily. Madame didn't agree. He, however, insisted he wouldn't go as far as calling us simple-minded, in spite of what everyone says. Although Creppe is only a short distance away from Spa, it might as well be in another country, you know."

"I didn't hear much of the rest of the conversation because I heard steps, as you well know, coming toward me, but as I left, I head Madame laugh and say that these men up in Creppe are like their wind-swept plateau. . . .rough, uncontrollable, and unpredictable. She also repeated simple-minded and with tempers that rose as quickly as boiling milk."

"That's not true. Our men are not like that. They are hard workers. They have little farms, work with wood, baskets and since we are descendants of Johan Hannon, our men are also miners. These are all hard jobs."

"Listen, Madame has a point there . . . . even if it is not true."

"What? I don't understand. What do you mean by she has a point there although it is not true?"

"You know, working outside of Creppe is new for you. You see things in black and white. A person is good or he is bad. Everything that happens is either one or the other for you There is nothing in-between."

"What would be between black and white?"

"Gray. Between black and white there is a lot of grays."

"So, what is this gray that I am not seeing?"

"It's simple really. If the Spa people consider us simple-minded, it is not only our fault, but it is also to our advantage."

"Alright, now you are making fun of me."

"Absolutely not. We have this crazy idea, you know, . . .which, at the end of the day is not so crazy. We learn more by looking stupid than if they were to see we are smart. It usually works. Everyone speaks in front of us without even being careful about what they are saying."

"So?"

"So, we know things. Because they think we are

simpleminded but good workers. Every time there is an important dinner where a delicate matter is going to be discussed, they prefer to have us serve them. After all, we are so stupid what could we possible understand?"

"And you are not making fun of me?"

"No."

"Well, I don't really care. I like working for Madame. She is very good to me. I am learning a lot from her."

Françoise smiles to herself as she remembers this conversation with Jean. True, he often opens her eyes to many things, but it doesn't change the fact that she likes the Nizets, enjoys working in the kitchen with Lambertine, and is always happy to help Madame with the children.

As the months go by, she realizes that Jean is right. She doesn't feel it personally, but she does notice it. Anyway, she likes working in Spa for another reason too. Listening to the conversations as she serves opens up a whole new world for her. She can hear about beautiful cathedrals like the one in Paris that fill you with the sounds of angels. There are also other things that she hears there that aren't so beautiful. One of those things is the name of that horrible sickness that swept through Spa and Creppe a few years ago and killed her Henry and baby. The man speaking of it called it by a strange name. Bubonic Plague. There are a lot of other things that she hears while serving, but sometimes they are so complicated or unbelievable that she can't understand them. Nonetheless, even though it makes you feel good to hear all these intelligent things, it is equally good to know where you belong.

# CHAPTER 3
# 29ᵗʰ November 1599

Thinking back on all this, Françoise can only agree that she belongs in Creppe, on this wind-swept plateau she calls home. She draws her shawl tighter around her shoulders and hastens her steps, thinking of the hot soup and the warm fresh bread Mam has prepared.

She listens to the calming, rhythmic sound of her footsteps in the snow. They are the only sounds in this silent, white universe she loves. Silence has a beautiful sound and she imagines it coming towards her from every direction, enveloping her it its magic.

"What's that?" she cries out as an unexpected sound breaks the silence. Some kind of a rustle followed by a twig snapping, Sounds bigger than a twig. Maybe a branch unable to bear the weight of the snow.

Françoise, waits to hear it again, but all she hears is silence. Just as she decides that it's probably nothing more than her imagination, there's another noise and this time it isn't stopping. There is definitely something moving and it is moving towards her. Closer. Closer. Then it stops again.

Her heart starts thumping in her chest and her throat tightens. The young woman knows that, whatever it is, she cannot stay where she is. With a bit of luck and if she hurries, she might be able to get home before it reaches her. What if that thing she heard is a wolf? No, running is not a good idea. On the other hand, she has to get as close to home as possible because at this distance no one could possibly hear her scream for help.

All her senses are on the alert as she decides to take the first step. Her right foot comes up slowly, forward and down.

Nothing.

She does the same with her left foot.

Again nothing.

Born and raised in the Ardennes, Françoise is no stranger to the dangers a hungry wolf represents. On the other hand, the mind can play tricks on a person out here on the winter roads. The young woman starts reasoning out loud with herself. "Sure, there was a noise. I heard it. There are always noises outside and especially in this area, but it doesn't mean it is something I need to be afraid of." It's probably, as she had first thought, just a branch, heavy with snow, that has finally cracked and fallen. What she took for movement coming towards her was certainly a poor scared animal running away from the branch as scared of her as she is of it.

With a shrug she takes up her former stride. Silence, except for her footsteps in the snow. All's well.

A mere ten steps further, the noise of something snapping breaks the silence again.

Coincidence? No, it can't be. Whatever made the noise stopped when she had and moved when she had moved.

"There is something out there. But what?" she says out loud. Henry once told her that it was easier to face fear when you are alone, if you speak out loud. It works every time he had said . . . .and it did for her.

"A wolf?" Fear fills her entire being and something like ice cold water seeps down her spine, legs and arms.

In a voice scarcely louder than a whisper she begins to recite the Hail Mary. As a little girl, the words of the prayer had both comforted and frightened her. "Holy Mary, Mother of God, pray for us sinners now and at the hour of our death. No, No, hour of our death, bad choice. Bad choice!"

"God fills the universe and hears all good Christians, right? And Father de Lazaar said Saint George understands people's fear. For sure, a slayer of dragons must be able to understand the fears of a simple country girl. Besides, if God wants her to live,

He will save her. Right?"

A scream slowly creeps up her throat and reaches her lips. Francoise's hands fly up to her mouth. But what if God's plans were for her to die right now? Would she be brave enough?

Another sound. This time she is certain it isn't a twig. "Pray, Françoise, pray! Pray", she repeats to herself. In a clear but stumbling voice she begins to recite a prayer her mother taught her as a little girl. "I…I…beg you wolf in the name of God not to have any p-p-power over me."

A few more timid steps bring her closer to the farm. "Not to have power over me." The more steps she takes, the more her throat and chest tighten. The few steps she does dare to take, leave her breathless. "Not to have power over me," she starts again, "…anymore t-t-t-than the D-D-D-Devil has on the p-p-priest at the altar when he is…"

The noise again.

Suddenly, the little noise turns into a loud rustle.

It becomes louder and nearer.

The sound enters her head and pounds at her temples. Nowhere to go! Stay still. Nowhere to go!

Tears roll down her cheeks, as she continues, "...any more than the Devil has on the priest at the altar when he is celebrating Mass."

She imagines the wolf's pointed teeth and its fetid breath coming nearer and nearer. The noise, loud and threatening, presses closer and closer behind her.

"In the name of God! In the name of God!" Françoise screams as she fights against the blackness enveloping her. "May Saint George seal your mouth," she screams "and Saint John break your teeth."

Her knees start to buckle.

"Our Father who art in Heaven", she whispers as she jumps from one prayer to the other. "Forgive us our trespasses." Françoise sends the words deep into every corner of her heart. She hopes they will save her from the wolf's sharp teeth

"I beg of you in the name of God. . . . May Saint

## The Drop of the Hammer

George seal your mouth!"[11]

Out of nowhere, a voice calls out "Françoise!".

The young woman freezes in place as bile rises up into her mouth. "A talking wolf," she whispers faintly to herself. Françoise frowns, and shakes her head. "Wolves can't talk. No wolf can talk unless it's something else. If it's something else, what is it? The Devil? The Devil, can disguise itself as a wolf, if it wants my soul. And if it can do that, then it can speak, too."

---

[11] These prayers that Françoise uses in the story may seem very childish to us today. However, they were taken very seriously back then in the Ardennes. The complete prayer goes like this:
>Wolf, she-wolf or wolf-pup,
>I beseech you in the name of the living God:
>You will have no more power over me
>nor over the animals in my charge
>than the Devil has on the priest who is saying the
>Holy Mass.
>May the Great Saint George
>Tighten your throat
>May Saint John
>Break your teeth

(translated from French)
Taken from: *Creppe sur la voie du temps passé* P. Gendarmes and J Lohest Originally compiled by Albert Doppage In his book entitled "Le Diable dans nos Campagne (The Devil in our countryside) Ed. Duclot.

"I beg you wolf in the name of God not to have any power over me. Oh! Dear God help me! Help me!" Salty tears run down her cheeks and slip into her open mouth as she screams over and over again. "Dear God, help me! Help me!"

"Françoise, it's me, Remacle Le Rosy. Don't you recognize my voice?"

Françoise turns towards the voice. At first, she can't see anyone, but then a man moves out from behind a tree trunk. A short, stocky, man with frizzy red hair, is moving toward her. He walks towards her like a shepherd or a tamer would walk towards a frightened animal. Remacle's steady and calculated footsteps make a soothing sound.

A steady murmur of words continually pours out of his mouth. Not one of his words sounds louder or softer than the other and his eyes do not leave her face for one second. "It's ok. It's me, Remacle Le Rosy. Don't be afraid. It's just me."

As he comes closer and finally stops a few feet in front of her, Francoise's fears turn to confusion.

The confusion quickly becomes anger as she realizes the affect he has on her. Although she recognizes the tactic, she also realizes that she cannot move away any more than one of his frightened sheep could.

"Come now, little Françoise. It's Remacle. You know Remacle, don't you?" The tone of his voice seeps into her mind and slithers in like a sly snake She takes a step backward.

Remacle takes a step closer in her direction. His voice becomes a soft whisper. It is so low that she needs to strain her ears to hear him. "Steady girl. Steady. Shhhh! Don't run away. Shhhh! It's me, Remacle. Steady." His voice wraps itself around her like a snake and holds her in its tight grip.

Françoise forces herself to snap out of the hypnotic grasp he has over her and starts shouting at him.

"Remacle,", Francoise screams at him as the blood drains from her face. "That was very stupid what you did. I thought you were a wolf. I thought I was going to die. Don't ever do that again."

Remacle Le Rosy, a distant cousin of the Hurlets, had always scared her. She had often asked Henry not to let him in because she felt uncomfortable in his presence. Although Henry neither liked or disliked the herder, he used to treat him just as he would have any other member of the family. Her husband used to laugh at her saying, "I wouldn't call Remacle my closest friend, but he is family. My door is always wide open for family. Besides, you're not going to be afraid of a harmless herder, are you? Not my little Françoise. You're too smart." In spite of Henry's gentle scolding, Françoise preferred to keep her distances whenever the cousin came by. In front of Henry, Remacle hardly spoke to her and treated the young woman with indifference. But, the second Henry turned his back or walked out of the room, Remacle's gaze would settle on her feet and linger up her body.

Remacle takes three more steps towards her. His eyes leave her face and travel over her body just like he used to do whenever Henry left the room.

Then silently and slowly he walks around her appraising her as he would a horse or another farm animal at the market.

A cold chill runs through Françoise and she pulls her shawl tighter around her shoulders.

"Et ben, well, Françoise. Don't tell me you are afraid of me." Their eyes lock. "So, you are afraid." His breath turns to steam as he laughs out loud.

"No, I'm not afraid. I am afraid of no man." Françoise answers angrily as she slowly eases away from him.

"Oh yes you are afraid, Little Françoise, I thought you had lost your voice since my cousin died. I guess you haven't. Must be lonely for you at times." Remacle grins lewdly.

"Leave me alone, Remacle. Henry's parents are waiting for me. I have to get home. I am already late. I am sure they are already worried and are looking for me." Françoise wants to turn and leave, but her feet won't move. Like a scared animal she stays in place.

Remacle doesn't say a word. Instead of

answering he grins lopsidedly keeping his eyes steady on her all the while. Every gesture, every look tells her he knows how successful his tactics are. Remacle licks his lips and grins that grin she hates so much. The gesture repulses the young woman.

"Come over here," he says softly.

Françoise doesn't move.

"I don't think you heard me. I told you to come over here," this time his voice is louder and harsher.

The change in his tone startles her.

"Why?" Asks Francoise feeling more and more uncomfortable. "I don't want to. Leave me alone."

"Why? Why? Because I have something to show you," is his irritated answer.

Françoise pulls her shawl even closer, sticks her chin out and says "You can show it to me from where you are."

"No, I can't. You have to come here." Remacle points to the space in front of him.

"No." She replies dryly.

"You're not interested?" Françoise hears the

mockery in his voice and fear or no fear, she would like to throw something at him, but what?

"No, I'm not interested."

"Not even a little?"

"Leave me alone. I have to get home," she says boldly as she tries to put up a front of self-assurance she does not have.

"In your shoes, I would be interested." He shakes his index at her like a parent scolding a child.

"Why?"

"Because it is something you lost. And I know the Hurlets will be cross with you if you lose it."

"That's not possible. Henry's parents are never cross with me. And I did not lose anything. I never lose anything."

He looks at her with that irritating grin again. His right hand goes up to scratch his nose. Then he says, "Oh, yes, you have."

"No. I am sure. I . . .have . . . not . . . lost . . . anything." Françoise stamps her foot emphasizing each word.

"If I say you did-then you did," comes his dry reply.

"Alright, so tell me. When did I lose it and what did I lose?" She realizes that he wants her to be angry and is succeeding.

"Ah, you see, you did lose something. Two days ago, in front of the house where you serve," he answers wetting his lip.

Françoise looks at him and realizes what she hates most about him . . . . after his stupid grin . . . .is the way he keeps wetting his lips.

"I don't believe you. I didn't lose anything," she says, her back ramrod straight and her chin high. She wants to go home, but maybe she did lose something and if it does belong to her, she wants it back.

"OK, if you don't want it back, I'll keep it," says Le Rosy stuffing something back in his shirt.

"Wait. If it is mine, as you say, you have no right keeping it. I want it back. If you keep something of mine, you are stealing. And if you steal, you go to hell."

"Ahh, but Françoise, it is not stealing. You said you did not lose anything. I found it. I keep it. I will take your word for it. You didn't lose anything. But I know you did."

"You said it was mine."

Remacle cups his chin in his hand, and looks up toward the tree tops as if thinking. "Hmmm. Yes. So, I did."

"Show it to me," she says stamping her foot in anger and hearing exasperation creeping into her voice. "Give it to me!".

"Come closer." Her husband's cousin beckons her to him with his index finger.

On her guard, Françoise walks towards Remacle. Her instincts tell her to run away, but if he has something of hers, she wants it back. When she gets to within a foot of Le Rosy, he grabs both her wrists in his big left hand and pulls her to him. "Let me go!" She screams, "You lied! I didn't lose anything. Let me go!"

Instead of letting her go, Remacle tears her

bonnet off her head breaking the ribbon that ties it under her chin. Then he frees her because now he knows she is not going to go anywhere.

    She should have realized what he was going to do. She walked right into the trap. The next few seconds seem endless. Françoise stands with her arms stretched out towards the bonnet which he is crushing in his big, rough hands high above his head. She takes a tentative step towards Remacle. He takes a step back. She takes another step towards him. He takes two steps back. "Give me the bonnet. How cruel can you be? You know it is Henry's last gift to me."

    Remacle brings his pudgy hand to his nose and smells the bonnet. "It smells like cinnamon." And with those words he sends the bonnet flying over her head, it lands in a pile of dead snow-covered twigs. From the corner of her eye, she notices the blue ribbon has fallen off the bonnet and is resting in the snow between them. She rushes to grab it, but the herder is quicker and he swoops it up just as her hand is about to touch it.

They stand there just looking at each other, Françoise with tears in her eyes and he with a satisfied look.

Suddenly, Remacle grabs her roughly by the waist, pulls her towards him, and pins her arms back. Françoise lifts her knee to hit him in the groins. A rough laugh escapes from Remacle's lips as he side-steps the blow. The young woman tries to run away, but he grabs a handful of her hair. She screams in pain. Once again, she is caught in his grip as he arches her neck back.

Cold hatred pours out of her eyes. He returns her look defiantly with an equally cold, but smug look. Remacle smiles mockingly "Where do you think you are going, Françoise Mathieu, widow of Henry de Creppe? You are not going anywhere."

The herder smells of the sheep he tends and lives with. The wet wool sheep-smell makes her stomach churn. His face hardens as he slowly runs the tip of his tongue across his lips.

In one quick swoop, he kicks her feet from

under her.

She lands heavily in the snow. He drops his full weight upon her.

Françoise opens her mouth to scream, but no sound comes out.

Remacle's hot and smelly breath upon her face coupled with the smell of his unwashed body make her heave.

She tries to break away, but the more she fights him, the more he is determined to have her, and the tighter he holds her.

He grabs her face between his hands and presses his fleshy lips against hers.

Her hands move up to push him away, as he forces her to part her lips. Remacle transfers his hands from her cheeks to her hands.

Terror fills her as he slides his tongue between her lips.

Fear gives way to despair. Françoise starts crying. Tears run down her cheeks as she gulps for air.

Remacle Le Rosy pulls back. Looks at her and

bursts into laughter as her tears both amuse and arouses him.

Between gulps Françoise tries to talk him into letting her go. "Remacle, please, Remacle. Please let me go," she cries between sobs. The taste of salt fills her mouth as the tears slip between her lips. "Please? Let me go. I won't tell the Hurlets, I promise. I won't tell them or anyone else. Please."

The pressure of Remacle's hands on hers disappear. Little by little, she is able to pull them out of his grasp. Her heart begins to beat wildly. She slowly opens her hands and places her palms flat on either side of her ready to get up.

Although she is relieved, Françoise finds it hard to believe Remacle has given in so easily. Is he really going to let her go?

"Too bad your precious Henry can't see this," Remacle says between his teeth.

Hot and cold waves of anger sweep through her body. His words echo through her head and send uncontrollable shudders up her spine. Françoise can't take it any longer. She gets up on her knees and lunges at him, her two hands up, fingers splayed-out. Her hands reach Remacle's face and she digs her nails down into his cheeks.

Remacle yells out in pain as he pushes her away from him. Blood runs down his cheeks. Without taking his eyes off her, he touches his cheeks. She sees the color drain from his face as he looks at the blood.

In one swift movement, he slaps her over and over again. Left. Right. Left Right. Françoise screams and the more she screams the harder he slaps her.

The first slap forces her face to the right. Her whole left side burns with pain.

The second slap makes her teeth rattle.

The third slap numbs her brain.

The fourth slap flings her backward onto the cold snow. Françoise tries to protect her head but to no avail. She hits something hard and pain zigzags through her head. Everything blurs over and she loses count after that.

Remacle pounces on her like a madman. He

grabs her by the shoulders and shakes her violently. She is completely disoriented. Her temples are throbbing. All she hears is screaming. Words that don't make sense! Words? Sounds? Where is all that screaming coming from? Then she realizes that Remacle is doing all the screaming. He sounds like a wild animal.

Screaming! Screaming! Words that don't make sense to her. Still screaming he comes close to her face. The cloud of his hot alcohol-laden breath covers her face. Little by little, Françoise is able to make sense of the words, but still cannot focus on him.

"How dare you hurt me. Me! Remacle Le Rosy. Me! How dare you scratch me! I'll show you what happens to little know-it-alls like you when they hurt Remacle Le Rosy. I'm going to make you pay for this. You will pay!"

Françoise tries to crawl away, but Remacle catches her by the leg and pulls her back towards him. He flips her over onto her back, again pinning her down with the weight of his body. His free hand roughly fumbles with her skirt and his cold hand touches her thigh.

Like a wild animal caught in a snare, she screams and twists to free herself. The only thing she can do to fight back is to bite the hand that is holding her down, Françoise twists her face to the left and is able to reach his wrist. She bites down as hard as she can. Screaming again, Remacle, reacts by repeatedly smashing his fist into her nose and mouth. She sees his fist coming towards her over and over again in slow motion She hears her nose crack. Her upper teeth bite into her lower lip. The taste of blood fills her mouth.

Françoise begins to pelt him with her fists. At least she thinks she is. Her punches don't seem to be connecting.

Deep down, she knows Remacle will never let her survive this attack. She puts her hands up expecting more blows.

None come. The screaming has stopped. Françoise opens her eyes and sees Remacle slumped over on his side next to her. Her vision is confused and bright spots dance in front of her eyes.

The last thing she remembers before darkness engulfs her is the coldness of the snow on her bruised face.

# CHAPTER 4
## 29th November 1599
## Almost dusk

Several high-pitched screams rip through the windswept plateau above Spa, startling a couple of crows on a branch. They fly off towards Spa, their wings woofing dryly into the distance.

They are not the only ones who have been startled. A young woman called Marie and close friend of Françoise who is walking beneath their tree has also been startled.

Marie, hears another scream and her heart skips a beat. "Françoise," she says out loud. "It's Françoise." Her lips go dry and the blood drains from her face. Should she run back to the Hurlet farm for help? Should she run towards the scream? If she runs back to the farm, she might lose precious time. If she runs towards the scream, those extra minutes might save her friend's life, but she will have to deal with whatever has happened on her own. Can she manage it?

It doesn't take her long to decide. Marie runs as fast as she can towards the road and the sound of the scream. Normally, her limp doesn't bother her much and usually it is so slight that it goes unnoticed. Now, stressed with the fear of not knowing what she is going to find, and hoping her decision is the right one, her bad leg becomes more and more of a nuisance. Pain shoots up her leg with every step she takes.

As she nears the rise leading to the road, Marie totally forgets her limp and the pain as she begins to run. Within seconds her feet get tangled up into each other and she falls face first into the snow.

Another scream pierces the silence around her.

She tries to get up, but falls back down again as the pain in her leg returns in full force. The young woman gets onto her knees and pulls herself up with the help of low branches.

Another scream. She checks to see that she can still put weight on her leg. The pain is there whether she puts weight on it or not. There is only one thing to do: walk on.

When she reaches the top of the rise, she sees two dark shapes struggling in the white snow. A man and a woman. She can hear the cries of the woman on the ground as she tries to fend off her attacker. It's Françoise! What's happening? Why is that man beating her? How is she going to stop the man from beating her!

The man, strong and stocky straddles Françoise. His left hand is pinning her down while he slaps her repeatedly with the right. Each slap echoes in the still air like the snap of a dry twig.

He stops momentarily to look around as if he has heard a noise. Marie pulls back behind a bush, and as he turns, she immediately recognizes him. Remacle Le Rosy.

Remacle is grinning and seems to be enjoying Françoise's loud pleading cries asking him to let her go. Marie's heart breaks as she feels helpless to help her friend. She should have gone back to the farm to get Jules. No, it's too late now to regret her decision. She has to act now.

Marie closes the distance between them. She keeps her eyes on him. Suddenly, the man stops hitting the woman on the ground. From where Marie is standing, she can see the young woman trying to sit up.

Marie comes closer. Slowly. Silently.

Maybe it is over. Maybe he will let her go.

Within seconds she sees, as if in slow motion,

# The Drop of the Hammer

Françoise bringing up her hands and digging her nails down both sides of the man's face.

The man screams like a wild animal. Blind with rage he doesn't see Marie as she inches closer.

He is screaming and screaming! She sees him put his face close to Françoise's.

"How dare you hurt me. Me! Remacle Le Rosy. Me! How dare you scratch me! I'll show you what happens to little know-it-alls like you when they hit Remacle Le Rosy. I'm going to make you pay for this. You will pay."

Françoise tries to crawl away, but Remacle catches her by the leg and pulls her back towards him. He flips her over onto her back, again pinning her down with the weight of his body.

In horror Marie sees his fist come swinging down into Françoise's face. Hitting her over and over again as Françoise screams and finally only whimpers.

Marie is only a few feet away now. She stops. A rock the size of her hand is by her feet. She picks it up with both hands. Only a few feet more and it will be over.

"Please God, help me do this," Marie prays as she stands behind Remacle, and heaves the rock above her head. The weight of the rock makes her lose her balance, and for a moment she thinks she is going to topple backwards.

Luckily, Remacle is still raving mad and is no longer aware of anything except revenge. Shifting her weight from her bad leg to the good one, she heaves the rock up again and throws herself towards him driving the rock into his head.

Once. Remacle's fist stops midway to Françoise's face.

Twice. He sways and groans.

The rock comes down a third time. Remacle Le Rosy turns his dazed eyes toward Marie, stiffens, slumps over Françoise's body and lands next to her.

Françoise, unaware of her friend's presence, continues to scream as the weight of Remacle's body crushes her to the ground.

Marie falls to her knees, grabs the man's left arm, and pushes him off Françoise. His limp body rolls over, and remained spread eagle in the snow.

After this everything is like in a nightmare.

Marie stares at the blood oozing out of Remacle's deep head wound. The contrast between the red blood and the white snow hypnotizes her. Part of her wants to look away, but another part of her cannot tear her eyes away. Totally hypnotized by the blood and by what she has done. Time stands still.

A slight movement to her left breaks the spell. Françoise has fainted. Marie tears her eyes away from Remacle's head wound, and scrambles to her friend's

# The Drop of the Hammer

side.

She is horrified by the damage Remacle has done to Françoise's beautiful face. There is no doubt her nose is broken. Blood is dripping down from her nose and one of her eyes is already starting to swell. Another cut on the side of her head is also bleeding.

They have to get away from here.

Marie cries as she tries to revive Françoise. If she can make her sit up, she might be able to get her back on her feet.

Little by little, Françoise comes to, but still thinks she is fighting Remacle. "Go away, go away," she mumbles between clattering teeth. "Don't touch me, don't hurt me. Please don't hurt me." She makes feeble gestures with her hands as if to push him away.

"Françoise, it's Marie You're safe now. It's over. He can't hurt you anymore. Calm down, please. You're not alone. I'm here." Marie holds her friend's head against her chest. "Shhh. It's alright. It's over," she whispers as she rocks Françoise gently.

"It's alright, Françoise. It's alright. It's finished." Marie says over and over again. Soon, she realizes her words are not getting through to Françoise who is becoming less and less conscious

"Françoise, wake up! Wake up, Françoise!" Marie rubs a little snow on her friend's face t wake her up.

"What? No, don't hit me. Don't hit me anymore. Please, no more. No more", cries Françoise, pushing Marie away, still half-dazed and unaware of her surroundings.

"No, Françoise. It's me. It's Marie. Remacle can't hurt you anymore."

"Marie? Marie? He's gone?"

"It's alright, Françoise. Yes, he's gone. He can't hurt you anymore."

Marie glances over to Remacle's still body. "Françoise. We have to leave right away. We have to get you home. Can you stand up?"

"It hurts, Marie."

"I know. But you have to help me get you back to the farm."

She helps her friend up and with her arm around her she starts leading her home.

Suddenly Françoise gasps. "My bonnet, my bonnet. I have to go back for the bonnet."

"Forget the bonnet, Françoise. We'll come back later for it."

"No, it's Henry's last gift. I want the bonnet."

"We have to get home."

"Please, Marie, please. Look, I can get it." Françoise pushes Marie away and turns to go back. Without Marie's support, Françoise knees buckled. Marie tries to hold her back, but her friend slips right through her fingers. Françoise gropes with her hands, and then falls face down in the snow.

"Françoise, it's alright. You're not alone. I'll go get the bonnet." Marie tries to lift Françoise up but fails.

Françoise starts crying again.

"Françoise, you have to help me, I can't do it alone." Taking Françoise's hands and putting them around her neck, she says, "Hold your hands together behind my neck. Now help me, Françoise. I can't do it without your help."

"My bonnet."

"I'll get the bonnet. But you can't stay in the snow like this. Here sit on this log." Marie tightens Françoise's shawl around her shoulders and checks her battered face again. The eye is totally closed now. Her nose is still bleeding but much less.

"I'll come with you. Don't leave me here alone."

"No. Françoise. Stay here. I can go there and back and I'll still see you."

Marie runs back to where Remacle is, looks around and sees the bonnet caught on the twig. She snatches it off then takes a quick look at Remacle and at the blood.

The two friends walk painfully back to the farm. When they arrive at the Old Cross at the crossroad both girls are exhausted. Marie decides to leave her near the Cross and tells her she is going to get help.

Françoise begs her not to leave her alone. "Remacle is going to kill me, don't leave me alone." Marie shakes her head, "I promise you, Françoise, that you are safe. He won't ever hurt you again."

Marie walks toward the Hurlet farm which is the first as you arrive in Creppe. She is exhausted and her leg hurts.

When she gets to the door, she can only lean against it and hit it with her fists.

The door opens briskly. A small, stocky man with an arched nose and a drooping moustache sticks his head out.

Jules' eyes widen when he sees Marie's pale face and the condition she is in. "Marie, Marie, what's happened. Are you hurt? Talk to me."

Marie tries to talk but at first is unable to utter a word. She just points toward where she came from and manages to mumble "Françoise. The Old Cross." Then she adds "J-j-jules. I killed . . . I k-k-killed him. He's d-d-dead. D-d-dead," before falling into his arms.

## CHAPTER 5
## 29th November 1599
## Dusk

By this time, Mam, a smallish woman whose black curly hair and lightly tanned complexion, even in winter, betray her Rom ancestry[12], has joined Jules and Marie. She is Mam (Mother) to everyone, except to her husband who has always called her by her first name: Honorine. When she sees the state Marie is in, she begins to panic.

What's happened, Jules? Marie, what's going on? Did you fall? Marie, what happened?"

---

[12] There is a very strange and interesting link between Creppe and the Gypsies. According to stories passed down from generation to generation, the Gypsies arrived in Creppe sometime in the 15th century when Creppe already existed. Interestingly, the young Crepplians and the young Gypsies got along better than their parents did. If these stories are true, when the Gypsies left the area, some Gypsies stayed in Creppe, and some Crepplians left with them.

There's no answer. Marie has fainted and is limp in Jules arms.

Jules carries Marie into the house all the while filling his wife in as quickly as possible. "Françoise is out there. Near the Cross. Something happened. I don't know what. Go out to the Cross while I lay Marie on the bed."

"She's at the cross? What is she doing there?"

"I have no idea, Honorine. Take a blanket with you. I will be with you as soon as possible."

"What about Marie?"

"As soon as I join you at the Cross, run back here to look after Marie. Ok? Hurry!"

Mam grabs a heavy blanket and runs off towards the Cross, calling out to her daughter-in-law. "Françoise! Françoise! I'm coming. Everything will be ok. I am on my way." As it is getting dark, she doesn't see Françoise right away, expecting to see her standing up. Mam turns towards the farm house, and sees Jules coming back out. "Jules, I don't see her." And then, "There she is. She is lying on the ground! Françoise! Françoise! We're here. Everything will be alright."

Françoise tries to get up when she hears Mam's voice, but falls back down. In that short period of time, Mam is able to register the state of her daughter-in-law's face, the blood, the closed eye, the bruises,

# The Drop of the Hammer

the broken nose, the look of utter desperation. "Françoise it's Mam. I'm here. Françoise, talk to me. Here, let me put the blanket around you. Françoise, don't fall asleep. Jules is on his way. I see him coming. We are taking you home. You're safe." says Mam as she tries, unsuccessfully, to hide her tears.

Jules catches up with his wife within seconds. He finds her cradling an unconscious Françoise in her arms, tears running down her cheeks. "This is not a fall. And it's not a wolf or another type of wild animal. Somebody did this to her. What happened to those girls? Who did this to them?"

Jules stops dead in his tracks when he sees the young woman's condition. His usual soft voice gives way to a hard and unforgiving one, betraying his emotions. "I don't know who did this. What I do know is that whoever it is, I am going to kill him."

Mam looks up into his face and nods.

"Go back to the house to take care of Marie. I don't think she is hurt, but terribly scared and weak. Oh, and Honorine, make some hot chicory coffee. We are all going to need it. This is not over. Believe me."

Jules bends over Françoise. "Can you hear me, Françoise? Say something." The only answer he gets are groans and incoherent words that sound like bonnet, nonette, sonnette, or something like that. It doesn't matter. What is important is that she is alive and can hear him. He takes her into his arms, carries her back to the farmhouse all the while whispering comfortingly, "You are safe now, Françoise. I am carrying you home. Mam is waiting for us. We are all going to take care of you. You're safe. Safe."

A soft "safe" escape from the young woman's lips and Jules is grateful because he knows she is still alive.

The door of the farmhouse swings open.

"I wanted Marie to stay in bed, but she insisted on getting up, so I brought her here near the kitchen fire. There you are, dear, drink this. It's hot chicory coffee. Drink this, please. It will help you." says Mam as she hands a bowl of coffee to Marie.

Jules comes in carrying Françoise. A conscious but still trembling Marie bursts into tears when she sees Françoise being carried in. The young woman tries to place the bowl of coffee on the table next to her, but her hand is trembling so much that Mam has to help her. "Everything will be fine now." Marie nods, tears still running down her cheeks as she stares silently into the fire, her cup of chicory coffee getting cold next to her.

After a while, Jules comes back to the kitchen. "Honorine, Françoise is lying on her bed. She is conscious now, but my heart breaks to see her in that condition. I looked at her cuts, cleaned and bandaged the one on the side of her head. Also, the slash under her eye. Her nose is broken. Otherwise, she is ok, I think. Scared and in pain but ok. She needs some of your coffee and the comforting words of another woman. I think it is better if she tells you what happened."

His wife nods. As she pours coffee into a cup for Françoise, Jules adds, "Honorine, on second thought, don't ask her what happened. Let her tell you. Don't force her and if she starts talking don't interrupt her."

"Did she mention any name? Do you have any idea who did this to her?"

"No. Not exactly. No name. I am pretty sure it is someone we know, but so far, I have no name and I don't want to press her. She is still very incoherent. Whoever it is, be sure, I am going to kill him. Now please, I need to talk to Marie, if she is able to do so now."

He watches his wife go off then turns to Marie. His voice pitched low, barely above a whisper, he says, "I think you and I have to talk". She nods silently.

"Are you feeling better? Is it ok to talk now?" Marie silently nods again.

He turns towards the fireplace. "Marie, was my daughter-in-law raped"? The hardness in his voice covers his emotions.

"No, but Remacle certainly tried. He. . . ." Marie starts crying again.

"What?" he says spinning around to look at Marie. Did you say Remacle? You know who did this?"

"Yes." Marie whispers

"Are you talking about Remacle Le Rosy?"

"Yes."

"That scum did that to Françoise? That animal did that to my Henry's wife? Did you see her face?"

"Yes, Jules, I did."

"Are you absolutely sure it is him? No doubts?"

"No."

"May God take his life and the Devil his soul!" Jules turns back to face the fireplace.

A soft voice hardly audible next to him says, "The Devil may very well take his soul, but God won't have to bother about taking his life."

A cold chill creeps up Jules' spine as he stares at the flames in the fireplace.

What is Marie trying to tell him?

Did she?

Would she?

# The Drop of the Hammer

Did he understand correctly?

Jules slowly turns back to face her. She is still sitting in the same chair. She is bent over looking at the floor and rocking back and forth. Her hair is disheveled, and wet from the snow. Her hands are together as if praying, palm against palm, fingers laced together.

"Marie?"

She looks up and her hard and cold eyes, usually so warm and laughing, lock with Jules'

"Tell me what happened. I need to know."

"I think I killed him. No. I know I killed him. I hit his head over, and over again with a rock. Then he fell sideways."

Jules doesn't say a word and nods.

"Jules?"

"Yes, Marie."

"I'm not sorry."

## CHAPTER 6
## 30th November 1599
## A little past midnight

Although it is night, the man's body creates a sharp contrast in the white snow. More snow is falling and the wind is picking up, swirling, circling and rapidly gathering strength.

From time to time, the man stirs and moans. Once he tries to turn over on his side, but falls back onto his face. He is definitely in pain and there is blood on the snow, next to his head.

Remacle is completely disoriented. It is dark and it is cold. His mind is blank. He can neither register where he is nor why.

He stirs again and slowly becomes aware of his surroundings. His head is throbbing and from time-to-time piercing pain on the side of his head paralyzes him. The first thing he is aware of is that the cold snow is clogging his right nostril. The second thing is the metallic taste of blood in his mouth. Other than this, he is closed to the world.

What seems to Remacle like several hours later, but actually is only minutes, he comes to again. Although the gash on the side of his head is still bleeding, a light crust is already starting to form over it.

There is something important, wandering around at the edge of his mind which he needs to remember, but can't. It's a vague, nagging thought. Whatever it is, it has to do with this constant pounding in his head. He is almost there. He can almost grasp it, and then the pounding comes and it disappears.

It's cold. He tries to push the snow away from his nostril. Why can't he? What's wrong with his hand? It's not doing what he is telling it to do.

He is floating between the cold conscious world and another, vaguer one. Is he dead? Could be. If he is dead, this can't be hell because hell is hot and it can't be heaven because it is way too cold. So, where is he? Purgatory?

Unexpectedly, he hears a sound and this time he knows what it is. He is immediately wide awake and he knows he needs to stay both awake and alert. The sound comes again from a distance. The sound he hears is a wolf, and in this weather wolves are hungry. Not only does he have to stay awake, he also has to get away from wherever he is.

A veil lifts and Remacle remembers everything: where he is, Françoise, the struggle between them and then total blackness. How long has he been here in the snow, unconscious and in the cold?

Another wolf howls in the distance. It is answered by a second one much closer to him and to his left. A third and fourth wolf take up the howling. It's impossible to determine how close they are. Are they circling him, getting closer and closer to their prey? If they have already spotted him, it may be too late to save his life. The wolves are on the prowl and food is scarce in winter. Remacle knows that, under normal circumstances, wolves do not attack humans unless they feel threatened or have the drooling disease[13]. In this case the smell of fresh blood can be very tempting.

He needs to get away. Cold fear runs through him like lightning. The fear turns into panic, starting at the soles of his feet, climbing up his spine and to every single part of his body. His emotional state tells him to run and scream. His mind tells him to neither

---

[13] Rabies

move nor make a sound.

There is an abandoned stable a little further where he had originally planned on taking Françoise--willingly or by force. It's not too far. Can he reach it quickly in his weakened state? Does he have a choice?

The wolves howl again and this time the herder thinks they are further away. Probably. Maybe. Wishful thinking? Anyway, he can't smell them. That bothers him considerably, because as a herder he should be able to detect them quicker than other people. And he has the reputation of being able to smell them out, if they are anywhere within six hundred steps. Well, maybe, he was boasting at the taverns when he said that. But it is a fact, boasting or not, he rarely has one of his flock lose its life to a pack of wolves. That's a lot more than the other herders can say.

The wolves howl again and this time he is certain they are further away and besides the wind is coming his way not going towards them.

Remacle le Rosy lifts his head and looks around. He is to the right of where he thought he was, but still close enough to the old stable. He can reach it even in his present state. The man bends a knee and puts his foot flat on the ground. He listens. He gets up slowly, slowly. Waits. He hears the wolves again and this time he is certain they are moving away from him.

There are no unexpected noises. He feels safe enough to get to the stable. Can he run? Yes. Not as fast as he would like to, but fast enough. He runs as fast as he can down the cold and deserted road towards the abandoned stable. He slips a couple of times but doesn't take much notice of it.

Once in the field separating the road from the stable, the going is more difficult. Several times he finds himself knee deep in snow. Once he falls into a ditch filled with snow . . . .only the length of a man away from the stable.

He reaches the stable. His heart is pounding. His head is pounding. The head wound is bleeding hard again. He must have scraped it when he fell in the ditch.

Remacle enters the stable and looks around. A shaft of moonlight shines on an old blanket abandoned in a corner. He has never been very particular and this is certainly not the time to start.

He huddles down onto the floor of the stable

and covers himself with the blanket. It smells like dung and, for sure, a colony of fleas call it home, but who cares. It's warm enough.

After a while, the pounding in his head calms down. It is replaced by a dull ache. He can live with that. Feeling both safe and warm, Remacle can start thinking clearly again and soon he remembers what that 'thing' was which had been wandering at the edge of his mind.

Françoise! She tried to kill him. Remacle shudders and blows a stream of fog from his mouth as he exhales. What did Henry's stupid cow think she was doing? Did she really think she could hurt Remacle Le Rosy? Hurt him? She didn't try to hurt him. She tried to kill him.

The more he thinks about it, the more Remacle is sure she wasn't alone. There had to be someone else. She couldn't have fought him off like that on her own. The scratches? Yes, she did that on her own. He remembers her hands coming up and the feeling of her nails digging down in his flesh. He remembers hitting her with his fist and breaking her nose. She definitely deserved that!

Could she have knocked him unconscious? No. Not possible. There was no way she could have hit him over the head while he was pinning her down and especially not after that last good whack. Anyway, why should she try to kill him? He wasn't trying to kill her or anything like that. All he wanted was to have a little fun. There are a lot of girls in Creppe and in Spa who enjoy having fun with him.

The big question now is: who else was out there with them? A man? Maybe. What kind of a man would hit him from the back? A real man faces his rival and looks at him straight in the eyes. A real man fights with his fists. Maybe one of those high and mighty rich visitors, a Bobelin, who come to Spa for the waters. Remacle thought for a while and then shakes his head. No, not a Bobelin. A Bobelin wouldn't even come up this road for two good reasons. The first reason is that Creppe is not known for its sources. So, no Bobelin would even think of coming up here. The second reason is the tough reputation people from Creppe have. No, no, it was not a Bobelin.

The more he thinks about it, the more he convinces himself that Françoise lured him up the road on purpose. Her intention was to kill him.

In the morning he will look around, but now he needs to sleep.

The last thought he has before falling asleep is, "Françoise, you will be punished for this. You will be so sorry."

## CHAPTER 7
## 30th November 1599
## A short while before Dawn

Mam is sitting at the kitchen table, her eyes following her husband as he moves around preparing himself. She is glad the girls are in their rooms.

The calm, soft spoken man she married thirty years ago is different this morning. He is nervous. The determination in his voice borders on a fierceness unknown to her.

"I have let my Henry down, Honorine. Minutes before dying he put his wife, our Françoise, into my safekeeping. I promised our son, she would always be safe with us. I have failed him."

"This is not something you could have foreseen. You are not responsible."

"I should not have let her go to work in Spa."

"Don't say that. You want to overprotect Françoise. I don't agree with your way of thinking, although I understand it. I know you always want to do the best possible thing. Let's face it, is safe and overly protected better than becoming a free and mature woman able to face life?"

"No," he says shaking his head sadly. "You are right. It's just my anger towards myself talking."

"Jules, I know you are going to follow your mind and nothing I can say will change it." Jules looks up at Honorine and smiles sadly. "But you don't have to go out there. The man is dead. Let him be."

"I can't do that. I need to protect the girls. I need to protect us."

"There is no way they can connect his death to us. Besides, we have done nothing wrong. Yes, I know, Marie killed him, but it was only to save her friend. He's the one who attacked our Françoise.

Jules, I have a bad feeling about all this. I don't like the idea of you going out to look for Remacle's body."

Her husband looks at her with his sad eyes, takes her by the shoulders and presses her to his chest. "I don't like the idea either, but Françoise did lose the ribbon of her bonnet during the attack. Luckily. Marie was able to find the bonnet. And besides, you know how they are. In today's world any excuse to arrest women for witchcraft is a good one. Maybe I am worrying for nothing, but I cannot take the chance of our girls being taken to Franchimont and being subjected to their questioning."

"This has nothing to do with witchcraft. Remacle has always been a good for nothing. If the hungry wolves get to him before his body is found at least we can say, that for once in his life, he served a useful purpose. No questions. No problems. The man isn't worth it." Mam wants to say more but Jules' stern look stops her. Her cheeks start burning, but her eyes do not waver. "I have loved and supported you from the first day I saw you. I am not going to change now. If you firmly think you need to do this, then do it."

"I do."

"I will just ask you one thing, please be careful and come back to me safely."

Jules smiles at his wife, takes her into his arms again and whispers, "That I promise."

## Chapter 8
## 30th November 1599
## Dawn

The body on the floor of the abandoned stable is stirring. The man is waking up. Slowly awakening and complaining. He is coming out of his last dream by degrees. It has not been a peaceful night for him. He spent the night either waking up from a feverish dream or from the pain in his head. Either way things were not going the way he had planned.

The colony of fleas that call the blanket home, are having a feast. Remacle automatically scratches his legs and arms between bouts of loud snoring, swearing and moaning. As the minutes go by there is

## The Drop of the Hammer

more swearing and moaning and less snoring. The man is awake.

The pain from his head wound seems to have calmed down, at least it isn't the piercing pain he had had when he regained consciousness on the road. Tentatively, he moves his limbs. He moves his head from left to right slowly. There is just a dull ache. It's manageable. He turns over onto his back to scratch his crotch, sits up and once again the piercing pain smashes into his head followed by heavy pounding.

This time he is wide awake. The speed with which the pain is coming back paralyzes him momentarily. He rises on an elbow and lets out a long string of blasphemy. . . . colorful enough to even shock a few of his drinking partners in Spa's seedier taverns.

Remacle sits sill for a few minutes. After a while, the worse of the pain goes away, and he is left with the manageable dull ache he woke up with. As he sits there in his dark, abandoned stable, the events of yesterday come rushing back to him. The herder is not used to being on the receiving end of pain. His shock turns to anger and then his anger turns to hatred.

No one can do what Françoise did to him and not pay for it. The question is, how did she do that? She was pinned down under him, and Remacle can guarantee she was not in any condition to hurt him. He chuckles when he remembers the sound her nose made when he broke it. Too bad her sweet Henry couldn't have seen that.

So, there must have been someone else. Who? Where?

He would get back to Françoise. She will pay. Oh, yes, she will pay for what she did to him. An idea is already taking shape in his mind and he rubs his hands together. But first he needs to take a look around. For sure, there was another person involved. Was it Jules, Henry's stupid father? No, he is more a man-to-man fighter.

What happened was more subtle. A weaker person taking advantage of a situation. Suddenly, he remembers a face. There was a woman. A woman holding a rock over her head ready to strike him and he knows who she is.

He gets up and slowly goes back to where he must have been when he regained consciousness during the night. The wind had picked up during the night, but there should still be enough traces for him to figure out things.

He walks over to where he first grabbed Françoise. She's a fighter, isn't she? He didn't expect that from her. He always thought she was a rather weak and silly woman.

The bonnet. Where's the bonnet? He remembers tearing off her bonnet and throwing it away. Well, there is no sign of it. Either Françoise picked it up before running off or the wind blew it away. Pity that. It would have served as proof of what she had done to him.

Remacle takes another look around. Gradually, his eyes discern an unusual color for this time of the year when everything is desolate and white. Blue.

Something the color of wild blue flowers is caught in some snow-covered twigs. He immediately knows what it is. It's the blue ribbon. There doesn't seem to be a bonnet anywhere, but at least there is the ribbon. He vaguely remembers putting the torn ribbon somewhere in his shirt. It must have fallen out during the night as he made his way to the abandoned stable. The stupid ribbon that fastened Françoise's stupid bonnet! Stupid woman, wearing it in winter! Stupid gift! Everybody knows it's Henry's last gift to her. He can even remember the day Henry brought the bonnet back from Verviers for his wife. He had said that although he was not a rich man, he only wanted the best for her. Blah! Blah! Blah!

Thank you, Henry. Now I have proof that not only your precious Françoise was here, but also that she attacked me, thinks Remacle sarcastically as he disentangles the ribbon from the twigs and fingers the torn end where it had been attached to the bonnet.

Remacle tries to work out the pieces of what happened. Things are coming backing back to him slowly and in flashes. He remembers sliding his tongue into her mouth and the way she struggled. He likes thinking about it.

Those flashes are not as clear as he would like them to be. He struggles to remember what happened next?

The headache is back. Pounding! Pounding! Pounding!

Another flash. Clearer and longer this time.

Françoise manages to free herself and tries to run away. Yes, it's coming back! He sees himself catching her easily and then throwing her onto the ground. "Hmmm, Françoise," he says out loud "you are a good fighter, but I guess not good enough for old Remacle, huh? Most girls wouldn't manage to free their hands at all."

He puts the ribbon up to his nose. There is still a faint smell of cinnamon on it. Françoise always uses cinnamon and when she walks by, the scent of cinnamon seems to swirl around you. "Well, after the cracking noise her nose made, she's not going to be able to smell cinnamon for a while," he says laughing.

The herder's cheeks start twitching. . . .a reminder of her nails digging into his flesh. He doesn't mind a little resistance, in fact, he even appreciates it. That doesn't mean he accepts having his face scratched. His friends will laugh at him when they see him. Only women scratch men's faces and he certainly is not going to let them think he let that happen. After all, what kind of a man lets a woman scratch him up like that, huh? Not much of a man.

The twitching and the memory of her fingernails digging into his skin angers him. "Henry, your precious Françoise deserved the whack I gave her and more. I swear, cousin, Remacle Le Rosy will see she gets more. Believe me, she will get more."

His toe hits something hard close to where he had regained consciousness. A rock. Picking it up, he sees there is blood in the snow where one end had rested. So, this is the weapon. He hefts the rock and decides a woman could have managed it. He is sure now. It is definitely a woman who attacked him from behind. That explains the hazy memory of a woman's face other than Françoise's that keeps coming up. "If it were a woman . . . . and I am sure of it now . . . . then I am a very lucky guy," says Remacle out loud. "A man wheeling such a weapon would certainly have killed me."

He looks around. The only clear footprints are the ones he is making now. Yes, yesterday's footprints can still be seen, but very faintly. This part of the road is very exposed and last night's wind and fresh snow did a good job of erasing them.

Remacle puts his hands on his hips and looks around. What would Françoise do. She was going home to Creppe when he stopped her. Even, if someone had joined her, she still would have gone home . . . . leaving him for dead. Remacle starts laughing, "Aren't you going to be surprised when you see me alive and well! Let's see what else I can find." As he continues his inspect, he reaches a more sheltered area. Remacle discovers a dozen or so clearer footprints!  Two people with small feet.

Women by the looks of it, walking close to each other.

What's that noise? Someone coming up from the village. Remacle hides behind the thick trunk of a tree.

# CHAPTER 9
## 30th November 1599
## Early Morning

Jules closes the door behind him and sets off. The sky is clear, but the light wind that started last night as he carried Françoise and Marie into the farmhouse has picked up during the night.

In spite of his heavy clothes, the wind chills his bones. Jules pulls his cloak tighter around him, grips his walking staff and turns toward the road to Spa.

Although the wind had erased many of the girls' footsteps during the night, there are still enough left for him to read and follow.

With each step he takes, both his anger and

guilt grow. He can still feel Henry's feverish hand clutching his and hear his own words, "Don't worry Henry. I will always take care of both Françoise and your little one. I've always been there for you and I'll always be there for them. I promise. I promise. I love them both. They are like my children."

As always when he thinks of his son, the pain that swells up in his soul completely overtakes him. His throat dries up and the thumping of his heart is hardly bearable. Paschal, Henry and Françoise's baby died a few days after his father and of the same illness. Many died in Creppe that year.

Jules recalls how he stood frozen behind Françoise as the child became weaker and weaker, gasping for breath and finally dying. The guilt has been tearing his heart to pieces ever since that day. The death of Paschal was the first promise to his son he failed to keep. Now, barely two years later, he again fails his son.

It is only thanks to Marie's arrival and action that Remacle did not rape his daughter-in-law. His anger toward Remacle burns hot in his chest, but the real anger is directed to himself. He balls his free hand into a fist and his nails dig into the palm of his hands. "I am sorry Henry. So sorry. Please forgive me. I did my best. Please forgive."

Jules retraces the distance the girls covered the night before. He reaches the cross where Marie no longer had any strength left in her to continue supporting Françoise. The only way to get help was by leaving her friend there at the foot of the cross. It is there that Jules, biting his lips and desperately trying not to cry, stops and kneels in front of it. The pain is so overwhelming that this strong man of the Ardennes, used to hiding his pain and suffering, succumbs. On his knees, head bowed to the ground, he is wracked by guilt and a torrent of hot, endless tears pour down his face. He looks at the cross and placing a hand on it he murmurs, "God, you must be so tired of me, so disgusted with me, and I don't blame you. But please, please, help me do what I must do."

Jules slowly gets up and continues up the road looking for signs left by the two girls. Again, and again he studies the traces left by Françoise and Marie, sometimes going back to be sure of his understanding. Some are deep because Marie had Francoise's added weight to support. About a hundred steps away from the cross, he gets down on one knee to examine the ground where the two girls stumbled, fell into the snow, got up and then stumbled again.

Further up there is an old log where the snow seems even more trampled. He slowly gets up and walks over to the log.

Last night Marie described the place where she had killed Remacle and this seems to be it. He can see where Françoise and Remacle struggled and Marie's footsteps as she came upon them and then the prints made by the two girls as they left.

He studies everything he sees and tries to put the picture together. There is the rock Marie used to hit Remacle. A small pool of darkness in the snow shows where Remacle bled. Everything is exactly like Marie said except for one thing. The body. There is no body.

Something is wrong. The skin over his cheekbone become taunt and a cold chill runs down his spine. It's too quiet.

A dry crunch of feet walking in the snow breaks the silence, and Jules reels around.

Remacle is standing a few feet away from him. The two men stare at each other in total silence. Remacle's hard and unweaving stare hits Jules like a slap in the face. The older man wills himself to hold the younger man's stare.

"Come to see whether the girls finished their job, Jules?" Remacle smiles, but his eyes stay fixed on his cousin.

Jules bites down on the inside of his cheek, and forces himself to stay calm before blurting out, "Evidently, they did not. But don't worry nothing is lost. I will kill you."

Remacle chuckles softly as he looks down at

his feet. Then he says, still as softly, "Yes, as you can see, I'm still alive. Disappointed, huh? You come here expecting a body, and there's no body."

Jules's anger grows with each one of Remacle's words. It grows and reaches every part of his body and soul.

"Is that it, Jules? Am I right? Do I understand correctly what you just said? An old man like you, thinks he can finish the job himself." At this, Remacle bursts into a crude and loud laugh. He starts to circle Jules slowly with his arms stretched out, his beckoning fingers inviting him to fight. "Come on, old man, try me. Cat's got your tongue or maybe you're just scared."

Jules feels the anger, he stubbornly holds in place, boiling over and ready to burst out. Heat and ice fill his world.

The heat of his hatred of Remacle makes him want to fight.

The icy coldness of his guilt makes him want to remain silent . . . .and hide under a rock.

The strength with which he clenches his jaws together sends waves of pain to his temples.

The dampness of his tightly closed fists contrasts with the cold dryness of his lips.

"Come on, old man. This is not like you. You always have something to say, and today I hardly hear anything from you .... except, of course, that you are going to kill me." Remacle lurches forward feigning an attack. In spite of himself, Jules puts up his arms to ward off the blow.

Remacle stops circling the older man. In a voice full of mockery and sarcasm he says, "Ohh! Did Remacle scare Jules? You shouldn't even be out here, old man. What do you think you are going to do to me, huh? Go home. Go sit next to the fireplace where you belong."

"Y-y-you tried to rape my Henry's wife. I can't and won't accept it. You're a s-s-scoundrel." Jules' face heats up as he realizes his anger is making him stutter.

Remacle less than an arm's length away from

Jules, places his hands on his hips. The herder's upper lip curls up as he leers at the older man. His feet set apart evenly balance the weight of his stocky body.

"W-w-what? Y-y-you w-w-won't a-a-cccept it? Is that what you said?" Remacle starts laughing. It starts as a low chuckle and develops into a high pitch sound.

Jules can hear the sound of his labored breathing and feel his heart pounding in his body. The mockery touches him in a way the earlier physical taunting did not. He looks down at his feet to hide the tears in his eyes. Jules takes a deep breath and swallows hard before speaking.

"It's not funny, Remacle. It's wrong what you did. In fact, 'wrong' is too mild a word to describe what you did."

"Funny? Do you believe I think it's funny? I don't think it's funny at all," the younger man says shrugging his shoulders and rolling his eyes. "It's not funny, old ma, it's pitiful."

"Pitiful?" Jules' voice echoes the herder's last

words.

"Yeah, pitiful. Here you are getting upset over nothing. It's all the time your Henry this and your Henry that. Henry is dead. Françoise is no longer your precious Henry's wife. She is his widow. So why get so upset, huh?" Remacle spreads his hands out and shakes his head. "We were just having fun."

Jules' head snaps up. "Did you say fun, Remacle? Did you see the state you put her in? You call that having fun?" The smug look on the younger man's face sends a surge of anger mixed with unexpected energy shooting through Jules' body. His mind shuts off and his body takes over. He rushes Remacle and tries to punch him in the face.

Remacle's stocky body moves deceptively fast, and he sidesteps the blow easily. Jules lands flat on his face. The younger man doesn't give him time to get up, and kicks him repeatedly in the ribs. Jules screams from the pain.

Remacle stands over him. "You're an old man, Jules. What are you doing? Not only are you trying to fight a much younger and stronger man, but you are doing it for a stupid reason. Go home. That kick should make you think. I feel no guilt about this. On the other hand, if you want to fight, I promise, you won't get up."

With great difficulty Jules starts to get up on his knees and then onto his feet, swaying left and right His side aches and each breath he takes sends spikes of pain throughout his body. He is aware of broken ribs. It is affecting his breathing. The effort he needs to stand is too much and he falls landing on his back. Jules hears himself making sounds which aren't words as he crawls towards a birch tree and painfully manages to get back on his feet.

The older man turns toward the herder and says as clearly as he can in spite of his pain "I will kill you."

The distance between the two men which seemed so short at the beginning now seems immense. Jules looks towards Remacle. Two Remacles are standing before him, and both appear vague and shiny. One of them is real. The other is not. Jules gathers his strength and attacks the herder, hoping he is attacking the real Remacle.

Remacle clasps both his hands together, and with all the strength he can muster swings them at Jules' head.

The blow paralyzes Jules from head to toe. He goes limp. He wants to get up, but his body refuses to obey.

The last thing he remembers before everything goes pitch black is a cold, hard twig as it scratches his face.

## CHAPTER 10
## 30<sup>th</sup> November 1599
## Several hours later

The hours are dragging by. Jules left the farmhouse a little past dawn. Its early afternoon now and he still hasn't come home. Something is terribly wrong. Mam can neither sit still nor concentrate on anything. After so many years together, she knows deep down when her Jules needs her. He has been gone a long time. In less the time, Jules could have gone to Spa and back twice even in this weather.

Marie is still at the Hurlet farm. As soon as Françoise had been taken care of, Jules told his wife he was going to go see Marie's husband. Johan

Hanchoulle and Marie live nearby and the two families are close. When Marie isn't home, Johan doesn't have to ask where she is. He knows Marie is at the Hurlet's, so he isn't worried.

When Marie learned that Jules was going to see Johan, she begged him not to tell her husband she had killed Remacle. What would he think of her?

Jules put his foot down. "How can you possibly think we can hide something like this from Johan? We can hide it from everybody else, but we can't hide it from Johan. We are one big family, Marie. Johan and I grew up together and we have always been there for each other. He needs to know."

"But what if he stops loving me because I committed this sin."

"Marie," Jules answered softly, "What are you afraid of? Your husband will always love you. I also want you to know that you did not commit a sin. You saved Françoise. You saw the state she is in. Without you, I am sure he was going to kill her. Never forget this. You saved Françoise."

"I am a killer. I will go to hell."

"You are neither a killer nor, are you going to hell. You saved a precious life. You saved Françoise."

Deep down Marie knows Jules is right. She did save Françoise. But how can her gentle husband ever accept the idea of his wife being a killer. Whatever Jules thinks, she did kill Remacle, and therefore she is a killer. She dreads the moment she will have to face her husband.

Voices in the kitchen. Jules is back and Johan is with him. It is not that she is afraid of her husband, but the idea he might not love her anymore is more than she can bear.

She can hear him walking towards the back room. The door opens and he comes in without a word. Hanchoulle walks up to her and silently puts his arms around his young wife and holds her tight against his chest. Then he whispers softly in her ear, "My little Marie, how can you think, for one single moment, that I could stop loving you. You brought me sunshine when I was in darkness. I am proud of you. You saved a precious life."

Marie pushes him away, "But Johan. I killed Remacle. I am going to hell. How can you still love me?"

Hanchoulle pulls her back against his chest. "You are not going to hell. You killed someone who was doing something bad."

All that, happened before Jules went out. Hours ago.

Jules has not come home yet.

Mam is pleased she and Jules insisted on telling Johan the truth. And now Johan has gone home, Marie is still with her.

But Jules has still not come home.

She is glad to have Marie at the farm. Françoise needs the company of her best friend. She promised Johan she would not let Marie put any weight on her leg. In reality, the pain is in her mind not in her leg, although it still aches.

Jules is still not home.

Mam knows Marie told Jules she was not sorry

about killing Remacle. Although Marie has not mentioned anything to her so far, she can feel that the young woman wants to talk to her about Remacle alone.

Where is Jules?

The door to the kitchen opens and Marie comes in. "Mam, is it alright if I come sit with you for a while? Françoise is sleeping."

"Of course, it is," answers Mam with a welcoming smile. "I was just going to sit down by the fireplace with some chicory coffee. Do you want some?"

"Yes, please."

At first, Marie is silent. Just sipping her coffee and staring into the fireplace. And then in a voice so low that it was hardly audible Marie said, "Mam, I need to talk to you. I did something terrible yesterday. I killed a man. I killed Remacle yesterday, and I am not sorry."

"I know. Jules told me everything before he went out to . . . . you know."

"I told Johan too."

"I know."

"Do you think I am going to hell?"

"No, dear. I am sure God will understand. You didn't do it to kill. It wasn't your intention. It's an accident because you wanted to save your friend."

"Mam, it was no accident. I knew what I was doing when I picked up that rock. And I don't feel bad like I should."

"Don't feel bad. Sometimes you need to do something that is bad to do good. You saved Françoise. If you hadn't gotten there on time, Remacle would have killed her. That's a fact. Look at the state she is in."

"Father de Lazaar always says you have to confess when you sin. I can't go to confession. How is God going to forgive me, if I don't go to confession? If I confess, Father de Lazaar is going to have me arrested. You know that."

"Marie, what happened is between you and God. What you did is not between you and Father de

Lazaar. I's not that Papist's[14] business. What did Johan say?"

"Johan said the same things you and Jules said to me. I was surprised. I thought he would no longer love me."

"Why did you think he would not react in the same way Jules and I did?"

"Well, he is a good man and a good husband, but you know how he is. Right is right. Wrong is wrong. There's no gray space in between. I thought what I did would break his heart, but it hasn't changed anything."

"That's because you married a good man, Marie."

---

[14] The term "Papist" was coined during the English Reformation to denote a person whose loyalties were to the Pope, rather than to the Church of England. The word soon crossed the English Channel and any reference to the Church of England was soon lost. The word, dating back to 1534, comes from the Latin word 'papa', i.e. Pope. Mam most probably doesn't know its background but she knows what a Papist is when she sees one and, for sure, Father de Lazaar is a Papist. She remembers her Gypsy grandmother very well and her true beliefs are perhaps not exactly what Father de Lazaar expects from one of his parishioners.

"Do we need to tell anybody?"

Mam shook her head. "Jules has gone to bury the body or maybe move it somewhere else. I don't know. If anybody finds out, both of you girls are in danger. No one has to know and no one must know. What happened last night has to be kept between the five of us. Let's not talk about it anymore. What's done is done. I wish Jules had already come back."

Marie gives her a sad smile and nods her head. "When do you expect Jules back?"

"Hours ago, Marie. I have a bad feeling in my bones. Something has happened to him. Marie could you . . . . would you . . . .?"

"Go ahead, Mam. If you need to go out looking for him, go ahead. I can take care of Françoise. Don't worry."

"Yes, I am going to go right away. I need to take along some things." And with those words Mam gets up and starts preparing the things she might need.

Marie looks at the older woman with affection. Strange what a few hours can do. Yesterday at this time, she was a young married woman leading a simple life. Today she is older and life will never be simple again. .

## CHAPTER 11
## 30th November 1599
## Mid afternoon

Now that she has decided to go out looking for Jules, Mam is getting more and more nervous. The feeling that something has happened to Jules is overwhelming her.

Marie continually wants to help her prepare to go out but she keeps being shooed up to Françoise's room.

"Marie, I think Françoise is calling you."

"No, Mam, she is not calling me."

"I am positive I heard her."

"Mam, you know it's not true. It's just an excuse

you are giving me. I really want to help you."

Finally, Mam convinces Marie to go back up when she says, "Yes, I know. But I really need to be alone to do this."

Honorine dresses as warmly as possible, grabs one of the wooden staffs in the corner, and on the point of opening the door she remembers to take a couple of blankets along. She hesitates. Are they really necessary? Yes, you never know. Something deep inside of her tells her that Jules is in big trouble and that he is calling her. She doesn't want to think about it, but if Jules is hurt, she needs to have something to cover him up with. Of course, he is ok. No use worrying. No, she can't fool herself.

Even when they first met, they had felt close. Over the years, a type of mental communication had developed between them and she knows for sure he needs her. This troubling mental nagging grows stronger by the minute. "Jules is out there and he needs me."

A half hour later, she reaches the old

abandoned stable. Looks in. The stable is empty except for an old blanket carelessly thrown in a corner. There are faint footprints leading to the stable and fresher ones leading away from it. She looks at the footprints. A man from the size of them, but they are not Jules' footprints. She can recognize his footprints anywhere as his right foot has a slight inward turn. She looks around but cannot see any others.

Going further up to the road itself, she quickly notices how trampled the snow is. She stops and listens. The silence is so strong that it is deafening. Again, cold fear clutches her heart. "He's not here," she murmurs to herself. "But he must be here. Where else could he be. Jules! Jules! Jules, it's Honorine," she cries out loudly. "Can you hear me? It's Honorine."

A faint sound breaks the silence and her throat tightens. "Jules? Jules? Is that you?". Someone is moaning. It's coming from the direction of a big snow-covered log.

She runs towards the sound and right after getting to the log, she trips over her husband's body. Panic! "Jules, Jules, can you hear me?" At least Jules is alive. What has happened to him? Can he hear her? Probably. Maybe. "Jules, It's Honorine. Can you hear me? Everything is going to be fine. Your Honorine is here."

The only answer she gets is more moaning. And then Jules lifts a hand towards her but his eyes remain shut. She grabs her husband's hand and tries to warm it, then takes the other one too.

"I'm here. Your Honorine is here. Everything will be fine." His face is cut up, swollen and bruised. The eyes are swollen shut and his lips are badly cut. "Hhho… nor'in. 'ere?"

"Yes, Binamé[15], I am here. I am taking you home." Tears fill her eyes and run down her cheeks. She doesn't want Jules to see her crying, but she can't stop. She feels his legs and they don't seem broken.

---

[15] Binamé is Walloon for 'beloved'.

She places her hands on his ribs and he screams with pain. Mam pinches her lips together. She has to act quickly. She takes his hands in hers "I am taking you home."

Jules squeezes her hand, "N-n-no, 'eavy. Hanchoul' 'elp you." Jules is right. He is too heavy for her. Yes, of course 'Hanchoulle'. She should have asked him to come along with her. "Yes, Binamé, Hanchoulle is strong and tall. I understand. I'm going to get him. But I can't leave you like this."

She is certain he has one or several ribs broken. Ribs are tricky. Sometimes they break and cut things up in the body. She looks at Jules' face. Honorine's heart breaks as she looks at the battered face she has loved for so long. She feels helpless. What can she do to protect Jules while she runs back to get Hanchoulle? Cuts heal and swellings go down, but her big worry is Jules' back. He is not complaining about his back. What if it is broken and he just cannot feel anything? All these thoughts are reeling in her mind as she looks around. There must be something she can do to shelter him. What? The abandoned stable is too far; besides she doesn't want to risk moving him that far even if she physically could. Can she move him a little? Where? It's a risk she is going to have to take. "Think! Honorine. Think.! One way or the other I can't leave him where he is. The only thing I can see nearby is the log."

The log?

It looks half embedded into the snow. Is she strong enough to move it? She tries one side. Then the other. No, it's too heavy.

Honorine's legs buckle under her. She sits down on the log to think.

She is half way between Creppe and Spa. Too far to go either way. The log didn't even budge a little bit when she tried to move it. What she needs is something to pry under it. What? She looks around. Her staff. There it is . . . . where it landed when she tripped over Jules. Using her staff as a lever Honorine tries to raise the log, but it doesn't budge. She needs something else. Jules had a staff too. Where's Jules' staff? She looks around and finally sees it at a distance.

Coming back with the second staff, she manages to thrust both of them under the log hoping to create some kind of counterbalanced lever. Her first try does nothing. At the second try, she thinks that maybe something moved, but is far from certain. It's only with the third try that she manages to dislodge the log enough to start digging around it to free it some more.

On all four, Honorine begins the slow work of freeing the log from the snow. Her frozen hands slip. She falls backwards in the snow. What's that in the snow? Blood is gushing out of a deep gash in her right palm.

She tears a long piece of material from her petticoat and wraps it, as well as she can, around her hand. "Another problem to put aside for later," she whispers to herself as she continues to release the log.

It may be the last day of November and it may be cold, but by the time Honorine is finished, she is dripping with sweat.

Over time the log's weight has created a hallow in the ground and the space is filled with old dry leaves. She sticks her arm into the hole and it goes down to her armpit. The log had been resting on a bed of dead leaves since fall.

Honorine silently prays to God that her husband's back is not broken and that she is not going to hurt him even more. Crawling over to where he is lying, she whispers to him, "Jules, can you hear me." He nods. "There's a hollow under the log there and I need your help to put you in there. Can you help me?" He nodded again, "Try."

"I need to put a blanket under you so I can pull you to the hollowed space under the log. Can you move your back?" Another nod. With her help and with a lot of pain, Jules manages to help her slide the blanket under him. Little by little, she pulls him towards the log. She can see he is trying not to moan or scream but twice the pain is more than he can bear and he lets out a long piercing scream.

Finally, she manages to settled him in the hallow space. The blanket she used to pull him along is under him. The second one is on top of him. The log serves as a makeshift buffer against the wind.

Honorine takes one of his hand between hers and kisses it. "This is the best I can do Jules. I'm off to get Hanchoulle. I love you." He nods as she squeezes his hand.

"Go," he mouths.

Without another word, Honorine gets up and runs towards Hanchoulle's house.

## CHAPTER 12
## 13th December 1599
## Evening

The man crossing the snow-packed street in front of the Hola Forge[16] has to stop every few minutes to loosen the snow caked underneath his wooden shoes.

---

[16] The Creppe-Hola connection: Most Crepplians described themselves as "cultivators" in official documents. Yes, they had a cow and maybe a couple of pigs, but on the whole the Spa region was not agricultural. However, they had something else. They mined iron ore. The foremost "ironmasters" of this early "steel complex" were the four main families of the region. In 1439, Johan Hannon, a member of one of these families and also an alderman of Spa at the time, was granted, by the Chatelain of Franchimont, the land where the village of Creppe later developed. Basically, the whole population of Creppe belonged to one family although divided into branches and were all descendants of Johan Hannon. In 1449, Johan Hannon inherited a quarter of the Hola Forge.

As he gets closer to the tavern, the noise of men drinking, talking in loud voices, and simply enjoying male comradery reaches out to him. He stops, chuckles, and smiles his cynical grin.

This is the first time he is back since that incident up on the road to Creppe. The scratches down his cheeks are healing well, but still visible enough for what he is planning. The crust covered wound on the side of his head is still visible and aches from time to time, but Remacle figures he has seen worse.

The wind is strong and ice-cold as it swirls in between the houses on either side of the road.

Remacle Le Rosy turns his back to the wind and holds onto a tree truck for support as a strong gust hits him right in the face. The cold stings his face, sweeps up his nostrils, and freezes the area between his eyes. He cups his hands around his nose and blows into them. That's better . . . . not great, but better. Beating his hands around his arms, he covers the short distance separating him from the tavern at a run.

Robert Storheau's tavern, within a stone throw of the Hola Forge enjoys its own particular clientele. The men who frequent it are rough, loud, and do not need a good reason to start a fight. In fact, an evening without at least one fist fight is unheard of.

Guillaume, Storheau's great-grandfather, came to Spa from Theux in the late 1400s at a time when the term 'coming for the waters' had not yet been used in connection with Spa. He soon became friends with the mayor, and opened a tavern a few months after his arrival. Within weeks, his tavern became a favorite with the Hola people. Soon workers from other forges in the area made it their favorite drinking place too. Robert Storheau's tavern prospered through harsh winters, rainy summers, peace, wars, epidemics as well as . . . . the good and the bad times.

Over the years, the tavern grew from a mere hole-in-the-wall to a two-room establishment with a name. It started out simply by being called 'Storheau's'. Recently, Robert decided his tavern should reflect its increasing popularity and amenities, such as they were, and started calling it ---as the sign outside attests---'The Storheau Tavern'.

The tavern has, like most taverns in these times a huge fireplace, wooden tables and benches. There is no privacy and what is said at one table is usually heard at all the other tables.

Beer, a cheap popular brew made according to the Flemish method with hops, is served in an earthenware pitcher and poured in pottery drinking vessels. In some taverns, not as prosperous as Storheau's, a full mug is simply served and shared around the table. Storheau will have none of that. He believes good service keeps the patrons loyal. If the patron is looking for something stronger and has the money to pay for it, he can order a shot of geniever distilled from grain.

He serves warm meals on request to hungry patrons as long as they are not too fussy. In winter and autumn, he advertises "Storheau's Special", consisting of pieces of chicken stewed in gravy along with carrots and onions. In summer and spring, he serves black bread, onions, and cured ham.

The patrons also come to Storheau's Tavern for the sweet attentions that Bella can offer for a reasonable price. Bella also serves and is, as can be expected, a great "favorite" with the patrons.

The Storheau Tavern is a real man's tavern where a man can drink his geniever or beer, and share his thoughts with people he knows and likes.

There are no panes of any type in the solitary window next to the door. At night, Ambroise, Robert's apprentice, closes the wooden shutters on either side of the window. During the day the window and the door allow natural light to come in. In good weather when benches are put outside, Robert passes the drinks through the window opening. And the times being what they are, over the years, more than one patron has used the window to escape from soldiers or from a jealous husband.

Robert Storheau, the current proprietor is closely or distantly related to most of his regulars and the majority of them are the descendants of the patrons his great-grandfather welcomed and served in his tavern.

Spa and Creppe (in the case of Creppe even more) live in two worlds. On the one hand, there is the "modern world" of the late 1500s and early 1600s. Well to do people have started coming for the curing waters of the various Spa sources. Spa is totally focused, or is at least in appearance, on the outside world. Money is coming in and an elite is starting to form. It can boast of having several hotels and good restaurants. These establishments cater to the rich people called Bobelins. During the 'season' the Bobelins act as if they own the town. They come to be cured of a variety of true or imaginary ailments, but they come mainly because . . . . it is the thing to do. The people of Creppe greatly share in this prosperity as they supply all the help.

On the other hand, Spa and again to a greater extent Creppe are still very deeply tied to the roots going back to the area's origins. It is this trait that made the Ban[17] de Spa such fertile ground for the Burning Times.

The newly established elite in Spa looks down their noses at the people from Creppe. As far as the people from Creppe are concerned, they are considered so stupid, by both the Bobelins and the Spadois, that anyone can discuss anything in front of them without any fear that they will be understood. The Crepplians are not overly perturbed by his as they have turned the situation in their favor. The Crepplians figure that if people think you are stupid enough, they are not going to be careful about what they say in front of you. And if people say everything in front of you . . . . you end up knowing everything that is going on.

The Bobelins stay in their "fancy" (as compared to the rest of Spa) hotels, eat in their "fancy" restaurants, drink water from the Sulphur

---

[17] Ban (Example Ban de Spa): A territory belonging to a Lord but run by a court of justice made up of a mayor and seven aldermen. Today it would be called in French an "Arrondissement" or a District in English.

smelling water of the Pouhon, drop names, enjoy being served hand and foot by the 'peasants' from Creppe, but they will never, never, never wander outside of the few streets they considered "proper".

And this is fine with Robert Storheau and his patrons.

## CHAPTER 13
## 13th December 1599
## Evening

As Remacle reaches the tavern, a small group of five men huddled together at the table closest to the fireplace are being particular noisy. These are the voices Remacle could here at a distance. All four of them . . . . five with Remacle . . . . have been close friends since childhood. They meet here as often as they can to enjoy not only the warmth of the strong fire burning in the fireplace but also the warmth of the geniever as it trickles down their throats.

Paschal, the eldest, works at the Hola Forge. Like many of the forge workers, he often talks about leaving Spa for Sweden where a handful of ironmasters have already immigrated with their families and knowledge. His friends, however, know Paschal does a lot of talking and very little moving. In ten years Paschal will still be sitting at the same table and still talking about leaving for Sweden.

Lubin, Paschal's cousin and brother-in-law, is considered short in an area where being tall usually does not go beyond five feet. When Gilles, who is a little over five feet two is out walking with his friends, he stands out like a giant. He finds being tall very gratifying because it makes him very popular with the girls. He is as silent as the others are rowdy. The type of person no one notices. He has come back from working in the mines in Germany, which of course, is the reason Paschal is again talking about leaving.

The fourth and last of the group is Leonard, who is in charge of the stables at one of the big houses. He has a long thin face, and a pointed nose. He is trying to grow a beard. Trying is the key word here because the results are anything except successful.

As Remacle enters the tavern, the cold to warm contrast stings his face. He spots the proprietor balancing a Stornheau's special in one hand and a jug of beer in the other, while making his way towards a Franciscan monk sitting near the fireplace. The monk is sitting quietly, at the end of the same table as Remacle's friends, staring into the fire and seemingly far away from the riotous atmosphere reigning around him. His hood is pulled well over his head hiding most of his face except for his Roman nose. When Storheau places the food and drink in front of him, he simply nods once and starts eating without a word.

"Salut, Robert!" shouts Remacle shouting over the buzzing noise of the tavern, with a wave of the hand. "How's business?"

Robert stops, looks towards the voice, smiles and waves back. "Your friends will be happy to see you, they keep asking me for you. We thought you didn't like beer or geniever anymore," he says walking toward Remacle with an outstretched hand. "What happened to you? Is that why we haven't seen you in well over a week? Oh, that looks bad."

"Robert, you cannot imagine what I went through last week. I was viciously attacked by a shapeshifting witch with long pointed fingernails. Can you take a few minutes off and come sit with us?"

"A shapeshifter? Here in the Ban de Spa? Yes, of course, I'll join you. Give me a moment. My cousin Colin is here. I'll ask him to give a hand to the apprentice. I'll have him bring us geniever too, on the house."

"Thank you, Robert, I do appreciate this," says Remacle putting his hand on the proprietor's shoulder. "I truly need to have your advice concerning what happened. It was so horrible." Remacle unconsciously touches his cheeks mumbling, "Don't worry, Robert. I am OK. Still in shock, however."

"Hey, Remacle! Where have you been?" shouts Lubin. "I told Storheau, the other day, you didn't like his geniever anymore. It's been a long time, Remacle. What . . . . " and his next words remain suspended in midair as he looks closely at his friend's face. "What happened to you? You are all scratched up. These scratches are healing, but they are still very visible. Ugly!"

The others at the table follow Lubin's gaze, and soon they are surrounding Remacle asking all types of questions.

"Did you have an accident?"

"When did this happen?"

"Why didn't you let us know?"

"Let's wait for Robert He's going to join us and he is bringing some geniever on the house. I don't feel strong enough to repeat the story several times."

"You, Remacle? You don't feel strong? I can't believe it. Everyone knows you are as strong as an ox."

With the appropriate look of weakness and despair, Remacle sits down. "Nice of you to say that, Paschal. But really, I have gone to hell and back. I never want to go through something like this again."

The monk drops his fork. His hood slips back

a little, revealing his steel blue eyes, as he leans down to pick it up. He and Remacle lock eyes. "Pray for me brother. I was attacked by a shapeshifter. Look at the shape I am in." The monk doesn't say a word, but nods once.

"What? A shapeshifter? Here in the Ban? Let me look at your wounds." Says Leonard as he gets up to get a good look at Remacle's wounds who is now sitting down. The light from the hearth gives Remacle a ruddier complexion than usual which makes him look even worse. His right eye is still swollen and some crust can still be seen along the deep and very noticeable scratches that run down his cheeks. The gash on his head is well on its way to healing but is not nice to see. Remacle winces as Leonard comes too close. "Don't touch that side of my head. You have no idea in how much pain I am." To be fair, even without taking into consideration the newly missing front teeth, his face is badly bruised.

At this point Robert arrives with the geniever. "You haven't started telling them what happened, have you? I want to hear the whole story.

Paschal puts his hand on his friend's arm and says, "Remacle, what happened to you? We are your friends," he says pointing to Robert and the others. "We have a right to ask you for details. Whatever happened is serious. I have never seen you in this state."

Remacle face takes on a painful expression as he looks seriously at each friend . . . . one after the other. "I cannot express in words how heartwarming it is to know that I have friends like you. I do need to talk to you. However, I don't feel strong to talk about it right now. Maybe I will after a couple of geniever, but not right now. Ok?"

Paschal nods and looks towards the others. "Look, it is clear the man has gone through a lot. If he doesn't feel strong enough to talk about it right now, we have to accept it."

Robert, stands up and with his index pointing towards the table, makes a circle indicating to his cousin he has to bring another round of geniever.

Contrary to their usual habits, the friends are silent.

When the geniever arrives, Robert asks pointblank, "Remacle, you told me as you came in that you had been attacked by a shapeshifter. Tell us what happened. We can't help you if we don't know what happened."

"I was attacked by a witch who transformed herself into a wild animal. A wild animal! What am I saying? She transformed herself into a gargoyle."

The monk stops eating and turns his head towards Remacle.

"I was talking to her. And you know, I like women and women like me. How could I know I was dealing with a witch? Suddenly, in front of my eyes, this woman turns into a wolf. No, not exactly a wolf. What I said before. More like a Gargoyle. She did have the teeth of a wolf. Claws like a cat. And the noise she made was like a bird. I have never seen this before."

"What happened next?" asks Leonard.

"Don't interrupt the man. Can't you see the state he is in?" retorts Robert. "Ambroise, another here!"

"She jumped on me with her claws out. I tried to defend myself, but I could not. This thing was so strong! It wasn't a woman any more. Her claws dug into the flesh of my cheeks. I screamed. That's when she . . . .er. . . I mean it . . . . threw its whole weight on me. I fell, I hit my head and I lost consciousness."

I heard about something like that happening in Pepinster not too long ago,"says Lubin. "I remember being told it happened to the cousin of my sister-in-law, but . . . . but . . . . but . . . ."

"But what?"

"Well, this changing into a wild animal is strange. I don't mean it can't happen, although I have never seen it or heard about it. Except, of course, for that one time in Pepinster and, I have to admit, I didn't get many details."

Remacle looks at him in shock. "What exactly are you trying to say?"

"Don't get me wrong. I am not saying it's not possible. I am just saying that I don't really know about these things."

"Well, Lubin, one day it may happen to you. When it does you will know a lot about it. If you have nothing to say, except what you don't know, then don't say anything." Lubin looks totally chastised by Remacle's answer and is relieved to see Ambroise arriving with the geniever.

"I swear on all the saints who have a statue in our parish church that the witch turned into a wild animal and then attacked me. Also, I am going to tell you one more thing. Not only, do we all know the witch in question, but she is going to burn for what she did to me. I will see to that. And whether she changed into a gargoyle or not, it makes no difference. She deserves to be garroted and burned."

Remacle's friends look at each other and then silently stare off in another direction. The only exception is the monk who is openly staring at Remacle.

"I, of course," continues Remacle "went to see Father de Lazaar immediately about this witch we all know and. . . ."

"What?" interrupts Leonard. "Did you say we all know her? Are you sure?"

"Of course, I am sure, Leonard. Do you want to hear the story or not?"

Leonard nods.

"Alright. So, as we are all aware, if anyone knows about witches, it's a priest. He opened my eyes to so much." He stops to drink his geniever and they all do the same. "So, I spoke to Father de Lazaar," says Remacle in a whisper and looking at each one individually, "and he explained a lot to me about this witch business. He talked to me about 'The Hammer'

"What hammer?" asks Lubin.

"You know. The Hammer they use to try witches.

Gilles, Lubin, Leonard, Paschal and Robert all look at each other. "What do you mean by a hammer, Remacle. How can they use a hammer to find out if a person is a witch?" asks Gilles.

"It's not a real hammer," answers Remacle in an exasperated tone. "It's a law book used to try witches. Did Ambroise forget to bring the geniever, Robert?"

"No, no, Ambroise, bring some more geniever," Robert calls out to his apprentice. Turning towards Remacle he says, "I have heard about that hammer but it has another name, doesn't it? It has a Latin name. It's a mali something or the other."

"Malleus Maleficarum."

"That's it"

"Ah, here is the geniever! Now, this book, according to Father de Lazaar, not only explains how to go about trying witches, but also explains how the witches go about their business."

"Really? All this is in a book?" asks Paschal unable to hide how impressed he is. "Do you remember anything specific."

"Well, I didn't read it personally, since I cannot read any more than you can, Paschal. But I do remember something about how a witch goes about killing animals and especially cattle.

"It's all in that book?"

"According to Father de Lazaar, it is. And I don't see why I should doubt a holy man. Especially, one we all know."

"Ok." Says Leonard, "So, how do they bewitch cattle?"

"The way they bewitch cattle is the way they bewitch men."

"Er . . . . and that is?"

"It doesn't matter if they are dealing with men or cattle. All they have to do is touch them, give them a certain look or . . . ., " and here Remacle stops for effect . . . . "by placing a charm near or under the threshold of a barn or door. And sometimes, they turn into wild animals and attack you with their claws."

Gloating over the apparent success he is having with his friends, the herder gestures them to get closer to him. "The witch will burn at Jonkeu. And I will even tell you her name. It is Françoise Mathieu, the widow of Henry Hurlet of Creppe."

Silence.

The monk's hand stops in midair as he reaches for a piece of bread. He turns slightly on the bench to get a good look at the man they all call Remacle.

As if by a common accord, all five men start talking at the same time.

"Françoise?"

"Are you sure it was her Remacle? Maybe it was somebody who looks like her."

"No, you can't mean Henry's wife."

"Françoise can't be a witch. I cannot believe this"

"No, no."

"Well," says Remacle looking around for Ambroise, "You forgot the geniever again, Ambroise!" The apprentice looks at the proprietor of the tavern for confirmation. Storheau gives him a discreet nod. "So, as I was saying, if I say she is a witch then she is. It will teach her to think I am not good enough for her."

The monk gets up and bumps Remacle's shoulder as he passes. Remacle looks up and for a split second the two men stare into each other's eyes. Remacle nods an "It's alright" and turns back toward his friends.

## CHAPTER 14
## 26ᵗʰ January 1600
## Late afternoon

Two months have passed since that terrible November day when Remacle attacked her on the road to Creppe. Her nose has healed but she still has problems breathing sometimes. All the bruising went through all the usual colors and finally disappeared. Well, almost disappeared. She can still see traces of them.

Jules's ribs are still hurting him sometimes but luckily his back has not been hurt. That was Mam's greatest worry.

They have not seen hide nor hair of Remacle in Creppe since then and by common accord, they decided to drop the matter. Or as Jules says, "Drop the matter, not forget it."

Today is, one of those beautiful cold but sunny winter days. Françoise leaves the Nizet's house with a basket full of material, old dresses Madame says she no longer wants. There's a nice blue one she can cut to make Mam a new kirtle. If she is extra careful cutting it, she thinks she might have enough to make herself a bodice, too. Something different for special occasions. The burgundy one is so beautiful. Of all of Madame's dresses, it's the simplest and easiest to alter. She would like to keep it for herself. All it needs is to be shortened and taken in here and there. At the very bottom of the basket is a prune dress, Mam's favorite color. None of these are new, but even Madame's old clothes look new. She can't wait to start altering everything.

Both Mam and Jules have told her several times to put her mourning clothes aside. She has been dressed in mourning since the deaths of Henry and her baby. Mam says black is not going to bring either one back so it is useless to go around in such a sad color. Françoise is young and needs color in her life. She feels a little guilty about it, but mourning is in the heart not in the clothes.

Her in-laws don't know what to do to make up for the nightmare she went through in November. Françoise doesn't understand why they feel like that. It's neither their fault nor hers. It happened and that's all there is to it.

She walks up Rue du Marché in the direction of the new Town Hall built in 1590. A group of people are already gathering at the Perron waiting for the Town Crier. Françoise cranes her neck in the direction of the Church to see if she can see him. No sight of him. It is still too early. She has a little time in front of her to take a walk in the market further on and look at all the lovely things. It doesn't matter if she misses the town crier. She can always catch up with him a little further down when he makes his next stop.

She turns back up the Rue du Marché to visit

the market. The Hurlets hardly ever buy anything in Spa. In fact, most of the Crepplians make and repair their own things. But coming here, like this, is a treat for her. Although the market is mostly for the citizens of Spa and the visitors, she enjoys greeting a few of the sellers from Creppe.

An elderly man with a beard, dressed in dull red and a black sleeveless jacket walks up to her. Françoise smiles at him. It's Walter. Hanchoulle's uncle.

"Well, little Françoise. Finished for the day?" Walter beams as he looks at her. Henry had been a favorite of his. When Henry died, he transferred his affection onto her.

Françoise nods her head. "I am. What do you have today Walter?" she asks pointing at the basket he is carrying.

"Eggs. I'm on my way to see Father de Lazaar. He asked me to bring him some. I have a couple of wild rabbits here," he adds lifting up his right hand. "Freshly killed. Maybe they'll interest him too."

## The Drop of the Hammer

Francoise smiles and wishes him luck.

"Françoise Mathieu," cries out another man. She turns around and sees Poncelet standing by his cart. His cart is full of baskets. Most are still full with the goods he is bringing to market. On the ground are a handful of empty baskets that need mending.

"Hello, Monsieur Poncelet. How are you today? Expecting a good sale?" asks Françoise with a big smile.

He points at five of the baskets on the ground and says, "Are you on your way back to Creppe?"

"Yes, as soon as I hear the latest news from the crier. Why?

"Could you stop by Louis's home and ask him to come pick these up. They need mending."

"I'll be glad to tell him, Monsieur Poncelet. I am sure he'll come as soon as he can."

Françoise looks back and sees that the crowd around the Perron has grown and decides it is time to go back if she wants to hear the Town Crier.

She turns quickly and bumps hard into a tall

hooded Franciscan monk. The force of the collision causes her to lose her footing and she falls down on her back side. Her basket has gone flying off to one side and the dresses spill out.

She immediately gets up and starts picking up the dresses. "I'm sorry, mon Révérend Père. I am terribly clumsy. Please excuse me." Françoise keeps her eyes down and hopes that by addressing him as Reverend Father he will overlook her clumsiness.

Unexpectedly, another pair of hands helps her gather the spilled goods. A large, strong hand takes her by the arm and gently helps her to her feet.

The monk's action embarrasses Françoise. Her eyes travel up from his hands to his face. She catches her breath when she reached his eyes. His steel blue eyes seem to go right through her. Her heart begins to beat strongly. She clenches her damp palms.

Flustered, she stammers her excuses. "I-I- please let me t-t-ake the basket. S-s-so sorry. So sorry. I-I- shouldn't. Excuse me, F-f-father. Really, I don't know...."

"It's nothing my child," the monk says interrupting her. "It's nothing. I too should watch where I am going. Please forgive me."

And without another word, he turns around and walks towards the other end of the market.

Françoise feels the heat in her cheeks as her face turns red. She curls her hands tightly around the basket handle and watches him walk away. Françoise pinches her lips together embarrassed by the strong feelings stirring deep inside of her. "Well, girl," she says to herself, "have you lost your mind? He's a monk. A holy man. How dare you?"

In spite of her harsh self-admonition, she looks longingly in the direction he has taken.

Françoise turns and runs towards the Town Hall.

When she reaches it, she joins the other people waiting for the Town Crier

Across the square, she sees Walter and Father de Lazaar talking in front of the church. Walter seems to be having luck with the rabbits because she can see Father de Lazaar handling them and nodding.

Françoise sits down on one of the perron steps. From where she is, she can see the Town Crier walking briskly up the street.

When he reaches Father de Lazaar, he stops to talk to him. Whatever it is they are talking about, it seems important. The Town Crier keeps referring to the parchment he is holding. Father de Lazard waves Walter away and from his gestures seems to be telling him to come back later.

Across the square she sees a dark-haired foreigner. It is clear he is not a Bobelin, but an artist. He has no interest in the Town Crier and, in fact, might not even understand him. At the moment he is drawing the mill across the square. The last time she saw him was at least 4 years ago, if not more. Someone told her he was from Italy. Françoise doesn't quite know where Italy is. The few times they spoke to each other, he was always very nice to her. He told her once that his name was Cantagallina. A strange name!

She had to ask him to repeat it several times before being able to repeat it. When she said she didn't know where Italy was, he told her it was shaped like a boot.

He was making fun of her, of course. She knew that and hadn't taken it badly. Even now, she laughs when she thinks about it. How can a country be shaped like a boot?

The Town Crier leaves the priest and begins to beat his drum. He walks past the perron in the direction of the water mill with a brisk military step. The crowd gathered at the perron follow him.

Françoise hopes he has interesting news today. Because she comes to Spa on a regular basis, it is her job to bring the news back to the others in Creppe.

She settles a short distance from him on the low wall in front of the mill.

Pierre Colson, carries out his duties as Town Crier with all the dignity he can muster. He is dressed almost like the mayor and, is probably, thinks Françoise, better known than the mayor. Colson plants his feet apart as he stands in front of the mill facing the people. He clears his voice loudly. A small group of young curists on the side continue to talk loudly.

Annoyed, Pierre looks at them from head to toe, evidently not caring if they see that he disapproves of them or not. And says loudly, "Gentlemen! Gentlemen! Your attention please. A little respect here, please."

Embarrassed the young men stop talking and give him their undivided attention.

Pierre Colson takes a moment to silently look them over before clearing his voice again.

"Hear ye! Hear ye!", he begins in his strong voice.

"Let it be known that the Governor of Franchimont has proclaimed the departure of all beggars from Spa, Marché, Polleur and Theux. No exception will be tolerated. They have forty-eight hours to leave the area. There is an outbreak of a fever in Polleur and no beggar will be tolerated in the area. If by chance, beggars remain, they will be jailed until further notice."

A murmur travels among the listeners. An epidemic is always a matter of great concerns.

"The governor of Franchimont has also requested a call for witnesses. Françoise Mathieu, the widow of Henry Hurlet de Creppe is accused of the crime of witchcraft. The court is interested in any information that will determine the seriousness of the crime committed by the suspect".

Françoise's head snaps up. She gets up from the low wall, chills running down her back.

"Primo, all rumors concerning the accused, Françoise Mathieu, widow of Henry Hurlet de Creppe are already being taken by the Sergeant-at-arms."

Françoise's knees buckle under her.

Her fingers become numb.

She falls back down.

"Secondo, as well as any details specifically concerning the vicious attack perpetuated by the accused on Remacle Le Rosy of Creppe on the road leading to Creppe on 29th November 1599."

Françoise's throat becomes dry.

Her heart pounds in her ears.

Her breathing becomes difficult.

Hot tears run down her face.

"Tercio, any other suspicious action on her part, especially concerning any acts of witchcraft, and shapeshifting have to be reported. To those who have information, let me stress that it is your duty to inform the authorities as soon as possible."

Françoise's vision blurs.

"Witnesses are requested to contact the Sergeant-at-arms at the Spa Town Hall as soon as possible."

Weakness and dizziness overcome her.

As in a dream she sees the Town Crier leave the square and the crowd disperses.

The drumming echoes in her head as if she were in an empty cavern.

In spite of the cold January weather, her body burns with fever and drops of perspiration roll down her face.

## The Drop of the Hammer

The last thing she remembers before plunging into darkness is her basket slipping out of her hands.

A few minutes later, a half an hour or perhaps an hour later, she comes to. An unpleasant taste of metal lingers in her mouth.

Upon opening her eyes, she sees Walter's familiar face.

"Are you alright, Pichounette[18]? Do you want me to take you home? My horse and cart are ready."

"Thank you, Walter. I'm fine. There's no need to take me home." She gets up stiffly. "I must have tripped on something. I'll be fine."

"Françoise, I can neither write nor read, but there is nothing wrong with my hearing. I heard the Town Crier as clearly as you did. And don't tell me it didn't affect you. I saw how pale you became. You are still very pale and you look uncertain on your feet I wouldn't bet a jug of beer that you are able to walk from here to that tree over there without falling."

---

[18] Pichounette is Walloon for 'my little girl'.

"No, Walter, I'm fine, It's. . . . it's. . . . it's. . . ."

"It's that your reaction is normal. I don't know how I would react in your place. What I do know is that you have to go back to Creppe as soon as possible."

"I didn't attack Remacle. It's the other way around. He attacked me. And look at what he did to Jules. What am I going to do?"

"I know you are innocent. Don't forget that it is my nephew who helped Mam take Jules home. We all saw the state he was in . . . . the state you were in that day. You are innocent."

"Thank you for believing me."

"Now, how about if you give me that basket, take my arm and walk down to the market where my horse and cart are?"

## CHAPTER 15
## 26ᵗʰ January 1600
## Late afternoon

Although, Françoise never complains about covering the distance from Spa to Creppe on foot, today she is very grateful to be sitting in Walter's cart. The even swaying of the cart and the regular clop-clop of the horse as it pulls them along calm her.

"We are almost there," says Walter cheerfully. "You are almost home. I can see the rooftop of the Hurlet farm."

"Yes, me too. Thank you again for offering me a ride. I am so happy I accepted."

"It was my pleasure. Whenever . . . .Whoa,

Suzette, Whoa. Look over there!" says Walter pointing towards the farm house

"Where? What am I looking for?"

"There beneath the trees. Several horses that don't belong to Creppe."

"Do you think . . . . ?"

"I don't know. What I do know, is that I am coming in with you."

"W-w-what's going to happen?"

"No idea. Just stay calm."

To their right are a couple of soldiers watching them. They neither intercept them nor talk to them.

"Who are they, Walter?"

"Men from the Marquisat of Franchimont on official business by the looks of them. Stay calm Françoise, and whatever happens don't argue with them."

Walter brings his horse and cart as close to the front door as possible.

No one stops them.

He stops his cart.

Gets down.

Helps Françoise down.

Reaches for her basket and gives it to her.

They enter the farmhouse. Everything done calmly and normally.

Inside, Mam is sitting on the bench near the fireplace sobbing. Jules is pacing the floor, his fists rolled up in tight balls. His usual calm face is red. His eyes teeming with anger.

Something is wrong. Very wrong. Françoise doesn't have to ask what is happening. She knows. She heard the Town Crier.

When Jules sees her, he stops pacing and spreads out his arms to gather her close to his chest. Françoise looks from Jules to Mam and back to Jules. "I was in town. The Town Crier is saying horrible things about me. They are asking for witnesses. I didn't do anything. I am not a witch. They say I attacked Remacle."

"I know, child, I know."

There's a movement behind her She hears a

man clearing his voice. Françoise spins around and comes face-to-face with three officers from the Château. One of them comes forward and says, "Are you Françoise Mathieu, the widow of Henry Hurlet de Creppe?"

"Yes, Monsieur," she answers in a voice barely above a whisper.

The officer turns towards his Sergeant-at-arms and stretches out his hand. The Sergeant hands him a parchment. "In the name of the Governor of the Marquisat of Franchimont, I arrest you Françoise Mathieu." He then unrolls the parchment and reads:

"Today, on the 26th day of January in the year of our Lord 1600, I, Thomas Bastin, Souverain Officer of the Marquisat at the Franchimont Fortress, mandated by Charles de Linden, Governor of the Marquisat of Franchimont, hereby duly arrest you, Françoise Mathieu, widow of Henry Hurlet de Creppe for the accumulated crimes of, but not necessarily restricted to these indicated below:

(1) Attack on the person of Remacle le Rosy on the 29[h] day of November of the year of our Lord 1599, causing him bodily harm.

(2) On the general charge of being a witch and shapeshifter.

Moreover, the arrest being immediate, you are to be brought to the Boverie[19], the seigneurial prison, located at the Marché in the Ban de Verviers. You will stay there until you are transferred to Fortress de Franchimont."

---

[19] "In those times there was a house located in the Ban de Verviers called *La Boverie*. It served as the Seigneurial prison. It was for people who were confined there by the court [...] and their stay could not last longer than three days. After this period, the prisoners had to be transferred to the Franchimont Fortress. From that moment on it was the Souverain Officer of the Marquisat who was responsible for them." Translated from French.
La Réforme Protestante á Verviers aux XVII siècle. G.Brasseur, E Fairon, P. Gaston, Dr. Hans, Eug. Poswick, Jos Thisquen, A. Weber.

## CHAPTER 16
## 28ᵗʰ January 1600
## La Boverie

Françoise is walking up the road to Winamplanche. The full moon lights her way. She is alone. The night is silent.

Silent.

Except for a faint beating sound somewhere in the distance.

"Where is it coming from?"

"What is it?"

She stops at a fork in the road, undecided about which one to take. Both are identical. So, does it make a difference which one she decides to take? Both roads stretch out like twisting ribbons bordered on either side by dark, swaying trees.

Something is wrong. This isn't the road to Winamplanche. There are no forks in the road between Creppe and Winamplanche. Besides the distance between the two villages is not that big, so why has she been walking for so long. She should be in Winamplanche by now. Where is she?

The soles of her feet hurt. Why did she go out bare foot? The road is full of jagged stones cutting her feet with each step she takes.

Deep down she knows she should turn around and go home, but there are wolves behind her. Their wild smell reaches her nostrils. She can't see them, but she knows they are there waiting for her steps to falter.

There is something else. Another reason she cannot turn around and go home. What is it? She has to get somewhere. Where? Over there. Where is there?

Françoise longs to be home in front of the

fireplace. Warm. Safe. What good is it to think about going home now, when she knows she has to continue. Something up ahead is pulling her forward. It controls her every move and her every thought. Only one thing really matters. One step after the other, towards whatever it is waiting ahead.

Up ahead and to the left there is something glowing in a field. It doesn't look like the bonfires the villagers light during the summer feasts. The beating sound is closer. It must be coming from there. The glow of the fire and the regular beating sound completely dominate her. Invisible threads pull her into its direction.

There's a narrow path that she hadn't immediately seen leading from the road up into the field and towards the glowing light. It isn't very wide, just enough for one person. As she walks up the path, the light grows stronger and the beating louder.

She walks quicker. She needs to get there.

Breathless.

Need to get there.

# The Drop of the Hammer

The force of the strange pull makes her walk quicker and quicker. Her feet hurt and she would like to stop for a while. Can't do that. The constant beat she hears keeps pulling Françoise, pressing her to go quicker and quicker. Françoise starts running.

From one moment to the other, the invisible threads pulling her along stop. Darkness engulfs her and she loses all sense of where she is or what she is doing. Darkness.

When Françoise comes to, she is no longer walking on the path, but lying in a clearing. The bonfire must be close because she can feel its heat. She hears the flames crackling. There is also something else that sounds like people murmuring. She opens her eyes. Why is she so close to the fire? The brightness of the fire hurts her eyes, and Françoise puts her hand up to shield them. The murmuring is still going on but it is much closer now.

There's a group of people walking in a circle. Moving always at the same steady, rhythmic pace.

What she had first taken for a bonfire is light

coming from many torches a group of people are holding up high in the air. The torches light up their faces and she recognizes many people she knows from Creppe and Spa. Here and there are a few unknown faces.

Her heart starts beating loudly. The more she watches them, the more frighten she becomes. It's difficult to focus, because the scene changes constantly. One moment, she can see them from one side and the next moment from the other side. At other times she is looking at them from above.

The murmuring has stopped.

The people gathered in the field are now silently walking along a single circular path of a stone labyrinth. Not a sound is made. Not a word escapes from their lips.

She is sure she is close enough for them to see her, but they don't seem to see her. She watches this strange procession for what seems to be a long time. Unexpectedly, one of the men holding a particularly bright torch cries out and points at her.

They have seen her.

The strange procession stops and within seconds they are all standing around her, hatred pouring out from their eyes.

The murmuring starts again, but it's not the same kind of murmur as before. Before it was as if they were reciting something now it is the murmur of people talking in low voices. At first it is barely audible and she can't make out the individual sounds. They are pointing at her. They are talking about her. Soon she is able to make out individual words, but not entire sentences.

Witch.

Henry Hurlet's widow.

Oneux.

Remacle.

Jonkeu.

Burn.

Burn.

The crowd is walking in a circle again, but now she is in the middle of the of the circle. Some of them start spitting at her.

An old woman shakes a fist menacingly. A little boy is making faces and sticks his tongue out at Françoise. They scream at her in shrill voices full of hatred.

"Witch!"

"Burn her. She made a pact."

"She must have the mark."

"Kill her!"

"Don't let the Devil's bride live."

"Burn her!"

Françoise puts her hands over her ears to block out the sounds and hatred coming from the people circling around her. Her feet buckle under her. She is falling. Moments before hitting the ground, rough hands hold her up and drag her to the center of the field where she is thrown onto the ground.

Françoise tries to get up.

A sharp pain in her side stops her from breathing normally.

Panting, she finally manages to stand up on her

own two feet.

She looks around at the people who are still around her, but now they have moved back a little. They don't seem to be thinking individually, it's more as a block response to some given order.

Remacle Le Rosy walks out of the crowd and floats up to her.

Françoise has problems focusing on him. One moment he is practically upon her and the next he is part of the crowd. Each time he comes towards her, it is from another direction. She swings around to avoid him. His smell, whenever he comes near her, overwhelms her and makes her gag.

The herder, suddenly, swoops down on her.

She wants to scream.

No sound comes out of her throat.

Remacle reaches towards her and starts fondling her breasts with his left hand while holding her tightly by the waist with the other.

She tries to free herself but the more she fights him off, the more his hands linger and explore her.

The need to scream becomes intolerable.

No sound comes from her lips.

Her breathing becomes rapid and her legs turn to jelly. Her legs buckle under her

Remacle holds her up, grabs her by the hair and presses his mouth to hers.

Her stomach heaves and she pushes him away.

This excites Remacle even more, just as it had on the road from Spa to Creppe in November.

He puts his rough hand behind her head and forces her face up towards his.

Françoise tries to keep her lips shut.

He manages to part them and slides his tongue in, exploring her mouth as he had earlier explored her body with his hands.

Françoise can take it no longer. She puts all the strength that is left in her into one last push and wrenches away from him. She falls backwards and hits the ground. She starts to retch and is on the point of passing out when a pail of water is emptied over her.

Françoise screams and looks about her. The

now empty and discarded pail is on the ground near her. Drops of water drip from her wet hair and her wet clothes cling to her.

She looks around and there no longer is any sign of Remacle. A feeling of dread engulfs her. Is she awake? Is she dreaming? Doesn't matter. Either way, she knows she can no longer bear it. Françoise feels her body sliding down to the ground. Her head rests on her hands. She starts weeping and crying out loud. "No more. Please, no more. Either wake me up or let them kill me, but don't, don't let it go on. No more. No more."

She senses rather than sees a figure kneeling beside her. Françoise's body tenses, unsure of what is going to happen next. She expects pain or Remacle's obscene groping---- instead her face is touched by soft, gentle fingers.

A strong smell of lavender fills the air and a strange peaceful feeling comes over her. In spite of what Remacle and the crowd have done to her, Françoise feels safe. Looking up she sees a young woman kneeling by her side. She instantly knows who it is.

"Jehenne! Jehenne Anseau!". Françoise remembers when Jehenne was burned for witchcraft. It wasn't so long ago. Jehenne was smiling at her. Françoise wipes tears away from her cheeks and smiles back.

"Do not fear little Françoise. Do not fear."

"I'm so scared, Jehenne."

"Don't give up. They can't do anything to you."

"But I'm so scared."

"You are strong, little one."

"No, Jehenne, I'm not strong. I'm not as strong as you are."

"The strength is there, Françoise. Trust me. All you have to do is ground yourself and the strength will move up your spine like the strength a tree extracts from the soil."

Jehenne puts out her hand again and caresses Françoise's cheek. "I remember you, Françoise. I will always remember you. You of all the people who were out there that day . . . . you are the only one who cried when they executed me. Of all the people there you were the only one who cared. Don't give up. You are not alone. Not alone"

Françoise puts out her hand but only meets empty space. Jehenne is gone.

Françoise swings around as another figure comes out of the crowd. He is holding a torch straight in front of him. She cannot see who it is. "Who are you?", she cries out. "Leave me alone."

The man holding the torch starts circling her like the crowd had done before. "Who are you?" she asks again bringing her knees up to her chin.

Instead of answering, he starts laughing. The crowd has moved back to clear the passage for him and now they join him. Their laughter becomes something solid, like a snake slowly wrapping itself around her.

The man holding the torch slowly lowers it and reveals his face to her. Françoise recognizes Father de

Lazaar, the priest from Spa. He is looking at her in the same cold way he had in Spa when the town crier announced she was accused of witchcraft.

He doesn't bother answering her. From time to time, he steps closer and plunges the torch towards her. Each time he stops just far enough not to touch her with the flames.

The crowd starts to chant. The sound itself frightens Françoise, but when she realizes what they are chanting she is petrified.

"Burn! Burn! Burn!" The quicker they chant the more Father de Lazaar plunges the torch towards her.

She begins to shake. She puts her hands up to her ears and starts screaming. This time the screams come out releasing all her fear.

Darkness.

She wakes up in the damp, cold cell at La Boverie.

Alone.

Frightened.

Frantic.

It was a dream after all.

The dream has exhausted her and she nods off as a gentle voice consoles her, "Don't give up, Françoise. They can't do anything to you. You are strong, little one."

## CHAPTER 17
## 15th February 1600
## Late morning

Roland de Bolland stops pacing and stands at the window of Count Charles' private apartment in the Hoogstraeten Mansion. His right hand beats a nervous tattoo on his thigh.

It has been snowing hard all week and today is no exception. From this second story window, he has a splendid view of the snow-covered Rue Isabelle. He can hear a group of young boys yelling and pushing each other down the street as they throw snow balls at each other. A hurried estafette riding a military charger comes galloping up Rue Isabelle. The boys scatter on either side of the road.

# The Drop of the Hammer

In the distance, he can hear, Saint Nicolas' bells filling Brussels with its joyful sounds. The magnificent view and the bells, however, do little to give Roland the peace he so badly needs.

"You know Roland, I am always happy to see you. However, today, you haven't come alone," says a middle-aged man sitting in an armchair behind him.

Roland turns around, puzzled at what the older man is saying. "Not alone? I came with no one."

"I agree. You came with no one but you haven't come alone either. You have come with a problem. And this problem is serious enough to convince you to travel all the way to Brussels in spite of the snow and the unexpected and particular late cold weather we are having."

Roland de Bolland stares at his friend Charles de Lalaing. Suddenly, he bursts out laughing. "How do you know that, Charles? In my profession you learn how to hide your thoughts and feelings. I am told I am very good at it. I am certain no one can know or even guess what I am thinking." Bolland crosses the room in three easy strides and sits down in the armchair opposite his friend.

"Don't worry, Roland," answers Charles as he leans towards Roland. "You are a master at hiding your thoughts. However, I know you too well. You can't hide anything from me. You know that."

"I can't?" Roland purposefully puts on an exaggerated expression of indignation on his face. "Hmmm, this is not only serious, it's very serious. Here is the High Magistrate of Liège being told to his face that he is not able to hide his thoughts. This is bad Charles. Maybe you should tell me how you can read me so well."

Charles de Lalaing unsuccessfully tries to suppress a smile from creeping onto his normally stern face. With a gleam in his eyes, he says, "No, I should not and I certainly will not. It's my secret." Charles sits back in his chair and looks across at Roland, "When did we first meet?"

Roland smiles, looks up at the ceiling and thinks. "Hmm, I believe twenty-seven years ago this month. Yes, in 1573. I was a young boy of eight." He lowers his eyes and looks at his friend with deep affection. "Yes, on that day twenty-seven years ago you opened your door and your heart to a very frightened and tearful eight-year-old boy. During all this time you have been my second father and my best friend. Always."

De Laing smiles and returns the look of affection. He nods. "I'll always remember the night your father brought you to my home. But, Roland," he says as he picks up a green Waldglas carafe, "tell me what you think of this new wine from France." He half fills two matching glasses and then fills the rest of the glasses with water from a clear carafe. "Drink up, my friend."

Roland brings the glass up to his nose and takes a deep whiff. He sits back to contemplate the aroma. "Excellent. Excellent. The spices are quite special."

Charles beams. "You think the aroma is

excellent . . . . wait until you taste this Claret."[20]

The Liégeois sips some of the wine and sloshes it around his mouth, swallows it and smiles. "Extremely commendable. An excellent choice. What is that aftertaste? Is it cinnamon?"

"Yes. However, from what I have been told, it is the mixture of the cinnamon and the honey that gives such a magnificent aroma not to mention taste. But, Roland, to get back to our friendship, twenty-seven years is long enough for two persons to get to know each other very well. Deep down in my heart, I know that a big problem is seriously bothering you. Am I right?"

---

[20] Claret is an old term for Bordeaux-style wines. It's meaning has changed over the years and when Count Charles offers Claret to Roland de Bolland, it is not the same thing as what we would call Claret today. Wine drinkers, well into the 17th century followed the old Greek and Roman custom of mixing wine with herbs, spices and honey. The following list of ingredients for a Claret recipe, called "The Lord's Claret", gives a good idea of what Roland smelled when he sniffed the wine: cinnamon, ginger, long pepper, grains of Paradise, cloves, galingale nutmeg, and honey.
Ria. Jansen-Sieben and M. van der Molen Willebrands, *Een notabel boecxken van cokeryen. The first cookbook printed around 1514 in Brussels by Thomas Vander Noot.*

Roland does not answer immediately. He puts his glass down and turns towards Charles. "But how did you know? I don't always come here with problems. So, again, I ask you, how did you know? Surely, such a long friendship gives me the right to insist on an answer, no?"

The count bursts out laughing. "For one, you haven't stopped pacing since you arrived. Secondly, every time you come here with a problem you stand at my window staring at the street as if you had never seen a street before. Thirdly, I know how hard it is for you to leave Liège. You stand at my window, and I know that internally you are cursing because you are not staring at the geometrically adorned columns in the inner courtyard of the Palace of the Prince-Bishops. Last but not least, you are unable to stand still until you find a solution. Am I wrong?"

Roland learns back in his chair and crosses his arms on his chest. He nods. "Very clever. And frightening too."

Charles smiles. "Now that I am so clever and

you are so frightened, maybe you can tell about this problem gnawing at you, Roland."

"Actually, everything is fine," answers Roland soberly.

"And now you are lying to your old friend. There's something nagging you and I want you to talk to me about it," insists Charles in his no-nonsense voice.

Roland silently gets up again and walks to the window.

"Also stop standing at my window," says Charles with his known directness. "In two seconds, your fingers are going to start a tattoo on your thigh, and that makes me nervous. Now, sit," he says sternly pointing at the chair in front of him, "And let me refill your glass."

Roland turns around and smiles at Count Charles. He has always liked this trait in his friend. "It is difficult to hide anything from you, isn't it?" He walks back to his chair and sits down still smiling. "It's true. I need to talk to you. I just don't know how and where to start."

"Oh! Finally, the man is going to talk. I thought he had perhaps come all this way from Liège . . . .in the snow, in the cold . . . . just to admire Rue Isabelle and drink my wine," his friend says dramatically, with a twinkle in his eyes. "As far as starting is concerned, take the advice I have always given you. Start at the beginning."

"It's all those witch trials that are cropping up in the Spa area," says Boland

"Oh, I see. Is the Court of the Inquisition busy earning its keep again?" The count leans back and presses his fingers together forming a steeple.

Roland wets his lips and thinks a moment. "No, not this time. You remember when the Inquisition Court tried Jehenne Anseau?"

"I don't remember the details, but I definitely remember you. You were very upset. Don't think that I don't understand why. If I did not, we would not be the friends we are."

"Charles, each new trial I hear about drives me

crazy. I don't like them. I hate them. I abhor all these witch trials and the endless torturing and sentencing."

"Everybody hates these trials, Roland."

"You are wrong. Not everybody hates the witch trials. Some take great pleasure in them. Even among the people. There's always a personal reason when one person goes out of his or her way to insist that another person is a witch. It is often an excuse to get rid of a bothersome person or simply to get material gains."

"Everyone knows there is always a certain amount of that going on. Not necessarily in witch trials."

"Yes, you are right. About Jehenne, well, I didn't agree with that sentencing, although, it was an open and shut case. Jehenne did not lift a finger to defend herself. It's as if she thoroughly enjoyed provoking them. It's her provocation more than anything else that sentenced her to death."

"Is there another similar case going on now?"

"Yes and no. This particular one, the case I

have in mind, is in the hands of the Court of Justice of Spa and will be tried at the Chateau of Franchimont." Roland stops talking as he realizes he is gesturing uncontrollably. Here with Charles, a man who over the years has become more a father than his own father, he feels free to let his feelings and indignation pour out of his soul.

"Isn't it being tried by the Court of the Inquisition?"

He springs up from his chair and then sits down immediately as his eyes meet Charles'. He crosses his right ankle onto his left leg and closes his eyes. "No, it's being tried as a criminal case."

"Roland, this sounds like a long and complicated story. Let's take another glass of wine. Will you serve this time?" The count pushes the carafes closer to Bolland. "Why don't you tell me how these two cases differ. And remember, I am not a magistrate. Don't use any of those fancy terms only magistrates understand and use between themselves. I have always suspected they do that so that no one else can understand what they are saying. Explain it in simple terms, please."

Roland de Bolland smiles and nods at his old friend. "It is good to be here with you again, Charles. I miss all our talks." He refills their glasses and hands Charles his.

"Thank you. I am all ears, Roland. You have a captive audience." The Count leans forward in his chair, his left hand rolled into a fist resting on his thigh.

"Well, as I said, Jehenne had a very provocative side to her. Strangely enough, the court could not accuse her of a specific crime other than witchcraft. Everything was hearsay, as usual, and the witnesses totally contradicted each other. However, her comportment, in and out of court, caught up with her and, of course, the fact so many relatives of hers, both males and females,[21] . . . . had already been sentenced

---

[21] In French, even in those times, there were specific words to indicate a female or male witch: 'Sorcière' for a woman and 'Sorcier' for a man. I have kept the word 'witch' here to refer to both as in the Middle English used in 1600 the word 'wicche' did not differentiate between the feminine and masculine. The use of the

for witchcraft. Unfortunately, her case . . . .whether one agrees or not . . . . typifies the classical trial against witches."

"Whether one agrees or not? Hmm, but surely, witchcraft is a crime?" Charles says, raising his eyebrows. He leans back in his armchair and toys absentmindedly with his wine-glass on the little table next to him.

"Yes, it is a crime, especially in a case like this where the woman is accused of physically attacking a man. By the way, don't think I don't realize you are playing the devil's advocate, Charles. I happen to know you hate them as much as I do. It is recognized as a crime by both the Church and our Civil Laws. However, no one ever accused Jehenne of killing anyone with violence. Jehenne's reputation sentenced her. I attended the whole trial. I remember how she tried to lead the court into believing her stories. I

---

word 'witch' to refer to a man, however, became less common in Standard English, as words like "wizard" and "warlock" were used more and more often.

remember how she entered the interrogation room at Franchimont. Arrogant. Daring. Mocking. And yet all her witnesses were heresay."

"What about this case which is bothering you so much? How is it different? You said, with Jehenne, you were upset in general. Now, this new case you are talking about does not upset you, it is making you furious. I have often seen you upset, but not furious like this. And by the way, I am not forgetting for one second how touchy you are about the subject."

Roland nods. In a very soft and low voice he answers, "Yes, you are right. I am furious. The situation is very different."

"Roland, I know you don't believe in the existence of witchcraft. I also think you need to be careful with your opinions. You don't want the church to come after you." Charles takes another sip of wine and looks at his friend over the rim of his glass.

Roland covers his face with his hands and rubs his cheeks. In a steady voice tinged with sadness he says, "I believe evil exists. If you tell me witches cause evil, I am unable to prove it is true or not. I don't know. Does their craft have any power? What I do know, is that many people are sentenced for witchcraft who not only do not deserve it, but are innocent of the crimes they are accused of." Roland closes his eyes and sighs. "Charles you say that I have to be careful about my opinions. I agree, if I were anybody else. I am not someone else. I am Roland de Bolland, the High Magistrate of Liège. If I do not react, who will?

## CHAPTER 18
## 15<sup>th</sup> February 1600
## Late morning

Roland begins, "Twenty-seven years ago," and then stops as his voice falters. He squeezes his eyes shut and presses the bridge of his nose with his fingertips. When he opens his eyes again, he continues, "Twenty-seven years ago was the first time I heard the words witch and witchcraft. It was two weeks before my father left me in your care. Aragon, the horse he had given me for my birthday, was lame. I don't remember how it happened, but I remember they said nothing could be done and Aragon had to be destroyed. I loved that horse. I ran away for three days. My father was frantic. He had everybody out searching for me. He told me later he had given precise orders that Aragon was not to be destroyed before I came back because he didn't want me to feel he had done something behind my back. When I came back three days later, I was not alone. I came back with Sasha, a gypsy who had found me wandering and crying in the High Fens. This man fed me and comforted me, and then took back to my father's home.

I remember my father taking me into his arms, tears running down his face. Today, as an adult, I realize how relieved he was to have me back alive and unhurt. But at that moment, I paid no attention to either the pain I had caused him nor his tears. I had so much to tell him. I looked around for Sasha. I saw my gypsy friend walking away towards Aragon's stables as if he had done it a thousand times before. I wiggled out of my father's arms and ran after Sasha.

When I finally caught up with him, he was in the stall with Aragon, kneeling next to Aragon's lame leg, rubbing it with a strange smelly ointment. All the while he was doing this, he was whispering to Aragon in a strange language. The words sounded so beautiful and also so calming. Within twenty-four hours my horse was as good as new."

Roland covers his face with his hands remembering the young boy he had once been. "This man not only saved me, but he also saved my horse whom I loved so much. I . . . . who owed him so much . . . . was unable to offer him any help when they arrested, tortured, and finally burned him at the stake. I was shattered both physically and mentally."

"Roland, don't torture yourself. You were a little child. What could you have done?"

"Sasha found me wandering. He took care of me. He brought me home and saved Aragon. And I was powerless."

Charles nods. "When your father brought you to me, I remember thinking that I had never seen an adult . . . . let alone a young child . . . . in such a devastated state."

"That day the sky fell on me. I remember the

tears rolling down my cheeks as I tried to stop them from taking him away. I clung to the gypsy's clothes and grabbed his hand screaming, *Don't take him away! Don't take him away! Sasha is my friend. Leave him alone.*

Suddenly, Sasha turned around and kneeled in front of me as he had done with Aragon. He spoke to me in his language. I can still hear the sound of his voice and those words I could not understand. This is something I never experienced afterwards. I could not understand those words filling me with inner peace. Something inside of me was taking the words into my heart. He looked me straight in the eyes and nodded. I let go of his hand."

Roland stops talking and the two men sit in silence. The younger man lost in his painful memories and the older one feeling his adopted son's pain, knowing there was nothing he could do or say to help him.

"Why are you bringing this up again, Roland. Why do you torture yourself so much? It has nothing to do with Jehenne's trial, does it?"

Roland shakes his head no. "No, it has nothing to do with Jehenne."

"Tell me exactly what is bothering you," says the Count in a voice both soft and hardly audible.

Roland looks up searchingly into his friend's dark eyes. He shakes his head from left to right slowly. "I do not accept people being sentenced to death for something we cannot prove and . . . . ," Roland pauses for effect, . . . . "may not even exist. Have you read the Malleus Maleficarum?"

"No, don't be insulting. I am a member of the nobility. I have much better things to do. I leave things like that to magistrates with problems." Charles adjusts his large ruff collar with a lot more affectation than necessary. He looks up at his friend and gives him a knowing smile. "Also, from what I hear, it is pretty rough reading. Tell me about it." He picks up his glass and sips the last of the wine.

The "Malleus Maleficarum, the Witches' Hammer, is a guidebook for trials against witches. It is supposed to cover every point in the trials.

Identification. Prosecution. Dispatching. Corporal searches. Dealing with witnesses. You name it, it is in there."

"What do you mean by 'supposed', Roland? Do you mean it doesn't do it?"

Roland places his hands back to back and interlaces his fingers. "In . . . . in my opinion, and it's my opinion only, the book is as stupid as its authors, Heinrich Kramer and James Sprenger. I believe . . . . do you know why they wrote it, Charles?

"No, but I have an idea."

"To silence the many scholars and theologians who either doubted the existence of witches, or regarded such beliefs as superstition. And even more than that, this book was a means of silencing and getting rid of free-thinking people, especially women. Included in their definition of 'witch' were female scholars, priestesses, mystics, herb-gatherers, Gypsies and midwives. Do you know why midwives are included in this list, Charles?" Roland asks as he get up.

Charles slowly shakes his head no.

The young Magistrate of Liège clasps his hands behind his back and starts pacing again from the table where Charles is sitting to the window. "Well, I will tell you. Midwives are included in the list because with their knowledge of herbs they are able to soothe the pains of childbirth. And, of course, ask anyone of those so-called just and holy men and they'll explain to you in detail that it is the punishment that God afflicted on women for Eve's sin!" He slumps back into his armchair drained of all his energy.

"Careful, my young friend. Those are heretic words and points of view coming from your mouth. I don't want to see you go the way of your Gypsy friend," scolded the older man.

De Bolland looks at his friend sadly. "I know," he says softly. "And I would not express my thoughts so openly on the subject to anyone other than you." He gets up and starts pacing the room again.

"Sit down Roland, and tell me, how is this present trial different? You keep going around the subject, totally avoiding the core of the matter. Is it different because it is being tried by a civilian court? Or is there something else?"

Roland continues to pace the room. Lost in his thoughts. He strokes his clean-shaven chin with his right hand.

"But please first, come back here to your armchair. You are making me quite dizzy with your pacing about," says Charles patting the armchair next to him.

Roland stops pacing, glances at Charles, nods and returns to his seat. As he stares at the richly colored tapestry of the Lady and the unicorn hanging on the wall behind Charles, he tries to collect his thoughts.

After a while he says, "Yes, it is very different from Jehenne's. Violence is one of the differences, but certainly not the main one. In fact, there are two main differences.

First of all, if you listen to gossip, town criers, people voicing their opinions, both in Liège and

Verviers, the trial concerns the danger of witchcraft on a member of the elite." Roland brings his left ankle up to rest on his right knee and absentmindedly fingers the top of his high boot.

"And that is not true?" Charles de Lalaing asks as he sits up in his chair. "I believe, I have heard something of this up-coming trial even here. A country domestic who changes into some kind of wild animal and who attacked a gentleman. Is that the case you are talking about, Roland?"

'Yes. No. I mean, yes, that is the one. But no, there is much more to this trial. It's not a country domestic changing into a wild animal at all. This girl doesn't change into a wild animal. In fact, she doesn't change into anything at all."

"Yes? No? Roland, life is not gray. Things are either black or they are white. Am I to understand that this man who is accusing the witch . . . ."

Roland puts up his hand.

"Let me go on, Roland. I know, you do not believe the girl is a witch."

"It's not what . . . .," Roland tries to explain.

This time it is Count Charles who puts his hand up. "Let me finish. The man, the main witness, is he or is he not a gentleman?"

"Remacle Le Rosy? A gentleman?" Roland can feel the repulsion he has for Le Rosy showing on his face. "No, he is not a gentleman. In fact, in my eyes, he is one of the most disgraceful creatures I have ever met." Roland hits the open palm of his left hand with his right fist and shakes his head.

Charles de Lalaing purses his lips and then asks, "A wolf in lamb's clothing?"

"Not even. He's . . . . he's . . . .disgusting."

"I see. At least I think I see. What is the second difference?"

"Vengeance. It is pure vengeance. This animal tries to rape a young woman and now wants her to burn simply because she defended herself."

"Are you certain of this?" Charles asks, his stern look back in place. "Absolutely certain?"

"Yes, he admitted it in a public place."

"You mean he told everybody? He just got up and announced it? What did he announce exactly? The fact she turned into a wild animal? That he wanted vengeance? What?"

"It wasn't like that. Yes, when his friends questioned him concerning the deep scratches that ran down his cheek and the gash in his head, he said the woman had turned into a wild animal and attacked him. In fact, he said she had turned into a gargoyle. Then he changed the story. He said he had followed her, tried to take her, and she refused. To use his words, 'to accept pleasure' from him."

"Possible. Do you really know, beyond a doubt, how he got those scratches and the gash in the head?"

"No, not exactly."

"But you have an idea."

"Yes. Of course, I do. The man clearly implied .– no, in fact, he implied nothing. He clearly stated that he could not accept women refusing him. Then he said something along the lines of 'I will see her burn on Jonkeu.' The witchcraft part came in as an afterthought. He is accusing her out of vengeance and nothing else."

"Roland, have you been walking around in your Monk's robe again?" asks Charles suppressing a smile, and looking up into his friend's face.

Roland smiles and rolls his eyes upward.

"I thought as much."

"I was, believe it or not, just sitting in a tavern having something to eat."

"In your monk's robe I suppose. What a coincidence. Oh, the poor wretched life of the travelling monk. How I pity it," says Charles dramatically. "Especially as you are not a monk. And I suppose you overheard the whole story."

"That's pretty much it."

"Roland, tell me if I am wrong. I remember you telling me that all the sentences from the Spa Court of Justice have to be counter-signed by the High Magistrate of the Court of Justice in Liège. Am I correct?"

"Yes."

"Well, you are the High Magistrate of the Liège Court of Justice. So? Why are you worrying? The final decision is yours."

"Of course, the final decision rests with me. But I want to be sure. I don't want to make a mistake and . . . ."

"And what?"

"You see, I don't want the girl to be subjected to torture. She has no chance of being allowed to go free and . . . ."

"Yes?"

Roland rubs his face with his left hand. He leans back and closes his eyes. Overwhelmed by the heavy load weighting on his shoulders. Sadness overcomes him. "Charles, I don't believe the girl can survive it."

"Have you seen her? Have you spoken to her?"

Yes, I saw her and I spoke to her once. I have neither seen nor spoken to her since her arrestation."

"Where did you see he?"

"In Spa."

"Roland, this is like getting blood out of a stone. Just tell me what happened."

"I saw her in Spa a few minutes before the Town Crier made the announcement asking for witnesses. We literally bumped into each other. Her basket went flying and I helped her pick up everything."

"Does she know who you are?"

"No, she thinks I am monk."

"How do you know it is her."

"She is so delicate and beautiful. I realized she was waiting to hear the Town Crier. So, I waited for him too and stood where I could look at her."

"And?"

"You should have seen the look of horror on her face when she heard she was being accused of witchcraft. She fainted, I started going towards her, but an older man... someone from the market... got to her first. He took her home."

"Am I to understand you followed them

home?"

"Yes, my horse was nearby. I followed them at a distance. Of course, I don't know what happened inside the farmhouse, but I saw her as they took her away. Charles, I wanted to go and intervene, but I could neither do that as a monk nor as the High Magistrate of Liège."

"I see. By the way, are there any witnesses?"

"Of course, there are witnesses. A lot of them always turn up after a public call for witnesses. You should hear all the stories the witnesses came up with. And the majority of these stories are based on could have, might have, possibly, looks like, seems like."

"There must be some bases to those stories. If there are so many witnesses, I presume she is guilty."

"Presume? Never presume, Charles. Most of those stories are impossible. Here I have the document accusing her. Listen to this. I won't bother you with the whole thing . . . .just the main parts."

Count Charles leans back in his armchair.

"The main accusation, of course, is the attack

on Remacle Le Rosy causing him bodily harm. She is also accused of causing her sister-in-law's miscarriage. This is followed by other accusations made by neighbors and even people who don't know her."

Roland taps on the parchment with his index finger. A man from Creppe saw crows flying over her house and then landing on the roof. It says, here, it started on a Sunday and lasted a whole week. Another neighbor said she saw Françoise Mathieu near one of the sources. She became suspicious when a frog acted strangely. And here is a man from Chevron who said he heard several rumors about the 'Creppe woman'. And listen to this one. A woman saw, Francoise Mathieu, the widow of Henry Hurlet of Creppe, talking to a strange-looking man dressed in black, in front of the Perron." Roland sighs and throws the parchments onto the table.

"The last one didn't have much imagination, did he?", chuckles Charles. "If I gave the order to my men to find ten 'strange-looking men dressed in black', they probably could do it in less than fifteen minutes."

Roland nods his head. "Besides, may I remind you, that I heard this Remacle fellow say he would see her burn because she didn't accept his advances. And he is the star witness on which everything is based."

"I see," answers the older man. He places his index finger on his lips and watches his friend. "So, Roland, do you have anything in mind? Seems to me that you are in an awkward position. You are both a witness for the defense and the Magistrate."

Roland nods. "Yes, I realize that. Actually, I have two plans in mind. First of all, I am going to set up a meeting between this Remacle De Creppe and myself. I believe with a little flattery and a lot of wine he will come out with everything. It will be a sort of confession which I can use without me having to divulge that I heard him as I was going around as a monk"

"I don't have to be a magistrate to realize this is highly irregular, Roland. Irregular but, I guess, not totally illegal. Go on. What about the second plan?"

"For the second I will need your help. The High Magistrate of Liège looks straight into the eyes of the Count.

"My help? What can I do?" asks Charles trying to follow Roland's reasoning.

"You can set up an appointment for me and Ferdinand of Baveria, the Prince-Bishop of Liège," answers Roland point-blank.

Charles de Lalaing does not answer right away. His gaze strays to the wall tapestry. To anyone other than Roland, he would seem interested in the design of the prancing unicorn. Only the movement in his jaws and the far-away look in his eyes shows his preoccupation.

Roland groans inwardly. Would his friend agree to this?

The Count turns towards Roland. "My friend, I need to remind you of a couple of facts."

Roland nods his head.

"First of all, you, Roland de Bolland, are a magistrate. Secondly, you are the High Magistrate of

Liège. Why are you coming here to me, in Brussels, to set up an appointment with such a high placed person as Ferdinand who is in your area and that you see on a regular basis. I don't understand. Why?"

Roland rubs his hands on his thighs. He looks down and studies the back of his hands. He lifts his eyes into Charles' and says, "Because Charles, as a High Magistrate of Liège or of anywhere else, I may not make the request I need to make. You see, I cannot make the request as a professional. I want to make the request in my own name, Roland de Bolland. And because I trust you more than anyone else, I need you to shoulder me."

Charles de Lalaing does not answer.

Roland continues. "Ferdinand is your friend. He will listen to you."

"Be careful, Roland. I have already warned you once today. I am doing it again now. Be careful."

"Will you help me?"

## CHAPTER 19
## 26th February 1600
## Late at night

It is late into the night and the rain is pelting down hard on two horsemen as they pass the chapel in Marché and proceed up the incline to the Chateau de Franchimont[22].

---

[22] Chateau de Franchimont   The chateau is first mentioned in 1155 as being a possession of the Catholic Church in Liège. Above all, it is a fortress and it played an important role during the many turbulent years the area has lived through. During the Burning Times, the Chateau was the sole prison for the 5 bans (Theux, Spa, Sart, Jalhay and Veviers) until the end of the Old Regime.

This is where the Court of Justice sat and where the men and women accused of witchcraft were tortured, sentenced and brought to Jonkeu to be burned at the stake.

The first horseman is Captain Joseph Dagley, a tall, thin man, with blond hair and blue eyes. He is one of de Bolland's men and he accepts orders from no superior other than de Bolland. Ask any soldier in Liège, in the Ban de Spa or at the Chateau of Franchimont, and they will tell you Dagley does not tolerate anyone who does not jump at the High Magistrate's orders. Those who don't jump, quickly find out that the Captain has a long arm and an excellent memory.

The second horseman, leading a riderless horse, is Sergeant Gustave Bastin. He is as devoted to the Captain as the Captain is to Roland de Bolland, the High Magistrate of Liège. The Captain and his sergeant are always seen together. It is well known that the Magistrate from Liège prefers to work only with men he trusts. In looks the Sergeant is the total opposite of the Captain. He is short, rather corpulent and dark haired.

"Sentinel! Open the gate for the High Magistrate's messengers. Be quick about it! We don't have all night," orders the Sergeant in a loud commanding voice.

The sentinel immediately recognizes the voice of the messenger who shouted the order and has no intention of getting on the wrong side of either the Sergeant or the Captain . . . . especially not of the Captain. He rushes to the gate and opens it as quickly as he can.

The sentinel grumbles under his breath as the two messengers ride through the open gates. He dislikes Captain Dagley and doesn't hide it when he talks with the other soldiers stationed at the Chateau of Franchimont. He considers him pompous, arrogant and too sure of himself. The thing that bothers the sentinel the most is that the High Magistrate of Liège's Captain knows he is not liked and doesn't care . . . . in fact, he takes great pride in it.

Captain Dagley is rarely at the Chateau de Franchimont. The only times he ever comes is when he is escorting the High Magistrate of Liège or when he is on a special mission for him.

Tonight, his orders are twofold. First of all, he needs to have the Governor countersign an order to pick up a certain Remacle Le Rosy and possibly keep him in custody. It is protocol and a question of mutual respect between the Magistrate and the Governor. Secondly, the Captain and his Sergeant are to proceed to Le Rosy's lodgings and take him to the Chateau de Colonster, near Liège, where Roland de Bolland is temporarily staying.

A half hour later, Captain Dagley and his companion, Sergeant Bastin, trot their mounts down the incline leading from the Chateau de Franchimont towards the hamlet of Marché on their way to the Ban de Spa. The signed summon tucked in the Captain's inner pocket is clear: pick up the herder known as Remacle Le Rosy, willingly or by force, and bring him to the Chateau of Colonster.[23]

The Pelting rain that they had arrived in seems

---

[23] The Chateau de Colonster is first mentioned in documents of the 14th century as a stronghold on a rocky spur of the Ourthe Valley near Liège. Over the years it was sold and bought several times. The last Lord of Colonster, Baron van Zuylen, sold it to the University of Liège

to have degenerated if that is at all possible. A shiver goes up the Sergeant's spine. He would be more than happy to find a shelter where they can stop until the storm lets up, but he knows this is only wishful thinking. First, they did not come across any shelter. Secondly, they are pressed for time. And thirdly, even if they had found a shelter and if they had a lot of time in front of them, Captain Dagley would not have stopped. When the Captain stops it is either because they have reached their destination or because the horses need a rest. Duty comes first with the Captain, the horse come second and in third place the men. Sergeant Bastin would have resented this except he knows that the Captain places his own comfort way below that of his men.

At the end of the day, the Sergeant is proud to be under the Captain's orders and therefore to also be considered as being 'one of de Bolland's men.' It is not a title to be taken lightly.

# CHAPTER 20
## 27ᵗʰ February 1600
## A little past midnight

Remacle's shelter, in which he lives all year round, but which he shares with his herd from the end of April to the first snowflakes of November, is small, and yet big enough for a man alone.[24] Of course, it doesn't have the

---

[24] In April or May, the herder would take the animals that had been put in his care into the Fagne (the Fens). Each one of the animals has a colored mark (black, red or blue) on its back indicating the owner's identity. There are two parts to the herder's hut. The first is a vast area to shelter his animals during the storms, the cold winter or in the autumn when the strong winds sweep through the Fagnes. The second part is his lodgings. A bag of ferns and a woolen blanket make up his bed. Potatoes cooked under the ashes, black bread, grilled bacon and, when in season, cranberries and blueberries make up the herder's frugal meal. In November, once the first snows started, he normally brings the animals back to their owners.' Henri

## The Drop of the Hammer

conveniences of the homes in Creppe and Spa and certainly there are no signs of a woman's touch, but it's home for Remacle. It is exactly what he needs. Thanks to his herd, it's warm in winter, cool in summer and its remoteness gives him the time alone he needs and wants. Whenever he needs company, he goes to the tavern for a drink with his friends. When he needs a woman's company, he either goes to Bella's at the Tavern or takes advantage of situations that put him in contact with pretty and willing girls.

Tonight, a particularly wild storm is raging outside. He had scarcely brought in the last of his herd when the rain started. Within minutes, the rain started pelting hard on his roof and the thunder and lightning were making his animals jumpy.

As usual, Remacle makes one last check of his sheep before preparing his evening meal and settling down for the night. Few people know this side of

---

George, Folklore Spadois. Vie et Moeurs d'Autrefois. Ed. J'Ose, Spa, 1935 p. 22

Remacle Le Rosy. His closeness to the herd entrusted to him and the care he gives it, are what makes him a good herder. Most people in Creppe and Spa know Remacle Le Rosy as a rough, coarse herder with a loud voice, but once he is with his animals his voice becomes soft and his hand light.

Normally he takes the animals back to their owners once the first snow flurries appear. This year one of the owners has asked him to keep his herd throughout the winter, guaranteeing that feed would be supplied. Remacle doesn't know why and he doesn't care. It will be nice to have them with him in winter.

As soon as the animals are taken care of, Remacle sits down to eat. He hungrily eats the black bread and bacon that usually make up his evening meals and rinses it all down with the hot chicory drink he brews. Afterwards, he settles down on the bag of straw that serves as a bed with a grateful "Ahhh", pats his belly, farts twice and falls asleep.

Out of nowhere comes another noise.

Someone is banging on the side of the shelter with something hard, "Remacle Le Rosy! Open the door. Remacle Le Rosy!"

Le Rosy's snoring hits a high note and then abruptly stops followed by a sleepy, "What? What? What's going on? Who's there? Can't a man sleep anymore? Who's out there?"

"Open up in the name of the law!"

By this time, Remacle is on his feet, grabs a heavy rock to use on anyone who dares to force his way in. "In the name of the law" is not going to work with him.

"Open the door, Le Rosy, and present yourself to the representatives of the High Magistrate of Liège, Roland de Bolland."

"No. No. You are lying. Why would the High Magistrate of Liège want to see me? I don't know him. Go away!"

"We have an official summons signed by both the Magistrate of Liège and the Governor at the Chateau de Franchimont. You will open the door or we will force our way in."

"I don't know who you are and I'm not responsible for what will happen to you if you force your way in. Go away!" he yells at the person on the other side of the door.

Captain Dagly hits the side of the shelter again and yells, "Remacle Le Rosy! I have orders to accompany you to the High Magistrate of Liège. You are not under arrest, but if you do not open the door and step out by the time, I count to three, I guarantee you will be arrested. One. Two."

The door to the shelter squeaks open, and Remacle sticks his head out. "I'm coming out. I'm coming out."

"Are you or are you not Remacle Le Rosy, the herder."

"Yes, I'm him. I am Remacle Le Rosy, the herder."

Remacle Le Rosy I hold here in my hand a summon from the High Magistrate of Liège and counter-signed by the Governor at the Chateau de

# The Drop of the Hammer

Franchimont. You are to come with us. I repeat you are not under arrest. We have a horse for you."

"Now? In this weather?," asks Remacle. "Can't we wait for morning?"

The Captain looks at the herder from head to toe. "If we could wait for morning do you think my Sergeant and I would be in front of your door at this time of the night and in a raging storm?"

"But Sergeant, I . . . ."

"Captain," Dagly corrects him.

"Er…yes, Captain. I don't go out so late when there's a storm because of the Beast of Staneux.[25]

---

[25] The Beast of Staneux: According to this very old legend, there lived in the forest of Staneux a terrible half-woman half horse monster that terrorized young and old in the region. It would attack chicken coops, herds and men who dared to go into the forest. A local cobbler noticed that the monster aped humans. He made boot to fit it, filled them with pitch and left them at the edge of a clearing. He then put his own boots next to them and waited for the monster to appear. The hungry beast appeared within a short time, growling dangerously and fiercely. The cobbler who had never seen the creature from so close up was terrified, but he was also a very brave man. He slowly put on his boots. The creature intrigued by what the man was doing stopped growling and looked at him. Everything went according to plan. It put on the big boots and immediately got stuck in the pitch. Of course, as it was not used to walking with any type of footwear, it stumbled. A group of men from the region and friends of the cobbler, who were hiding in the

"What?" asks Captain Dagly clearly getting tired of all this.

"They found the man who was the herder before me dead early one morning after a storm like this. Some said it was the lightning that killed him, but everybody knows it was the Beast."

"Remacle Le Rosy, I am giving you a choice. Either you get onto the horse, we have for you, and come along peacefully or we will not only arrest you, but we will also tie you up and throw you on the horse . . . . head down and feet dangling. What do you prefer?"

"Where's the horse?" asks Remacle.

---

bushes, jumped up and killed the Beast of Staneux. Jehenne Anseau as well as the real Françoise grew up with this legend and would have understood the herder's fear.

# CHAPTER 21
## 29th February 1600
## Early afternoon

By the time they arrive at the Chateau de Colonster, the rain has stopped and it is early afternoon on the 29th February 1600, a leap year.

To Sergeant Bastin's great relief, Captain Dagly decided that the distance they needed to cover in pelting rain was not good for the horses. They stopped at a farm where the farmer took pity on the three thoroughly drenched travelers who came to his door and allowed them to sleep in the barn.

Up on a hill, sometime after noon on the 29th, Captain Dagly reigns in his horse and points at a castle in the distance.

"Chateau de Colonster," he says with that satisfied smile Sergeant Bastin has long known means 'Mission Accomplished'. He understands the feeling and, to be fair, he shares it more that he cares to admit.

Once they get to the Chateau, the Captain and the Sergeant turn the herder over to the guards, along with the signed documents from Franchimont. "The Sergeant and I will be in the kitchens. We are famished," says Dagly as they start going up a staircase to the right of the guards' room.

Remacle starts to follow them out and the guard bars his way. "Where do you think you are going?" asks the guard.

"To the kitchens," answers Remacle innocently. "I am also very hungry."

"So?" The guard looks Remacle up and down as if he were yesterday's fish.

"So, I would like to eat something and also to drink something warm."

"Tell me, what are doing here?"

"I don't really know, but I was invited to come."

The guard crosses his arms and with clear exasperation in his voice says, "Invited? You have been invited to the Chateau of Colonster and yet you are in the guard room"

"Yes, but I don't know why. I am not a prisoner. I am a herder. From Spa. I was invited. And I am hungry."

"I see. Why don't you sit down and wait there on the bench? I'll be right back."

As he leaves the guard room, Remacle hears the lock on the door being turned. Soon afterwards another guard comes in and sits down without a word.

"Er . . . . do you know how long I have to wait?"

Silence.

"I think they are going to bring some food for me."

Silence.

"You see, I'm hungry and thirsty."

Silence.

"Er . . . .am I under arrest?"

Silence

"Do you know why I am here?"

Still no answer

"Do you think they are going to bring me something to eat?"

Again, no answer.

Remacle starts humming to himself. The he gets up. Stretches his arms a little then his legs. The guard does not react. Then he decides to make faces at him. Still no reaction. He is starting to worry. If no one can see or hear him, maybe he is dead.

Two other guards enter and the taller of the two says, "The High Magistrate is ready to see this man. He said to take him to his office." Then turning to Remacle, "The High Magistrate of Liège will see you now. Follow us." They lead him down a corridor to a large room. He goes in. They tell him "The High Magistrate will be with you shortly. Don't touch anything," and close the door behind him.

Remacle turns around and takes a good look at the room he is in. At least this room is more comfortable than the guard room and more beautiful, too. There are so many things to look at and he doesn't know where to begin. His attention is drawn to the warm flames in the fireplace across the room. The guard room was dry, but far from warm. He starts crossing the room. Then he realizes he is stepping on the carpet and decides maybe the carpet is not made to walk on. The carpet is big but doesn't cover the whole of the room as it is set on very polished black and white tiles. The tiles should be safe to walk on, he figures, as he starts walking around the room to get to the fireplace.

The herder is not a man easily impressed, nor is beauty important. For him everything has a value. If it brings him money or could bring him money it is good. If something has no value, it is of no interest to him. This richness surrendering him, however, does fascinate him. It is something quite new to him.

Remacle gets down on a knee to take a better look at the carpet. His friends at the tavern will never believe him when he describes this room. The carpet is a rust-red field of rows after rows of strange looking flowers and the whole thing has a border of green leaves. He nods as he looks at the design.

He is no longer that far from the fireplace. Would it be safe to step on the carpet now? Deciding that he really wants to warm himself he takes a first step and then a second. Steps back. Has he left a mark on the carpet? No. So, no problem. It might be safer anyway to take his shoes off.

To get to the fireplace he has to pass by a table. A rich man's table. Looks heavy. He tries to lift it up. It doesn't even budge a little bit. He rubs his hands on the carved lions heads on the table's arched supports. His attention is then drawn to the top of the table. It is full of parchments, quills and something else. The something else is a gold brooch showing a bird with its wings spread out and all around it are rubies. He brings it close to his mouth, breathes on it

## The Drop of the Hammer

and rubs it on his tunic. Now, that's impressive and beautiful and especially it is worth a lot of money. He checks around him and satisfied that no guard has reentered the room without him knowing it, he hides it in his tunic. "Anybody who lives here and has all of this wealth will certainly not miss anything as small as the brooch."

And acting as innocent as possible, he finally walks up to the fireplace to warms his hands.

During all this time, Roland de Bolland, seated in a dark corner of the room, is watching Remacle's every move including the theft of the brooch. He stands up and clears his throat.

Remacle jumps with surprise and turns around slowly.

"Good day. I am Roland de Bolland, the High Magistrate of Liège Have you been waiting long?"

"No, Monsieur .... er .... My Lord." Answers the herder sure now that the theft of the brooch was still unknown. For a moment there he thought the man might have seen him steal it.

Roland goes to his desk and sits down. He then points to a matching chair on the opposite side. "Sit. There."

"Oui, My Lord." Answers Remacle as he walks to the chair. Looks at the High Magistrate and points at the chair "There?"

Roland nods, staring at him.

Remacle sits down and looks around him uncomfortably.

Without removing his eyes from the herder, Roland says, "As you probably know we are going to have an important witch trial soon. I am doing some research and thought it might help me if I spoke to one of the main witnesses, in private, to get a better idea."

"Ah, I see," answers Remacle. "You want to talk man-to-man."

"Yes, that's pretty well what I had in mind. Would you like a little shot of Geniever or two? And, by the way, put the brooch back on the desk."

## CHAPTER 22
## 10th March 1600
## Château of Franchimont

The harquebusier presses his charger forward as they walk over the frozen terrain. He can feel his horse's warm body through his leggings, but also the horse's tensed muscles. The path is not easy even for an experienced charger like Crusader. Both the rider and the horse are tense, and the acrid, gamy smell of the animal's sweat reaches the harquebusier's nostrils.

Even at the best of times, in good weather, the way to the Chateau of Franchimont is treacherous. The rider has been on the road for three days and during that time the road had more than outdone itself. The freezing cold numbs his senses. The falling snow hides the holes in the ground where a horse can easily break a leg.

Twice, during the journey, the strong military horse had stumbled. Twice, the horse and Captain Dieudonné Lejeune fell perilously close to the ravine edge.

A half foot closer to the edge and the jagged rocks would have lacerated both their bodies. A half foot closer to the cold bare trees, the impact would have broken their bones.

Captain Dieudonné Lejeune and Crusader have been a team for the last five years, and he hates to think of the consequences with a less-experienced horse.

Dieudonné's head begins to throb with the cold. He moves his fingers and toes to keep the circulation going.

They reach the Hoegne river and they stop. The Captain stiffly makes the sign of the cross and murmurs a short prayer of thanks. At this point the

# The Drop of the Hammer

Hoegne is only a small creek. Nonetheless, small or not, the Hoegne is still dangerous.

The frozen water mirrors the grey sky above. A bird is flying overhead. Its wings flapping sharply and loudly. As the harquebusier looks at the frozen creek, he sees the reflection of a crow. A big, black crow. A bad omen.

The soldier shudders as his soul registers the sign. His heart pounds. All his senses are alert.

He pulls a cross out of his vest with trembling hands, brings it to his lips, and kisses it. Then he sighs and presses his knees into Crusader's sides."

Suddenly, he hears a twig snap behind them. The horse rears and pulls away from the creek. The big charger's eyes are wild. He snorts and warm foam from his mouth hits the harquebusier in the face.

The two of them have been working together too long, for Captain Lejeune to ignore the horse's warnings. "Easy, Crusader, easy", he whispers calmly.

His military instinct leaps into action. He tightens his left hand around the rein, and feels the taunt leather around his fingers.

On foot he would have relied on his long harquebus and the hooked staff on which it rests. On horseback he has no choice other than his sword.

His right hand unsheathes his sword. The cold metal of the hilt nesting comfortably in his hand.

Together, man and horse join their experiences to face the threat. Crusader is still agitated although totally battle ready. An emaciated grey wolf is standing a few feet away from them. It's two hard, hungry eyes staring menacingly. The animal's ears are pulled back as it growls. Dieudonné is certain he can overcome the animal, but it doesn't mean that the wolf will not cause fatal injuries before it is killed.

Dieudonné carefully watches the hungry animal for any sudden change in his body movements. At the same time, he tries to take in his surroundings. A thought keeps nagging him. The wolf watching them is not acting according to its natural instinct. A lone wolf will rarely attack a potential prey that is stronger than he is which is the case here. In spite of their reputation, they are intelligent but not very brave. A lone wolf always calculates his chances and it only attacks people or other animals that are weaker than he is. Unless…unless… it has the drooling sickness.

Captain Lejeune slowly leans close to one of his horse's ears and again whispers softly, "Easy, Crusader, easy." The Harquebusier feels his horse tense beneath him, both of them ready to react to the smallest movement in the animal's eyes.

Unexpectedly, the wolf backs away and runs off.

Dieudonné Lejeune lets out a sigh of relief. It is a hungry wolf and hungry wolves, similar to hungry men, can do the unforeseen.

The harquebusier returns his sword to its sheath and gives another pat to his horse. "Good boy, Crusader, Good boy." Not a day goes by that he does not admire the strength and sure-footedness of his charger not to mention his battle readiness.

The rider and his horse continue on their

journey. Both are dead tired. The soldier left the Prince-Bishops' palace three days ago as the first three bells of the morning Angelus started pealing. As a military officer under the command of the High Magistrate of Liège, he never has problems commandeering quarters when on a mission and he had done so twice since leaving Liège.

Now, within sight of Marché and the road leading up to the chateau, the evening Angelus begins to sound.

Taking advantage of a better road, the harquebusier decides to do the last few miles at a galop as he wants to reach the chateau as soon as possible.

Captain Lejeune reaches the small village of Marché, the free market at the foot of the chateau and reduces his speed to a trot and then to a steady pace. He turns his horse towards the incline leading to the Chateau of Franchimont. The closer he gets to the chateau, the steeper the road becomes. Halfway up, the road makes a hairpin turn to the right.

## The Drop of the Hammer

The drawbridge leading to the chateau appears before him and he spurs his horse forward.

"Let me through! Let me through! Urgent messages for Cedric Boniver, the magistrate of Spa from Frederic of Bavaria, the Prince-Bishop of Liège and Roland de Bolland, High Magistrate of Liège for the High Magistrate of Spa. Let me through!"

At the drawbridge several soldiers armed with swords and crossbows run towards him. A soldier takes hold of the horse's bridle. "Do you have a laissez-passer?" barks another soldier.

Dieudonné Lejeune reaches inside his vest and hands a rolled parchment to the soldier.

The heavy wooden doors open and the commanding officer joins them. "Does the messenger have a laissez-passer?" he asks drily. The soldier snaps at attention and hands him the laissez-passer signed by both the Prince-Bishop of Liège and the High Magistrate of Liège."

The officer takes the laissez-passer and looks at Dieudonné who introduces himself, "Captain

Dieudonné Lejeune from the Visé Harquebusiers, Sir. I'm on an urgent mission for the Prince-Bishop of Liège and the High Magistrate of Liège."

The officer quickly looks at the Laissez-passer, nods to Dieudonné Lejeune. Turns towards his soldiers and yells the command, "Let the messenger through. Take him to the High Magistrate of Spa right away." Then pointing to one of the soldiers, "You there, see that the Captain's horse is taken care of and that quarters are available for the Captain afterwards."

The doors of the château open immediately and the Harquebusier and his horse pass through the gate. As he enters, he glances up at the three-frontal coat of arms carved above the entrance.

Once inside, a tall, lanky Sargeant joins Lejeune. "Let me take your mount, Captain. A fine charger, Sir. Looks like he could do with a rest though."

The Haquebusier looks at the Sergeant and smiles. He always appreciates a man who knows horses. "Yes, Crusader is a good horse. Can't tell you how often my life depends on him. Take my horse, Sergeant, and take good care of him. Water and feed." He pats Crusader and smiles again at the Sergeant.

"Yes, Captain. And with all due respect, Sir, may I add, Crusader's owner also looks tired and in need of rest. After your business with the High Magistrate of Spa you might like to walk down to the kitchens. They are in the keep. To the right of the main door. I will also see that quarters are available." He snaps to attention and says another "Sir" before leading Crusader away.

## CHAPTER 23
## 10<sup>th</sup> March 1600
## At the Château of Franchimont[26]

Dieudonné follows a second Sergeant across the yard. They pass the casemates used as prisons.[27] They turn into the inner courtyard and walk towards the keep.

As they enter the keep, Dieudonné glances towards the right where a tempting smell is floating

---

[26] Although in ruins, the Chateau de Franchimont is still standing today. A visit of the official website, set up by the Compagnons de Franchimont (Friends of Franchimont), who are responsible for the safeguarding of the castle gives a good idea of what it once was like as well as an idea of the country side. www.chateau-franchimont.be

[27] Although a casemate is an armored structure from which guns are fired, the word originally referred to a vaulted chamber in a fortress and it is used in that sense here

out of the kitchens. His stomach starts to rumble. He hopes it won't do so in front of the High Magistrate of Spa.

A silent guard is told to escort the Captain down the hall towards what he knows are the torture room. Hopefully, he has reached Franchimont in time.

Half way down the hall he sees a young disheveled woman slumped on the cold stone floor. She is dressed only in a dirty and ripped shift that once was white, but no longer was. Her vacant eyes stare out into nothingness. Her hands are clasped together as she tries to control her constant shivering.

"Is that Françoise Mathieu, the widow of Henry Hurlet of Creppe?" he asks the guard in a low voice.

The guard snaps at attention. "Yes, Sir. That she is. I expect we'll be hearing her scream in a little while. They say she is a witch."

"Why isn't she covered? She has nothing under that old shift. The woman is freezing. Get her something right away!"

"I am not allowed, Sir."

"And why not?" asks Dieudonné drily.

"She is a witch, Sir. They don't feel the cold. Besides, she is going to be executed anyway."

Captain Lejeune looks at the guard from head to toe. "One, she feels the cold like you or I do. Two, she has not yet been sentenced. Your job is to guard, not to sentence."

"Yes, Sir." Answers the guard not bothering to hide his distaste at being told off by a 'stranger'.

Dieudonné walks over to Françoise, goes down on one knee and places his gloved hand under her chin. As he lifts her face up, he feels her trembling under his fingers. Their eyes meet. Her eyes are like that of a doe cornered by hunters. Distraught, in complete disarray, her shift dirty and torn, the Captain still thinks she is the most beautiful woman he has ever seen.

"Françoise," he says softly in her ear, "I cannot give you names, but you have friends who are trying to help you." She looks up at him seemingly not understanding. Dieudonné takes his cape off and puts it around her shoulders. Françoise holds on to it tightly and tears roll down her cheeks.

The harquebusier from Visé stands up and takes all this in. He looks at her for a moment longer, and then turns towards the guard. "Carry on, Guard, carry on."

The guard pounds on the wooden door. "Messenger from Frederic of Bavaria, the Prince–Bishop of Liège and the High Magistrate of Liège. Messenger requests to see the High Magistrate of Spa, Cedric Boniver."

A young guard opens the door. Behind him Dieudonné Lejeune can see four men sitting at a heavy oak table. To their right in the shadows, a surly looking man leans against the wall.

Captain Lejeune, the harquebusier of Visé, and definitely one of de Bolland's men, marches in the room with a military step. He faces Cedric Boniver, seated at the oak table. "My Lord, I have an urgent message for you from the Prince–Bishop of Liège, Frederic of Bavaria and the High Magistrate of Liège, Roland de Bolland."

Dieudonné takes an instant dislike to Cedric Boniver and he quickly picks up that the sentiment is mutual.

Although no stranger to the horrors of war, he recoils not only from what he knows this room represents but also from the man sitting in front of him. He involuntarily takes in the shackles and weights around the room. Disciplined as he is, he quickly averts his eyes and stares at an imaginary point above Cedric's head.

The Magistrate of Spa put out his hand for the parchment. Once in his hand, he tosses it upon the table. With a wave of his hand at the messenger, he says without looking at him, "You may go."

The harquebusier stiffens. "Beg your pardon, My Lord, but I have to remain for the answer."

Boniver's head snaps towards him. "I said you may go. I----have—no—need—of---you." The hard tone of Cedric's voice increases with each word. As he speaks tiny drops of spit reach Dieudonné Lejeune.

"With all due respect, Sir, the message is urgent and needs to be looked into immediately."

Boniver abruptly stands up. "Are you giving me orders?"

"No, Sir, I would not allow myself to do so. I am simply giving you the message I was told to give you."

Boniver moves from behind the table and walks up to the messenger. He notices with satisfaction the difference in height between the two of them. The High Magistrate towers over the harquebusier by half a head. He smirks and looks towards the other judges.

The man from Spa looks the harquebusier over and asks coldly, "You are a harquebusier from Visé?"

"Yes, My Lord. I am a harquebusier from Visé." The captain's pride shows in both his demeaner and his voice.

"Do they not teach you discipline in Vise? I

will make a full report of your behavior to both your commander and the Prince-Bishop. You are a disgrace to your uniform."

He turns his back to the messenger and once again waves his hand in a sign of dismissal. "You may go. I have no need of you. I will deal with the message once I am free. As it is, I am about to do an interrogation. I have no time for this," he says pointing to the parchment he has thrown onto the table.

"With all due respect, My Lord. This message concerns your interrogation of Françoise Mathieu, the widow of Henry Hurlet of Creppe . . . . "

Cedric spins around and looms over the messenger staring at him.

"I have strict orders from the Prince-Bishop of Liege, Ferdinand of Bavaria and from Roland de Boland the High Magistrate of Liège to remain in your presence until you have signed the parchment. Your signature is Prince Frederic's certitude his order will be followed to the letter. With all due respect, My

Lord, I must draw your attention to the fact that Françoise Mathieu, the widow of Henry Hurlet of Creppe may be questioned but may not, under any circumstances whatsoever, be tortured." Dieudonné adds "Sir."

The magistrate's face turns purple. The shadow from the candles makes his face grotesque. His eyes bulge out. He sucks in his cheeks. "Very well."

He turns towards the other judges. With both his palms up, he says, "This interference into our affaires is grotesque! Unbelievable! Did you hear that? We're being told how to carry out our interrogations." He starts pacing the room in front of the table where the other judges are sitting.

Cedric stops in front of the harquebusier. The soldier is standing as still as a statue. Not a muscle is moving in his face nor in his body. He does not even blink an eye as he stares at a point somewhere beyond the Magistrate.

Cedric is enraged. The soldier's self-discipline

unsettles him.

The magistrate puts his hands on his hip and shouts, "Very well. We have received an order to refrain from torturing this woman .... this witch. And how does Liège suggest we obtain her confession? I suppose you don't have another parchment hidden somewhere explaining that?"

Dieudonné Lejeune does not answer and does not move a muscle.

"I did not think so." The Magistrate smiles scornfully. Once again, he turns towards the other judges. "Well, what do you think of all this, Johan?" he asks the oldest judge at the table."

"Cedric, I agree with you. This is unacceptable. We cannot, will not accept this. This is unheard of. The Governor of Franchimont will never accept such stupidity." His hands flutter about nervously as he speaks.

Cedric Boniver purposely and insolently looks the messenger up and down trying to intimidate him. "And I suppose you know what is in the message?

Have you read it? Can you read? Do you know the punishment for a messenger who dares to open an important message or any message at all?"

Cedric looks at the harquebusier with distain. He points his index at him and snarls. "Do you, huh?".

Dieudonné's own anger grows by the second. "With all due respect, My Lord. I had no need to read it. I . . . ."

"Are you one of de Bolland's men?" Cedric interrupts.

"I beg your pardon, My Lord, I am a harquebusier from Visé. And I am presently in the service of the Prince-Bishop of Liège Ferdinand of Bavaria. He . . . ."

Cedric again interrupts him. "And I suppose that gives you, a simple, uneducated soldier, the right to open messages?" He stands, hands clasped behind his back, away from the harquebusier.

"My Lord, I . . . ."

"Speak up, man. Don't mumble." Cedric roars

fiercely turning towards the messenger and looking at him straight in the face.

"With all due respect, My Lord. I am Captain Dieudonné Lejeune. Yes, I can read. I am here today under the orders of both the Prince-Bishop of Liège, Ferdinand of Bavaria, and Roland de Boland, the High Magistrate. No, that does not give me the right to open any message confided to me. I neither opened it nor read it. I did not need to read it in order to know its contents. My mission was explained to me in detail before I set out."

Dieudonné sees through the magistrate's strategy. He knows this type of man. He also knows he speaks clearly. He never mumbles. A soldier and especially a harquebusier from Vise values discipline above all things.

"What?"

"With all due respect, My Lord, the Prince-Bishop and the High Magistrate wanted us to realize the importance of the message. They explained the mission to us before our departure and told us exactly what to say. My lord, Frederic of Bavaria also explained to us the resistance our mission would be facing."

"Us?" asks Cedric with sarcasm. "I only see one of you."

"With all due respect, My Lord. Us. Two messengers. The Prince-Bishop and the High Magistrate sent out two harquebusiers from Visé. Both messengers were given the same message and the same instructions. This one destined to you and the other destined to Roger de Linden, the Governor of Franchimont."

The High Magistrate of Spa looks at the harquebusier. "Roger de Linden is not here. He is away and has been away for a while."

"Yes, my lord. Roger the Linden is in Cologne. He went there three weeks ago."

Cedric walks back to his seat and sits down. He wills the harquebusier to look him in the eyes but the soldier continues to stare at a point above him.

"I am to remind you, My Lord, that it is an

urgent message from the Prince–Bishop Ferdinand of Bavaria and the High Magistrate of Liège. They have requested your signature upon the parchment."

Dieudonné continues to stand at attention. Not once do his eyes stray from the imaginary point. He never allows himself to look at Cedric Boniver. He deeply distrusts the man. Given half a chance the man would accuse him of insubordination.

The messenger takes a step forward and retrieves the parchment from the table. He hands it back to the magistrate. "My Lord."

Cedric snatches the parchment from the harquebusier's hands.

The messenger immediately takes one step back and continues to look at the point.

Cedric Boniver's hands shake with anger.

He takes a quill from the oak table, dips it in ink and signs his name to the parchment. Dieudonné sees anger surging in ugly waves across the magistrate's face. Cedric's lips are pressed together. A frown creases the area between his eyes.

With hatred in his eyes, he looks at the harquebusier from head to toes. Cedric rolls up the parchment, then tosses it to the harquebusier as he would a bone to a dog. The parchment falls short of the Captain and drops to the floor with a thud.

Dieudonné does not flinch. Thanks to his military training, he keeps his face as empty as a clean slate. Not once can Cedric Boniver find the messenger's eyes upon him. Yet, Lejeune's training enables him to take in each and every one of the magistrate's gestures and looks.

For a few seconds, the parchment remains unrolled on the stone floor. Neither one of the two men moves.

Cedric wants to see the Captain explode. He knows the anger is bubbling under the messenger's calm exterior.

Instead, the messenger picks up the parchment with care, rolls it up carefully and secures it with a ribbon.

As if nothing unusual has happened, Captain

Dieudonné Lejeune snaps at attention and says, "My Lord, my homages." He does an about-face and walks out of the room with a stiff military stride.

Once out of the room, the soldier feels the door slam behind even before he hears it.

The dark and damp hall seems light and airy compared to the interrogation room. Again, he thanks his military training for his self-control.

As he walks down the hall, he passes the young woman again. She is sitting against the wall. Her arms are holding her drawn knees close to her breast. She is still clutching Dieudonné's cape.

The arquebusier slows down as he comes near her. He hopes his small insignificant part in this tragedy will save her from torture. He does not kid himself. Even without torture, those men in the room will give her a hard time.

Dieudonné Lejeune shudders. To hide his disarray, he turns towards one of the guards. "Go check on my horse. I want to be certain he has sufficient water and feed." He orders gruffly. "And then take me down to the kitchens. I want to fill my belly before starting off again."

With one last look towards the young woman he follows the guard out.

## CHAPTER 24
## 13<sup>th</sup> March 1600
## Three days later

"Outrageous! Never have I seen something like this" yells Cedric Boniver as he paces the room.

Three days have passed since, as the Magistrate of Spa has so well said, the outrageous incident with the messenger and meddling of Liège. Cedric Boniver and the three black robed judges, Norbert Gosselin, Désiré de Soiron and Michel Dupont are meeting again in the torture room.

Outrageous or not, the mandate has to be respected: Françoise Mathieu, the widow of Henry Hurlet de Creppe can be questioned but not tortured.

# The Drop of the Hammer

The Magistrate of Spa is livid. Never in his whole career has his judgement been overruled or even questioned.

They are sitting at the long heavy oak table in this tragic, windowless torture room lit only by candles and torches. A multitude of parchments are scattered on the table before them. They have been discussing the situation for hours and have come up with a method of procedure which they are convinced will deliver the expected results.

"Of course, this plan will be successful. It cannot fail," assures Michel Dupont, "but it is a waste of time."

"There's no doubt about it," agrees Norbert "This woman is weak. If we hadn't had our hands tied by Liège, this whole thing would have been over and done with in less than an hour."

Cedric Boniver taps one of the parchments on the table with his index finger. "That is the essence of it, Norbert. Your reasoning is exact, as always. This Françoise Mathieu is a weak woman and she will break faster than even we think."

"I had a good look at her yesterday and she is no Jehenne Anseau, arrogant and provocative," adds Desire de Soiron. "There's no comparison between the two, but in the end, we did prove she was a witch and had her burned for her sins."

"I have taken upon myself to request two preliminary actions which should help us gain time. First of all, I have had her examined from head to toe for a Devil's sign. I would be very surprised if they didn't find one. Secondly, I have made her witness the torture of that man who was brought in yesterday."

"Which man was that, Magistrate?" asks Desire de Soiron.

"The man who was accused of stealing a horse."

"Oh, I thought that case was already closed. He admitted the theft right away, didn't he?"

"Yes, but I believe, he could serve a greater purpose by being tortured in front of that woman. After all, there are so many thieves . . . .one more or one less makes no difference."

All three judges nod their agreement.

"Guard, have the executioner come in," calls out Cedric. And in an aside to the judges, he adds, "I thought it best for us to have our discussion in private. Any way I have put him in charge of my two preliminary actions and he will report back to us. He is very good at his job."

"My Lord." says the executioner as he comes in. He is a squat man practically as wide as he is tall. A black leather patch covers his left eye and when he speaks, one notices right away that many of his teeth are missing.

"Gaston, tell us about last night's torture. How did it go? And what about the examination?" And to the judges, "As I have already said, Gaston is very good at his job and after listening to his results we may not even need a trial." Looking up at Gaston, "Tell us."

"Yes, My Lord. First of all, she has the Mark of the Devil on her body. It was not difficult to find."

"What and where was it?" interrupts Norbert.

"On her right ankle, My Lord. A brown spot There was also another one."

"Two?"

"Yes, My Lord. The second confirmed the first. She has the same brown spot on her elbow. Also, on the right."

The three judges begin to talk loudly between themselves, agreeing that indeed this was good news. Even Jehenne didn't have such good signs.

"And what about the torture last night, Gaston?" asks Cedric smiling.

"My Lord, you had a very good idea. It affected the woman immensely. Unfortunately, she did not confess. In my opinion, she is not far from breaking. It is regrettable, that I could not administer some torture."

"Gaston, we could not agree with you more. Tell us how you proceeded?"

"Yes, My Lord. First of all, we brought her in and stripped her. She gave us some problems there as she was clutching a dark woolen cape. She wouldn't let go of it. I don't know where she got it, because we removed everything from her except the old shift she was given upon her arrival. She began screaming when we took it away. We then strapped her down, as you had ordered, and left her there for a while . . . . again as you had ordered."

"What was her state of mind when you came back?"

"Not very good, My Lord. She sounded like a wild animal that had been wounded to death. However, after witnessing the torture of the thief she was in a much worse state."

"You didn't leave any marks on her?"

"No, My Lord, you were very clear about that. I did not touch her. Anyway, just strapping her down and letting her watch seemed enough. The torturing of the thief went on for a long time. By the time, we were done he was fatally hurt and he died within a few hours once removed to his cell."

"From your experience, do you think she is

going to confess?"

"My Lord, as I have already said, she is not far from breaking, but I am not sure she is in any state to confess or even to say she is innocent."

"What do you mean?"

"She is broken. I believe, before she witnessed the thief's torture, only a little prompting from me would have resulted in a confession. Now, after seeing what was being done to the man, her eyes are dull, can't seem to focus. She doesn't say a single word and no other sound comes out of her except a continuous moaning. Her whole body seems to be a total wreck. She trembles and is, I believe, not far from having convulsions. You won't get anything from her."

"I see," answers Cedric Boniver. He turns to the judges sitting at the table with him. "Gentlemen, I think we will be better off conducting the trial and, of course, the sentencing here among us. We won't even need the accused. The sooner all this is over, the sooner we have Liège off our backs."

"Gaston, one more thing. Please see that she stays alive long enough to get to Jonkeu."

# CHAPTER 25
# 14th March 1600
# Witness One

## Declaration - Office of the Governor of Franchimont

Examining Judge: "What is your name?"

Witness: "Gilson Froidville of Spa."

Examining Judge: "How would you describe yourself? Are you a God-fearing man?"

Witness: "Yes, your honor. I swear that I am a God-fearing man. I swear on the heads of my children. All six of them."

Examining Judge: "On what do you base your

affirmation?"

Witness: "My affirmations, your honor?"

Examining Judge: Yes, can you confirm that you are a God-fearing man?"

Witness: "Yes, your honor."

Examining Judge: "And?"

Witness: "And, your honor?"

Examining Judge: "Yes, tell me why I should believe you are a God-fearing man?"

Witness: "I attend Mass every Sunday, and I confess my sins every week."

Examining Judge: "Did someone force you to come as a witness?"

Witness: "No, your honor. I came forward of my own free will, before the officer of the Governor of Franchimont in order to make a declaration in the case against Françoise Mathieu, the widow of Henry Hurlet de Creppe."

Examining Judge: "Very good. What can you tell us about Françoise Mathieu, the widow of Henry Hurlet de Creppe?"

Witness: "Françoise Mathieu, the widow of Henry Hurlet of Creppe is a witch and has been one for at least six years."

Examining Judge: "Are you making this declaration on your honor?"

Witness: "Yes, your honor. On my honor and on the heads of my six children."

Examining Judge: "Please go on."

Witness: "Last summer I went to Desnié with my hunting dogs. Suddenly, the dogs became very agitated and started snarling and barking."

Examining Judge: "Did you go to investigate why they were so agitated?"

Witness: "Oh, yes, your honor."

Examining Judge: "Well, can you explain?"

Witness: "Yes, your honor. I went to investigate why my animals were so agitated."

Examining Judge: "Did you find out what was bothering them?"

Witness: "Oh, yes, My Lord. It was Françoise Mathieu."

Examining Judge: "What was she doing?"

Witness: "She was gathering some plants."

Examining Judge: "Do you know what plants she was gathering?"

Witness: "Yes, your honor. I recognized them right away. She was gathering lilies-of-the-valley and oleander leaves."

Examining Judge: "And did you ask her why she was gathering lilies-of-the-valley and oleanders leaves?"

Witness: "Yes, your honor. I asked her what she was doing and she answered me rudely."

Examining Judge: "You sound worried when you say Françoise Mathieu was gathering lilies-of-the-valley and oleander leaves. Is there a reason for this?"

Witness: "Yes, your Honor. Both plants are highly poisonous."

Examining Judge: "Are you absolutely certain?"

Witness: "Of course, I am. And especially because I never trusted her, I specifically looked at what she had gathered in her basket. I am an Ardennais, your honor, and it is difficult to fool me."

Examining Judge: "What happened after that?"

Witness: "A few months later a neighbor of Françoise Mathieu's, whom she was tending, unexpectedly died. I put two and two together."

Examining Judge: "And what was your conclusion?"

Witness: "I realized that the day I saw her on the road to Desnié, she had been collecting poisonous plants."

## CHAPTER 26
## 14th March 1600
## Witness Two

## Declaration - Office of the Governor of Franchimont

Examining Judge: "What is your name?"

Witness: "Etienne Querlin"

Examining Judge: "Do you confirm that you have already sworn that you are a God-fearing man. Also, that you not only attend mass, but confess your sins regularly?"

Witness: "Yes, your honor. I confirm and I swear it."

Examining Judge: "Have you come forward of your own free will before the officer of the Governor of Franchimont to make the following declaration in the case of Françoise Mathieu, widow of Henry Hurlet de Creppe?"

Witness: "Yes, your honor."

Examining Judge: "What do you have to declare?"

Witness: "That Françoise Mathieu is a witch."

Examining Judge: "How do you know that she is a witch?"

Witness: "I know for a fact that she is a witch because of what I saw and what I heard during the execution of Jehenne Anseau."

Examining Judge: "Can you tell the court exactly what you saw and heard?"

Witness: "Yes, I can, your honor."

Examining Judge: "Well, what did you see and hear?"

Witness: "The sympathy she openly showed at the burning of Jehenne Anseau was an absolute scandal. She . . . . Françoise Mathieu . . . . was standing next to me. I saw tears running down her cheeks and

# The Drop of the Hammer

I heard her say 'Poor Girl' referring to Jehenne Anseau.[28]"

Examining Judge:"What is your conclusion?"

Witness: "The way she acted is proof that Françoise Mathieu is a witch! No God-fearing person, a good Christian woman would ever feel anything for a witch except contempt and revulsion..

---

[28] Anybody who would have shown a sign of compassion of any type towards an accused witch, would have quickly been singled out. The hard-working farmer, the loving mothers, the Pious priest quickly turned into a blood thirsty mob. I am including in the Annex a translation of Pierre Den Dooven's "The Chapel of the Damned Knight where he describes the mob "accompanying" a witch to her death. The Chapel in the title is, of course, the Chapel of Marché at the foot of the Chateau of Franchimont

## CHAPTER 27
## 14th March 1600
## Witness Three

### Declaration - Office of the Governor of Franchimont

Examining Judge: "What is your name?"

Witness: "Catherine Ogier."

Examining Judge: "Are you from Spa or Creppe?"

Witness: "From Creppe, your Honor."

Examining Judge: "Do you confirm that you swore in good faith before the judges that you are a God-fearing woman?"

Witness: "Yes, your honor, I confirm."

Examining Judge: "Do you also confirm that

you attend mass and confess your sins regularly?"

Witness: "Yes, your honor, I confirm."

Examining Judge: "And have you come to testify against the accused, Françoise Mathieu, of your own free will?"

Witness: "Yes, your honor, of my own free will."

Examining Judge: "Do you know, Françoise Mathieu, the widow of Henri Hurlet of Creppe well?"

Witness "Yes, your Honor, we are from the same village. We used to play together as children."

Examining Judge: "Tell us what you know."

Witness: "I was there. I saw her give an apple to Henry Badrulle's ten-year-old daughter. I was there."

Examining Judge: "How is that bad?"

Witness: "The little girl died a few days later."

Examining Judge: "In your opinion, is there a connection between the apple and the death of the little girl?"

Witness: "Of course, your Honor. The little girl

had never been ill a single day since she was born. I mean, until she ate that apple and died."

Examining Judge: "Do you have anything else to add?"

Witness: "Yes, your Honor. My cousin's next-door neighbor told my mother that one day he was in the forest gathering wood, when he came across Françoise Mathieu. Although she spoke to him politely, she had a strange look in her eyes. By the time he had gathered all his wood, he noticed that his horse was lame. He had a hard time getting back to Creppe."

Examining Judge: "Is there a connection between the lame horse and this case?"

Witness: "Oh, yes, your honor."

Examining Judge: "What is that connection?"

Witness: The horse only started limping after the man saw Françoise Mathieu. It's that strange look in her eyes that did it?"

## CHAPTER 28
## 17ᵗʰ March 1600
## The Sentencing

"On this seventeenth day of the month of March in the year one thousand six hundred of our Lord, We, the Court of Justice of Spa, declare that Françoise Mathieu, widow of Henry Hurlet of Creppe, herself living in Creppe and therefore in the Ban of Spa and the Ward of her father-in-law Jules Hurlet, is indicted on the bases of detestable acts of witchcraft, conjuring spells, conspiracy with the devil to destroy the Christian World, wicked behavior, murder, shape-shifting, and having viciously attacked the person of Remacle Le Rosy causing grave injury.

We, Cedric Boniver, the High Magistrate of the

Court of Justice of Spa, as well as judges Norbert Gosselin, Désiré de Soiron and Michel Dupont, all three of the Court of Justice of Spa affirm that:

- All procedures were carried out as specified by the law,
- All witnesses were heard and questioned as intended by the law of our land,
- A physical examination of the accused Françoise Mathieu, the widow of Henry Hurlet of Creppe, was carried out prior to the trial and that the mark of the Devil was found on her body and attested by all officially present,
- That the accused continued to claim her innocence in spite of all the charges against her and all the witnesses of her foul deeds.

Therefore, We, the Court of Justice of Spa, put forward the sentence of death by burning for Françoise Mathieu for the above-mentioned acts on and prior to 29th November 1599.

We graciously request the High Court of Liège to comply with our wishes and our ruling by affirming its authorization upon this request as it sees fit.

Cedric Boniver
High Magistrate of Spa
Chateau de Franchimont

Norbert Gosselin
Désiré de Soiron
Michel Dupont
Judges of the Court of Justice of Spa."

## CHAPTER 29
## 26th March 1600
## Evening

Jules is sitting at the big oak table in front of the fireplace in Hanchoulle's home. Both his elbows are resting on the table, his head bent and buried in his hands. Salty tears fill and sting his eyes. Biting his lips, he tries his best to hold back the tears.

It is one of those cold and humid nights so common to the Ardennes, but this one is different because Jules knows he will remember it for the rest of his life. A cold shudder runs through him in spite of the warm fire burning in the fireplace. The cold in his body doesn't come from the outside but the despair growing in him. The coldness filling him is deep-rooted and spreads into his bones, muscles and nerves.

Jules' mind is racing around in circles. One moment he thinks he can see a way out and the next moment he sinks even deeper in his desperation.

The sound of Hanchoulle's heavy steps precede him into the room. Taller than most of the other villagers, Johan Hanchoulle's long legs bring him next to his friend and cousin in three easy strides. He places his hand on Jules' shoulder and presses it. Jules does not look up. Although he tries to control his grief, tears run down his cheeks and he is ashamed of what he considers a weakness.

"It's time to go, Jules. They'll be waiting for us at the forge." The tall man bites his lower lip, when he sees his cousin's tears. He turns towards the fireplace and says roughly, "Better attend to the fire before we leave. Otherwise, it will be out and it will take a long time before we can warm the room up again." He hopes his deep and hash voice will cover the pain he shares with Jules. The men from Creppe are proud and they don't like to show their feelings.

Hanchoulle and Jules are cousins. Most of the people in Creppe are related and those who are not direct family are related by marriage. Jules and Hanchoulle go back a long way. In many ways, they are closer than brothers. All their lives they have been there for each other, sharing their sadness as well as their joys . . . . but always hiding their emotions. For the men of Creppe, emotions are things that need to be dealt with internally and in private.

Hanchoulle walks back to the table. He sets down a couple of clay glasses and a jug half full with geniever. "I've been keeping this geniever for a special occasion. I feel today is special. Let's take a little drop before meeting the others. It will bring us luck."

Jules does not move.

"Drink it, Jules," says Hanchoulle in his gruff voice.

"Can't," answers Jules with difficulty.

"Drink it. It will warm you up and bring us

luck." Hanchoulle pushes the glass closer to Jules' hand.

Jules sits back, looks at the geniever and picks up the glass. He drinks it slowly, savoring the subtle juniper taste mingling with other familiar spices. He stares into the fireplace.

Hanchoulle picks up the jug to refill their glasses.

Jules shakes his head. He lifts his sad eyes towards Hanchoulle and says, his voice barely above a whisper, "I've let Henry down again. He left both Françoise and his baby son in my care and I failed in both cases. The baby died from the same cough that took his father and now---and now this."

Hanchoulle stands up and puts his arms round Jules' shoulders. Jules' trembling hands fly up to his face. After a moment the man continues, "Johan, I couldn't stop them from arresting her and now I am unable to save her from being burned for witchcraft at Jonkeu. I am a bad father."

This time Jules is unable to hold back his tears

and he collapses on the table in front of him. His body shakes with each sob that escapes him.

"Drink your geniever, Jules, and let's go. This may be her only chance. You didn't let anybody down. You especially did not let Henry down. Now drink this second geniever. You need it. We both need it."

The two men empty their geniever and leave Hanchoulle's house. The meeting is at the Hola Forge.[29]

The easiest and fastest way to get to the Hola Forge from Creppe is by taking the narrow path to the right of the Wooden Cross. As they reach it, Hanchoulle puts his hand out and stops Jules. Jules quickly looks at him, but doesn't say a word. Hanchoulle is holding his index up to his lips. "Shh. I think we are being followed." He points to bushes along the path.

---

[29] The Hola Forge did exist. Many of the men from Creppe worked there. In a roundabout way, they considered it theirs, since Johan Hannon, their ancestor and founder of Creppe, had inherited a quarter of it in 1449

The two men quickly hide behind the bushes and wait.

Minutes tick by.

Nothing.

Just as Hanchoulle decides that maybe it was all in his imagination, they hear a twig snap and then a second. They wait some more but all they hear is silence.

Hanchoulle puts his lips close to Jules' ear and whispers, "That was no four-legged animal. We are being followed. Let's go through the woods and cross the Barisart stream. We'll reach the forge from the other side. We'll be late, but it doesn't matter. Better to be safe than sorry." Jules nods and both men are soon lost from sight in the welcoming safety of the woods.

When they get to the Hola Forge everyone else has already arrived.

"Expected you over an hour ago." Says one of the men, a miller, getting up from his seat as Hanchoulle and Jules enter. "What happened? Were you followed?"

Hanchoulle and Jules nod.

"Figured it was something like that."

"Someone followed us, for sure from Creppe to the Big Cross, and probably up to Barisart. We're pretty sure we lost him," continues Hanchoulle as he sits down and stretches his legs out before him. "So, let's get started."

Luke, the younger of the Lezaak brothers, brings his face close to the candle, and hits his fist loudly on the table to make a point. "We're here to help you, Jules! Just tell us what to do and we will do it."

Jules smiles sadly at him.

René Bredar puts his hand up to silence Luke. "Jules, what Luke means is, we are all friends and relatives of yours. We are going to do what we can. However, we need to be very careful. We don't want another Maroie episode on our hands."

"René," Louis Mathieu breaks in, "You can't compare Maroie to Françoise. Maroie talked to everyone about her plan to escape. She .... "

A loud knock at the door interrupts Louis in mid-sentence.

Hanchoulle quickly blows out the candle. The men stand up and wait without making a noise.

A second loud knock follows and a low, raspy voice said, "Let me in. I know you are there. Let me in, please. I am a friend."

Wilkin mouths "Please?" He looks around, "What do we do?"

René sighs and slowly walks to the door, looking back at his comrades one last time before lifting the bar off the hooks.

No sooner the bar off, a strong hand flings the door open. A broad-shouldered man fills the doorway. "Don't be afraid. I am a friend."

Louis Mathieu relights the candle. At that moment and for the first time, they get a good look at the stranger who for all intents and purposes has forced his presence on them. Jules gasps as he realizes they have allowed a hooded Franciscan monk to come in.

Although the monk keeps his hood up, the strength of his hooked nose and the steadiness of his steel blue eyes transfix them.

The monk turns towards the miller and in that raspy voice of his says, "Lock the door." To the men around the table he says, "Sit down".

The men sit down without a word. The arrival of a Franciscan monk scares them. The Inquisition? They look at each other, fear gripping their hearts. No, it can't be the inquisition. This is not the way they act.

The monk sits down on Wilkin's empty stool. He reaches out with one hand, to take one of the clay glasses in the middle of the table. With the other hand he reaches for the jug full of geniever and pours himself a drink.

He drinks it and smacks his lips with the gesture of a man who appreciates the fruits of the earth.

The monk puts his glass down with a thud. He

looks around at the men sitting around him.

They are all staring at him, their mouths agape, not knowing what to expect.

"I represent someone who, like you, wants to see Françoise Mathieu, the widow of Henry Hurlet of Spa, freed.".

## CHAPTER 30
## 2nd April 1600
## A prison cell
## Château of Franchimont

A rough hand grabs Françoise's left shoulder and shakes her like a rag doll. Her hand shoots up to remove it. Instead of letting go a second hand joins the first, and holds her shoulders in a tight clamp. Pain radiates throughout her shoulders as fingernails dig into her skin. Something slams into her cheek, and jolts her senses.

Her mind switches with difficulty from the recurrent dream of Jehenne and the chanting in the field to the stark reality of the rough, bare floor on which she is laying. Françoise flip flops between the two states, not quite sure which one is a dream and which one is reality.

Pain spreads along her arms into the fingers.

Françoise can no longer hear the chanting. She glances up. A moist fog surrounds her. A strange, haunting music comes out of the fog and the priest floats in front of her. Father de Lazaar holds two pointed rods in his hands which he waves in the air as his body sways sensuously to the music.

The music fades, and the chanting starts again. The fog lifts. The villagers' bodyless faces circle around Françoise. Hatred pours out of their eyes. A gruff voice yells at her. She can't make out the man's words, but their sharp tones are like a sharp knife slicing its way through her head. Each word plunges nails into her temples, and each nail sends burning flashes into her eyes. The chanting and the words break into each other.

The priest floats by her again, and thrusts a rod towards her. The jagged point of the rod catches on the front of her kirtle and tears it open. Françoise's hands shoot up to her breasts, and she tries to scramble away. When de Lazaar sees her embarrassment at her exposed breasts, he starts laughing. His laughter becomes louder and louder until it fills her head. When she thinks she can no longer stand it, his face turns into a grotesque mask, and shatters into pieces.

A woman's shrill and mournful scream rips through the night. A cold tremor snakes up Françoise's spine. She closes her eyes to escape from both the sound and the scene. A second scream slashes the darkness. As the second scream rips through her, she realizes whose screams are echoing in her head. The screams are hers.

A strong smell of onions mixed with fetid breath breaks through her nightmare. It floats up her nostrils, settles in her mouth, and seeps into her lungs. Nausea swells up her throat, and she retches.

"Hey, wake up you! And stop all that crying and screaming. Where do you think you are? I said shut up," shouts an angry voice at her. Françoise forces her eyes open, and unexpectedly finds herself staring into the furious, bloodshot eyes of Guillaume Nicolet, the jailer.

As his voice and foul smell fade away, the nightmare engulfs her again. Father de Lazaar stands bigger than life in front of her. He is holding a large flaming torch in his right hand.

Fear and panic gushes up in Françoise as tears roll down her cheeks. The more she panics the more she cries. She put her hands up to protect her face certain Father de Lazard will burn her with his torch.

"Don't....don't....please don't! Don't touch me! Go away! Leave me alone," she screams. The group is no longer circling her, and the chanting has stopped. Individual faces zoom toward her before withdrawing once again into the crowd.

Frantic, she looks around for a possible escape. Every time she thinks she has found one, a giant flame pushes her back. The priest is standing a few feet away from her. Françoise now understands how cornered animals feel as she tosses about like a wild animal caught in a hunter's net.

In her dream, Remacle leaves the chanting group, and grabs the torch from Father de Lazaar's hands. The herder's eyes glance from her to the torch several times. Suddenly he plunges it towards her. Her skirt catches on fire. Françoise tries to put the flames out, but they kept getting bigger and bigger. The flames quickly spread to her hair. The flames jump from one strand of hair to the other. Within seconds fire swallow up her whole head.

"I said shut up," growls the jailer as he slaps her hard across the face.

Françoise screams. She puts her hand up to her cheek as the searing flames engulf her face. Her heart races. She can feel the fire piercing into her cheeks. Fear leaves her breathless. She gasps for air as the flames consume her.

The jailer's coarse voice slices through her brain like lightning. The rough voice makes her seesaw between the horror of her dream and the dreadfulness of jail.

## The Drop of the Hammer

Part of Françoise wants to keep her eyes shut, another part wills her to open them.

The jailer's face hovers inches from her face. His foul breath makes her heave.

"You're in jail. You're not at one of your witches' sabbat. You hear me? Huh? What you do there with your cloven foot friend is none of my business. It's yours. What you do here is mine. Within these walls I am the master and you do what I tell you."

Françoise can't take her eyes away from his disgusting mouth. When his lips move, his mouth reveals black, broken teeth. The more she looks at his mouth, the sicker she feels.

"Well, do you hear me," he continues pointing a finger at her. "Did you hear what I said, huh? And what are you staring at anyway? I am the master here. Me, Guillaume Nicolet is the master, and I want to hear you say it. Let me hear you say it. Guillaume Nicolet, you are the master. I am nothing but the whore of the cloven hoof devil, and you are the master." The jailer steps closer to her, grabs her chin with his rough hand, "Yes, the devil sure knows how to choose them."

Françoise presses her lips together not only to stifle the scream caught in her throat, but also to calm the rising nausea. The jailer's closeness makes her stomach turn. With one hand she pinches her nose shut, and with the other she holds her torn shift closed.

"What? I don't smell good enough for you? Of course, you prefer sulfur. I know your kind. Believe me, I know your kind. So many of you are sent to my casemate, and you are all alike." The jailer leans his face closer to Francoise's, puckers his lips, and blows air across her face.

Françoise scrambles against the wall. She covers her face with her hands and cries, "Leave me alone! You stink! Get away from me!"

Nicolet pulls back as if he had been slapped. He pulls one of her hands away from her face angrily. Their eyes meet. Françoise sees his eyes narrow, and her tears became uncontrollable. Nicolet looks at the young woman crying desolately on the bare casemate floor. His eyes fall upon her breasts. He licks his lips in anticipation, and throws himself on her. His hands couple her breasts roughly as he tries to separate her legs with his own.

Like a wild animal, cornered in an impasse, her whole body retracts. She tightens her hands into fists and strikes her tormentor with all her strength.

Guillaume Nicolet tries to grab her wrists but only succeeds in getting his face close enough for the young woman to scratch him across his cheeks and nose.

He jumps back screaming. Guillaume puts a hand up to his face, and fingers the wetness covering his cheeks. He lowers his hand and looks at the blood. Françoise follows his gaze. She looks up at his face and stares with satisfaction at the three deep scratches across his nose and on either side of the jailor's face.

He lowers his hands to his side, and wipes

them on his trousers. Although deep inside she feels defiant, she knows this time she has gone too far. Guillaume looks down at Françoise. He stares at her with an icy glare full of hatred. She hears him clear his throat seconds before he spits at her. She lifts an arm to protect her face, and the yellow spittle hits her hand.

Françoise wills herself not to react. Frozen in place, she cannot move her eyes from his.

Suddenly, some ancestral instinct of survival makes her react to a flicker in the jailor's eyes. Françoise rolls up in a ball just in time to thwart a kick. The kick he had aimed at her ribs lands on her thigh. Françoise screams. She screams more from shock than pain.

This time Nicolet manages to grab her wrists and brusquely pulls her up to her feet. He grabs a handful of her hair, and pulls her head back. Françoise tries to move, but the more she moves the more he pulls her head back. She knows he can see the fear in her eyes and to her horror she realizes her fear has aroused him.

A muffled voice from somewhere behind the jailer breaks into her world. "Stop it, Guillaume. Save it for later. De Bolland wants the witch brought to his office immediately." Nicolet steps back and she slowly slides face down to the floor. Françoise coughs as she tries to breathe in, and slowly her breathing returns to normal. Her whole body aches. Her face hurts. Every part of her hurts.

The jailer kicks her over onto her back with his foot. A wicked sneer spreads across his face as he says, "You are a lucky little witch, Françoise Mathieu. A very lucky one."

Françoise feels the blood rising up her face from both embarrassment and anger.

Nicolet pins her against the stone floor with his foot. "Ohh yes, you are very lucky. Very lucky the High Magistrate of Liège probably wants you for his pleasure and I doubt he likes damaged goods. Otherwise, I would carve your face like meat. You would look so bad even your mother wouldn't recognize you." He takes out a knife from his boot, and waves it in front of Françoise's face. "They may all have the mark of the devil on them when they arrive, but when they burn, they all have Guillaume Nicolet's mark."

The young woman lifts her arms to push his foot off her. Just as she is going to reach his foot, he removes it and pulls her up to her feet. Just as swiftly he throws her against the wall, and holds her there with one arm.

Françoise struggles to free herself. Nicolet again pushes her roughly against the wall. The jagged edges of the stone cut into her back. A groan escapes from her lips.

"Come on, Guillaume," insists Sergeant Richard, "I don't like to keep de Bolland waiting. You know how he is." He takes a step toward Françoise, cups her chin, and turns her face from right to left. "You're talking about damaged goods? Look at her. She's a mess. You damaged her. You are going to take her to him. Not me."

# The Drop of the Hammer

Guillaume takes his eyes away from Françoise and looks at the Sergeant. "I haven't even started, Sergeant. I can't help it if the witch is in this condition. They all arrive here in bad condition. You know how thorough the men from the inquisition can be. Terrible! Terrible!"

And with those harsh words he grabs her by the hair, pulls her behind him, and violently hurls her out of the cell.

Françoise screams as he propels her into the hall. She tries to steady herself with her right hand but misses. The whole of her weight falls on her hand and forearm. A broken tile slices into a finger and the cut starts to bleed

She feels his two hands reach out to stand her back on her feet. When the jailor sees her hand, he became furious, and starts yelling at her. The words don't mean anything to Françoise. At the point where she is, physically and mentally, everything is just noise.

He grabs her wounded hand by the wrist and brings it inches from her eyes. "Look what you did.

Didn't I tell you I didn't want to damage the magistrate's goods, huh?"

The sergeant put a hand on Nicolet's shoulder, and says in a low voice, "Let her go, Nicolet. You'll have a lot of time later. Take her to de Bolland now. That's all I'm asking you to do."

Nicolet turns toward the Sergeant and grins. "It's not my job."

"It is now."

The jailor's eyes harden as he looks back at Françoise. His right arm swings up and slaps her face forcefully. The slap flings Françoise against the staircase wall. With her arms over her face and head to protect herself from Guillaume's slaps, she is unable to steady herself and she slides to the floor. The pain and the fear become intolerable. Loud sobs escape from Françoise's lips. She can no longer hold anything back. "No, please, no more. Don't hurt me. Please no!"

"Oh, now you are pleading with me, are you? Witches are sly I hear. And if I do hurt you, what are you going to do, huh? Turn me into a toad," Nicolet asks with a mean glint in his eyes.

In a calm voice surprising even herself, Françoise answer, "No, I'm not a witch. Please believe me." All the fight has runs out of her. Françoise's shoulders slump as the weight of her pain and state she is in crush her.

"You're not a witch? Then why are they going to burn you. Can you tell me that? Don't try to put up a sweet, little frightened front for me. I'm too smart for that. You can't hide anything from me."

Françoise realizes the uselessness of answering the jailor. At the end of the day, does her innocence matter anymore?

"I have nothing to hide from you, the people of Spa or Creppe and even less from God. I am innocent. I am no witch."

"I don't care. You are going to burn anyway." The jailer laughs mockingly at her. "Now up the stairs."

Françoise looks up at the flight of stairs in front

of her. How can she go up all those steps? She can hardly put one foot in front of the other.

The Sergeant steps in between Nicolet and Françoise. "Guillaume, stop now. De Bolland has been waiting long enough, and I have to get back to my post. Do what you are told to do. Your wants can wait. Take her to him now. That's an order."

Guillaume nods his head. "Well, if it's an order, I guess, it's an order. I'll take the witch up to the mighty de Bolland right away. Can't let the gentleman wait, can I?" He winks at the Sergeant.

The Sergeant nods, and without another word goes up the stairs two by two.

A sharp burning pain tears at her lower chest, and a bitter taste fills both her throat and mouth. Françoise looks around her. Everything looked shiny. Her knees buckle under her.

"Up," Nicolet shouts as he pulls her up unceremoniously by the arm. "Go up the stairs," he says pointing at the long flight of steps.

Francoise tried to climb, but falls at the second

step.

Guillaume grabs her by the arm, and pulls her up behind him. Françoise scrapes her arms and legs against the sharp stones, but she can no longer feel pain.

At the top of the stairs, he pushes her towards a door leading out into a courtyard. The door swings open under her weight, and she topples across a wheelbarrow. She holds on to the wheelbarrow, and takes a deep breathe. The fresh air helps clear Françoise's head. She looks up towards the sky. From the position of the sun, she assumes it is midafternoon. The sun and the fresh air give her added strength.

Because she wants to put up a strong front, she gathers all the energy she can, and swings around to face her tormentor.

"Where are you taking me?" Françoise steadies herself against the wheelbarrow, and hopes her voice sounds steadier than she feels.

"That's none of your business, witch, But,"

says Nicolet in a tone which does not even try to hide scorn, "this is one of my good days. So, I guess I'll tell you. There's a gentleman over there who has strange tastes. Wants me to take you to him. Hope I haven't damaged the goods too much."

Françoise feel the blood drain from her face. "No, no, I won't permit it. Take me back to my cell," she orders.

"What? You're giving me orders. You?" The jailor looks her over with disgust and spits at her again. The spittle misses her by a couple of inches. The young woman looks up at her jailor's amused expression. She knows he can read on her face the revulsion she feels. He probably will kill her before the end of the day, but at least he will know how much she hates him. "Now walk," he says indicating the direction with a nod of his chin.

Icy fingers of fear run up her back. She presses her lips together; balls her fists and turns towards the direction he indicates. Although her back and legs ache, she considers hiding it from him is a victory.

They cross the courtyard in silence.

They reach a heavy, wooden door. Guillaume Nicolet starts chuckling. "You're still insolent, aren't you? Really difficult to break, aren't you? You think I can't see through your little game. You think hiding your pain is a victory?" Françoise's heart sinks. He cups her chin hard between his fingers, and whispers, "But you're still going to burn." Françoise's back stiffens. "Let's see if you are still as insolent when you come back to your cell," he jeers. They reach a door and he says mockingly, "After you, my lady."

Guillaume Nicolet opens the door, and shoves her roughly into a room. Françoise's foot catches under a carpet. Her arms waving about to steady herself, she dives straight into the center of the room where she falls once again on her injured arm.

She doesn't want to get up.

She wants to blend into nothingness.

She wants to go back to the way life used to be.

She wants the nightmares to stop.

She wants peace and safety.

Francoise does not bother getting up.

Oblivious to the room around her, she gives free rein to the misery bubbling inside of her. Her eyes begin to burn and hot tears of anger and disgust cascade down her cheeks.

## CHAPTER 31
## 2nd  April 1600

The force of the jailor's trust sends Françoise diving into the room. Her right foot gets caught under the rug and she plunges face down on the floor. Françoise puts her arms out to stop the fall. Instead of stopping her fall she land on the arm that had been hurt on her way up. The pain shoots straight into her shoulder. The young woman remains motionless as she feels tears well up in her eyes.

Hurt.

Desperate.

Embarrassed.

Angry with herself because she keeps thinking she is stronger than she really is, Françoise abandons herself to her despair and cries.

Somewhere in the background, she hears the jailor's crude laugh. In spite of her tears, she holds her breath. It is only once she hears the door slam shut, and the jailor's steps walking away, that she allows herself a deep breath.

The room is quiet, so quiet that she can almost touch the silence. Françoise thanks God for these few precious minutes of silence that give her the strength to get a grip on herself. Calmer but still too stunned to even move a muscle, she tries to block her thoughts. Every time she thinks about what is happening fresh tears threaten to surface.

How did all this even happen? She never hurt anyone. Why doesn't it all stop. The worst part is being alone, not being allowed to see her family. Do they even know where she is? The last time she saw Mam and Jules was the day they arrested her. An eternity ago. Just get it over with. Let them do what they want to her. But here's one thing they won't make her do and that is to confess to what she hasn't done.

Her eyes focus on the tiny white and blue flowers of the carpet inches from her eyes. She decides to try a trick she used as a little girl when she didn't want to cry. She used to tell herself, "Concentrate on the little white flowers, Françoise, the size, the color, the number of petals the distance between the flowers. The size of one as compared to the others."

The childish game dries her last tears, but do not change what is happening. Françoise is so exhausted that the tiredness fills every part of her mind and body. The simplest movement is agony. Pain shoots through her head, and when she closes her eyes bright flashes blind her as if her brain is going to explode. Her eyes begin to sting as tears well up again, but this time she is able to stop them.

Françoise starts trembling from head to toe. She can feel her teeth clattering and her face throbbing as silent uncontrollable grief pours over her.

Suddenly, she hears a small noise. Someone else is in the room. Is the jailor back? Or is it that de Bolland she has heard of every day since her arrest. The jailors say he is arrogant and cruel.

Maybe it is just her imagination.

Françoise focuses on the flowers again. The young woman starts mumbling uncontrollably, "I have been slapped, kicked, physically humiliated. I can't and won't go through this again. I don't care what they do. Why don't they just kill me now. Everything will be over soon anyway. Why should I even put up a strong front or even fight. Let them do whatever they want to do with me. There is nothing I can do one way or the other. This de Bolland will use me and then send me back to the casemates where the jailor is waiting for me."

Why even fight it? It will start all over again. Maybe if she puts up no resistance, they won't hurt her too much. All she has to do is avoid as much pain as possible until they take her up to Jonkeu. And then what will happen after that? They will burn her at the stake. Françoise coldly analyzes her coming execution as if it were happening to somebody unknown to her. Will they garrote her first? What does it matter? If only she could be at Jonkeu now. It would be a blessing to know that everything will be over in a matter of minutes.

A noise breaks the silence surrounding Françoise. It was not her imagination. She can hear steps coming towards her. The young woman wants to distance herself from this intrusion. At the same time, she needs to know. Keeping her head down, Françoise partially opens her eyes . . . .just enough to know what is happening. Be strong, Françoise, be strong. In a few days all of this will be over. Death. How welcoming it seems today.

A pair of leather riding boots stops close to her face. Although her plan is not to show she knows he is there, her survival instincts take over. Françoise's hand automatically swings up to protect her face. She knows she is going to be kicked . . . . but the kick does not come.

The man bends down on one knee. He stays like that for what seems an eternity to Françoise. The longer he stays the greater the panic in her. She starts trembling. She has never felt so cold. Be strong, Françoise, be strong.

Unexpectedly, a gentle hand touches her shoulder. Part of her reacts in fear and she stiffens at the touch. Another part of her reacts to the unexpected gentleness in the touch. Anger immediately boils up in her as she realizes that she is so starved for any show of kindness whatsoever that she is actually wallowing. And yet, the gentleness of the hand touching her is like a soothing balm, sending a series of burning waves throughout her body. Her emotions begin to flip flop. She swings from wanting to relish it to wanting to banish it; from wanting to give in to the pleasure to being paralyzed by fear.

Her mind takes over, pushing her emotions away. It's a trick, Françoise, nothing but a trick. Her hands become cold. Her mouth goes dry. She expects the kick to come at any second.

Not daring to meet the danger face-to-face, she keeps her eyes riveted on the flowered carpet. It's a trick she keeps reminding herself. They can't get me to confess with brutal force, and they think a change of tactics will do the trick. Why? Why? They've already sentenced her. Why don't they leave her alone?

The hand gently presses her shoulder.

Slowly the hand turns her over on her back.

She comes face to face with him.

HIM is what she mentally calls the man in front of her. HIM who is going to use her.

HIM who will throw her back downstairs into the casemates for the jailor to enjoy.

Their eyes meet. He puts out his hand to move away a lock of hair partly covering her face. Françoise recoils from the touch as the jailor's crude words flash again through her mind. She feels trapped and helpless like a trapped deer.

She tries to sit up and in doing so she puts too much weight on her wounded arm. She winces and cries out. HIM, the man, looks surprised and full of sympathy.

Françoise is momentarily touched by this but then like a slap in the face, she remembers why she is here. The jailer made it quite clear. Instead of compassion he is just probably concerned that his goods, as the jailor said, might be damaged.

His hand goes slowly up to her face. He cups her chin and slowly turns her face left and then right. When she looks at his face again, the compassion is gone. Instead, boiling anger pours out of his steel blue eyes. Is this directed towards her? Because he considers her damaged goods?

Just as slowly as he had touched her face, his eyes go down to her torn clothes and her exposed breasts. Françoise pulls up her knees and clasps her hands around them. She then lays her head on her knees.

The man gently picks Françoise up in his arms

and places her in an armchair. He gets onto his knees in front of her so that their faces are at the same level. She tries to cover her breasts. He stops her hands gently. He looked at her breasts again and then looks up at her face. In spite of herself she is fascinated by his eyes. There isn't any trace of the crudeness she had seen in the jailor's eyes. This is something else. Something she doesn't understand. She looks at his face. His eyes are taking in the rest of her bruised body. His lips are pressed together and his eagle nose seems to dominate his whole face. He takes her by the hands and turns her arms around. He lifts her shift and she gasps. He stops and once again his eyes meet hers. He shakes his head slowly and returns to inspecting her legs. His eyes take in every scratch and every bruise.

The man sits back on his heels and looks at her. Their eyes meet again, hers brown and fearful and his steel blue and steady.

In a low and raspy voice, he murmurs, "Most of these are new, little one. When did they happen?"

Françoise presses her lips together. Can she trust him?

He moves his hand up to touch the side of her face and she flinches thinking he is going to slap her.

The man pulls his hand away quickly when he sees her reaction, and then once again returns his hand to her cheek. He caresses her with the back of his fingers. "I'm not going to hurt you, Françoise Mathieu, but I do expect answers when I ask questions. Is this absolutely clear between us?"

She nods and begins to tremble again. This man's ways are even more frightening. At least the jailor is coarse all the time. She knows what is coming all the time. This man is different. He is being gentle and compassionate but she feels that deep inside there is deep anger. The gentleness and compassion must be a trap to bait her. It can't be anything else. It is just his way. After all, she is a prisoner accused of witchcraft and sentenced to die at Jonkeu. He is a gentleman with soft hands and other ways. He still wants the same thing as the jailor does. Once satisfied

## The Drop of the Hammer

he will throw her back to the jailor like one throws pieces of meat to household dogs.

She turns her eyes toward him and catches him looking at her breasts. She is ashamed of the bruises and the fact this man is seeing them. His eyes look into hers. "Who did this, little one? These are new cuts and new bruises. They don't come from any mistreatment you received when you arrived at Franchimont. Who did this? Is it the jailor?"

Françoise bites her lips. She wants to answer but at the same time there is something in the back of her mind telling her that if she does, she will be giving in. Don't trust him, Françoise, don't trust him.

He gets up and walks to the corner of the room to get something, but she doesn't see right away what it is. He comes back with a warm cloak which he places around her shoulders. Something jars in her mind. This has happened before. Where? When? Out in the corridor before they sentenced her. Fingering the material, she looks up at the man in amazement. "I . . . . er . . . .another man . . . . another cloak. There was a man before the sentencing he gave me his cloak. I . . ."

"Ah, so you were aware of him. You saw him. He wasn't certain you knew he was there."

"It was a dream", answers Françoise. "It was a dream."

"No, Françoise, it was not a dream. He was my messenger. He stopped their plans to torture you. His name is Captain Dieudonné Lejeune. He is one of my men."

"Messenger? One of your men? It's not a dream? He said something to me, but I don't remember what."

The man's face comes close to hers. She expects a fetid breath but instead the smell that comes from him is clean. He looks into her eyes. "Your cuts and bruises are new. Some are still bleeding. Little one. So, I will ask you again. Did the jailor do this?"

Françoise is caught in his eyes. Her mouth goes dry and her throat is knotted. She nods.

Francoise sees something stir in his eyes and

she panics.

The man moves closer to her and, whispers softly in her ear, "Little one, did he forcibly take you?"

Françoise turns her head towards him and looks into his bottomless steel blue eyes. She searches his face. She wants so much to trust him. A part of her says trust him and another part says run away from him. Run? She is a prisoner condemned to be executed, burned to the stake . . . .and she wants to run away! She shakes her head. "No. The Sergeant stopped Nicolet."

"I see," says the man stiffly as he stands up.

Françoise feels weak and she hates it. It is clear that is the only thing that concerns him. How can she be so stupid? This man with his nice boots, soft hands and steel blue eyes is no different. He just doesn't want left overs. The jailor was right. The man will use her and throw her back into the casemates and the jailer. Her cheeks begin to burn. She is angry and embarrassed even toward herself.

The man turns and walks to the window. He

stands with his back to her. His hands are clasped behind his back. Françoise catches sight of a dagger on his desk and jumps to grab it. Her movements are clumsy and slower than they normally are. He spins around, runs to her and manages to stop her seconds before she can plunge the knife into her heart.

He holds her tightly from behind against his body. His strong left arm around her waist. His right hand holding her hand with the knife tightly.

He lowers his head until his cheek is against hers and whispers, "Drop it."

Françoise holds on to it and tries to resist his strength.

His big hand tightens around her wrist. Her fingers loosen. The knife falls to the floor. With his foot he kicks it away.

Deep down, Françoise knows he is going to make her pay for her defiance. In what seems to be one movement, he lets go of her wrist, spins her around and holds her tightly against him. A ragged breath tears through her lungs as she tries to regain control of herself. A faint stream of defiance snakes up her legs and zigzags toward her mind. She balls her fists and barely able to control her anger she says in a voice so low the man has to lean his head closer to hear, "Enough! Enough! Kill me if you wish. I don't care. I have been sentenced. I am going to be executed anyway. Why did you have to stop me? It would be all over now. You can't hurt me anymore. You accuse me of being a witch. You throw me into your filthy jail. You torture me, insult me, humiliate me, and hurt me. And now you think you can take me for your pleasure? You'll wish I had killed myself, because there will be no pleasure for you. You'll have to kill me first. I swear, there will be no pleasure for you. I will fight you from beginning to end."

She feels more than hears the man's sharp intake of breath as he pulls his hands back.

From instinct, she takes a step back.

She looks up into his face. There is no gentleness or compassion there, but then no lust or anger either. The only thing she can see is strength.

He points to the armchair and says one word, "Sit."

True to her word, Françoise starts protesting. "No, I don't want to . . . ." He steps closer to her, puts a finger on her lips and repeats "Sit."

# CHAPTER 32
# 2nd April 1600

Roland keeps his eyes on Francoise's face as she steps back and moves towards the armchair. He notices that, she too, does not move her eyes away from him. He likes that. He has no doubt her spirit has given up several times since her arrest, but no one needs to tell him how resilient she is. Even in the face of death, and even knowing that her death is inevitable . . . .she is rebellious.

Somehow, he knew the first time he heard the herder talk about her in the tavern that she was something special. She is beautiful. Beautiful and rebellious. He looks at her eyes, her face, her body.

Even bruised and cut the way she is, she is beautiful.

Françoise, still with her eyes on his face, suddenly feels vulnerable and tries to cover herself. Her large, shapeless shift which was given to her after the sentencing was totally ripped apart from her struggle up the stairs. She holds her torn and dirty shift together and Roland's cape tightly around her. Roland feels himself blush and chuckles thinking this must be the first time he has ever blushed, and because of a woman's body too. He smiles to himself and turns towards his desk.

Françoise instinctively turns toward the opposite direction but both stop in their track.

"Françoise Mathieu. That's your name, isn't it?"

"Yes. Why are you asking me? We both know you know my name."

He smiles sadly at her. "I wanted to know simply if your family calls you by another name. That's all."

"They call me Françoise. That's my name."

"Françoise, you are beautiful. You must know that."

Françoise looks at him with open distrust. "I am a simple peasant girl from Creppe. I work hard. I should say . . . .I worked hard. Now, I am simply an injured and battered peasant girl from Creppe, dressed in a soiled and torn shift, waiting for the executioner at Jonkeu. I do not see what a gentleman like you can find beautiful in me. If you have any kindness in you, you will stop making fun of me."

Well, Françoise Mathieu, I think you should get used to the idea of being beautiful. Any man who lays his eyes on you takes pleasure in just looking at you. I understand the jailor wanting you. I'm not going to lie to you. I am no different from him in that respect," says Roland in that raspy voice of his. "However, there is a difference between being a jailor and being the High Magistrate of Liège."

Françoise's abruptly turns her face towards him.

"So that is who you are! The High Magistrate

of Liège. Don't you have enough to do in Liège that you need to come to Creppe to make fun of an innocent woman who has been wrongly accused and sentenced to burn?"

"I respect you. And whatever my body feels for you that is my problem . . . .not yours. Is that quite clear between us?"

Françoise swallows hard and nods, looking at him furtively. I suppose I have to thank you for your respect, but it's not going to help me at Jonkeu, is it?"

"Françoise, please stop fighting me," he answers dryly. "Can you at least do that?"

She nods silently.

"Good. Now that all this is clear between us, do you think you could sit down in that armchair, while I take care of a few things?"

Françoise silently nods again.

A glint, both mischievous and amused, passes through his eye as he winks at her and says, "By the way, I am not asking you to become a mute. You may speak, you know."

Françoise nods.

Roland looked at her sternly.

She says, "Yes."

He looks around to where he had kicked the knife away. He spots it, gets up, and picks it up. Back at his desk he automatically wants to put it back where it had originally been, and then having second thoughts about it, decides to stick it in his boot. "Stay put. Let me do what I have to do. As soon as I am finished, we are going to tend to your cuts and bruises."

"What is it that you need to do that is so urgent?"

Roland looks at her and says softly, "I need to gain your trust. You don't trust me and I understand that very well. But you have to trust me."

Françoise looks at him defiantly.

"Don't look at me like that! You can trust me. Will you give me the opportunity of proving it?"

Françoise just looks at him without a word.

"Well?"

She nods and then adds, "I suppose I can do that. I have nothing to lose, do I."

Roland de Bolland covers the distance to the big wooden door in three easy steps. He flings it open and steps into the corridor. "Sergeant Richard," he bawls out loud and clear. "I want you here on the double." He then turns back into his office and stands by the fireplace.

They can hear hurried steps coming up the corridor. Soon afterwards, Sergeant Richard appears at the door. When he sees the High Magistrate, he stands at attention and salutes.

"Sir?"

"Did you bring the prisoner to my office?" A hard gritty voice replaces his usual raspy one.

"Sir, did you not want the prisoner here?"

"Sergeant that is not the answer to my question. I want a simple yes or no. Did you or did you not bring the prisoner to my office?"

"No, Sir. I did not."

"Then who did?"

## The Drop of the Hammer

"Er . . . . the jailor, Sir"

"The jailor?"

"Er . . . .yes, Sir, the . . . .er . . . jailor. "

"I presume, this jailor of yours has a name?"

"Yes, er . . . .Guillaume Nicolet, Sir," answers the Sergeant definitely ill at ease.

"But you saw the prisoner in her cell, did you not?"

"Yes, Sir."

"I presume you can now also see the condition she is in?"

"Yes, Sir."

"Well?"

"She's a prisoner, Sir."

"I did not ask you if she were a prisoner or not. Answer the question I asked you. I presume you can see the condition she is in?"

"Yes, Sir. I see the condition she is in."

"And you saw her yesterday. Am I right?"

"Yes Sir."

"Was she in his condition when you saw her?

"No, Sir."

"So, something must have happened to her in between."

"Yes. Sir."

"Do you have anything to do with the condition she is now in, Sergeant?"

"No, Sir."

"Sergeant, do you know who I am."

"Yes, Sir. Of course, I know who you are. We all know who you are. Sir."

"Good. Tell me who I am."

"You are Roland de Bolland, the High Magistrate of Liège. Sir."

"Fine. Get the jailor up here immediately."

"Yes sir." The sergeant salutes, does an about face and practically runs out of the office.

Roland turns towards Françoise. Both her hands are grasping the arm of the chair with such force that her knuckles are turning white. She looks at him with her mouth open.

Roland looks at her and says, "As a child when

my mother saw me with my mouth open, she would always warn me that bats could come in and turn me into their home."

Françoise snaps her mouth shut. "Are . . . are . . . . you sending me back to the j . . . .jailor?"

Roland walks up to her and leans over her, his two arms resting on the arms of her chair, "Have you not understood a word of what I have said? Trust me. You are not in danger with me or from me."

Françoise looks up at him. "But. . . .but . . . you're the High Magistrate of Liège."

"I know who I am. You don't have to remind me. Trust me."

She lets out a soft ironic laugh. "I am a poor peasant girl not only accused of witchcraft, but also already sentenced to die, and you are telling me to trust you? You?" She points at him every time she says 'you'. "You! The High Magistrate of Liège! You are telling me to trust you?"

Roland looks up as he hears footsteps coming towards the doorway. The first to enter is the

Sergeant. He stands at attention and salutes. "Sir. The jailor is here. Will that be all, Sir?"

"Bring him in. Stay. I still have something for you to do."

The Sergeant moves aside and motions to the jailor to come into the office. Behind him, Roland hears Françoise utter a faint cry.

"Name?"

"Guillaume Nicolet, Sir."

"What do you do here?"

"I'm the jailor, Sir."

The fetid smell of the jailor's breath floats toward him. His eyes move to the jailor's large hands, and settles on his dirty, jiggered fingernails.

"Do you know this prisoner?"

Guillaume looks towards Françoise and smirks as he answers, "Yes sir."

"Have you noticed the condition she is in?"

"Oh! Sir! Those inquisitionist are rough people. Especially with witches and other heretics. Some of their torturing is bad."

"Yes, I know. However, this prisoner was not tortured. Do you know why she was not tortured?"

"No, Sir."

"Because I gave the order not to torture her. That is why."

"Oh."

Roland looks at him sternly.

"Sir, she is a witch and she is going to burn in a few days. I'm sure she went through some torture."

"No. She wasn't tortured. At least not physically. I can guarantee that. I can also guarantee that those cuts and bruises are new and are due to you."

"Me?"

"Sergeant?"

The Sergeant, who up to now was standing on the side, as far away from the jailor as possible, steps forward. "Yes, Sir?"

"Sergeant, when you entered the cell was this animal trying to bed her?"

"Er . . . .pretty well, Sir, I mean . . . er, yes, Sir

. . . no. No. Er . . . .I didn't see him bedding her. You see, er . . . . what I mean . . . . er . . . .was, yes he manhandled her . . . . yes, er . . . . actually, he had no time to do so. Sir."

Roland looks at the Sergeant with mock astonishment. "What do you mean by he had no time?"

"Sir, I interrupted him because you asked me to bring her here. Sir."

Roland looks at the jailor.

"Sir, I'm sorry. I didn't know she was being kept for you. I mean . . . . er, I usually . . . .well, we all . . . . you know."

In one swift movement, Roland steps forward, balls his right fist and sends it flying straight into the jailor's face. The jailor falls back, practically into the Sergeant who moves away just in time. He tumbles into the wall, hits his head and goes flying out through the open doorway where he lands in an unconscious heap. Followed by the Sergeant, Roland steps over to the jailor, leans over his body to check the damage.

"Sergeant, take care of him. He has a broken nose, definitely a few more teeth missing, but he'll live." With that he stands up, turns back to the office and slams the door behind him.

Françoise is standing as rigid as a statue in front of his desk staring at him.

Then she faints.

# CHAPTER 33
## Official Message
## dated 4th May 1600

To: Cedric Bonive

The High Magistrate of Spa

Chateau de Franchimont.

From: Roland de Bolland

The High Magistrate of Liège

Palace of the Prince-Bishop Liège

We have received your request for the countersigning of the document confirming the sentencing and the forthwith execution of Françoise Mathieu, widow of Henry Hurlet of Creppe.

We are, however, unable to do justice to your

request.

The Court of Justice of Spa has not supplied sufficient proof of the crime the prisoner has been accused of to allow The High Court of Justice in Liège to neither confirm this sentencing nor offer our competent interpretation of the case until a retrial has taken place.

The High Court of Justice in Liège wishes to draw the attention of the High Magistrate of Spa that during the above-mentioned retrial the Defendant will have the opportunity of presenting her case.

Furthermore, we wish to inform you of our decision to allow Françoise Mathieu, widow of Henry Hurlet of Creppe to return to her home in Creppe to await the retrial.

Roland de Bolland

High Magistrate of Liège

# CHAPTER 34
## Petition
## dated 4th May 1600

To: The Honored High Court of Justice of Spa

Right Honored Gentlemen,

We, your humble petitioners, whose names are written below would not wish to trouble your honors except to present the distressed condition we are faced with, before you and beg your honors' favor and pithy.

It is the tormented condition of my daughter-in-law and relative, Françoise Mathieu, widow of Henry Hurlet of Creppe, that compels us to write to you, the High Court of Justice of Spa.

We humbly make our address to your honors that Françoise Mathieu may be granted the right to return to her home in Creppe until the retrial at which time we humbly beg the high and just court of Spa to allow her to defend herself point-by-point.

We humbly beg your honors favor and pithy for us and ours herein.

Petitioners:

Jules Hurlet (Father-in-law)

Johan Hanchoulle

Giles de Creppe

## CHAPTER 35
### 6th May 1600
### Early afternoon

**The High Magistrate of Spa's office in Spa.**

A valet enters the Magistrate of Spa's office with a tray on which he is balancing two glasses and a carafe of wine. Thiry de Monville, the Magistrate's Deputy and cousin, nods at him, and points to the massive mahogany table that serves as the Magistrate's desk.

Thiry de Monville has been silently observing Cedric Boniver for well over an hour. Boniver has not uttered a single word during all that time.

De Monville and Boniver grew up together,

## The Drop of the Hammer

and although he knows his cousin never directs his anger towards him, he also realizes, it is more prudent to leave him be until his anger evaporates. So, he sits back in his armchair and watches the Magistrate pacing the floor.

He presumes his cousin still knows he is present, but he is far from certain of it. When Boniver gets into one of his boiling rages everything tends to disappear except for his fury. The strength of his anger is overwhelming and becomes something solid :...almost tangible. In his lifetime, de Monville has witnessed many of Boniver's temper tantrums, but he is positive he has never seen it quite this bad before. With a sigh, the Deputy, a calm man in any situation, reflects that the magistrate's red face, wild eyes and constant pacing would drive a saint up the wall.

One of two things are bound to happen. Either the anger will burst followed by loud shouting, or Boniver will leave the room without a word. In either case, Monville knows there isn't much he personally can do.

When faced with a problem, Cedric Boniver does not want someone with whom he can discuss it. At the limit, he simply wants someone to sound off to, and perhaps agree with him. That, however, is only secondary as he really doesn't care.

All of a sudden, Boniver turns toward the desk, sees the carafe of wine, presses his lips together, and lifts his eyes to his Deputy. Something in his eyes warns de Monville that Boniver's rage is about to explode.

The Magistrate of Spa storms up to the desk, and sweeps the carafe and glasses off it with one wild swing of the hand.

With one last look at the broken carafe and the spilled wine on the floor, the silent Thiry de Monville, who had half gotten up from his armchair, sits back down. Too bad about the wine. Spiced wine would have helped the afternoon in Boniver's company go quicker.

Boniver bangs his desk with an open palm. "Damn the man! Damn him! Damn him to Hell," he shouts. Turning to his cousin he says, "Oh, Thiry, have you just come in? I didn't hear you."

"Well, no you see, I . . . ."

Cedric Boniver turns his back on him and starts pacing again, not really caring about his cousin's answer.

As de Monville watches him pacing the floor again, gesturing wildly, and grabbing his head between his hands, he can hear the floor creaking on the other side of the door. "Hmm," he thinks, "It's probably the valet debating with himself. Should he come in to pick up the broken glass, or wait until later?" He silently advises the valet to disappear for a while.

The High Magistrate of Spa returns to his desk, throwing himself onto his armchair with so much anger and force, that the chair tips on its back legs.

From instinct, Thiry puts his hand out, as the chair slams back onto its four legs.

The creaking outside the door is louder, and then de Montville can hear footsteps quickly walking down the hall.

Cedric Boniver grabs a couple of parchments from his desk and waves them at de Monville. "Everybody agrees," his voice thunders. "This issue with Françoise Mathieu is a an open and shut case. She is accused of-of-of-." The High Magistrate's face turns purple as he looks for another document which he can't find.

The Deputy spots a rolled parchment on the floor a few feet away from him. It most probable fell when Boniver swept the carafe off the desk. He picks it up and hands it to the Magistrate without a word.

The Magistrate tears it out of his hands without a thank you. He holds it in front of him, and reads from it. "Francoise Mathieu, widow of Henry Hurlet of Creppe, guilty as charged, of shapeshifting, an attack on a citizen of the Ban de Spa and various things to do with witchcaft and sentenced by the Court of Justice of Spa to be burn within a week of the sentencing."

He looks up at Monville. "Did you hear what I said? Sentenced to burn within a week of her sentencing. There is nothing vague about this case. Reliable, God-fearing people came before us and accused her of shape-shifting, commerce with the Devil, giving off an odor of Sulphur, gathering herbs with the intention of using them for harm, attacking Remacle Rosy de Creppe on the road to Creppe, using her witchery to incite Remacle de Creppe's normal male carnal desires, killing her husband Henry Hurlet, causing the death of her sister-in-law's unborn child." Says the Magistrate as he punctures each one of the accusations by striking his index against the parchment.

Monville nods hoping he is conveying some kind of agreement.

Boniver tosses the parchment across the room. "We planned the execution for a week after the sentencing. All we needed is de Bolland's signature. Just a simple signature. Did we get that? No! The week has come and gone many times and during all that time the High Court of Justice in Liège gave no sign of life."

Palms out, Monville shrugs his shoulders and nods.

Boniver rises and walks up to his Deputy. He leans toward his face. "Not a word from Roland de Boland. Not a word", he shouts. Monville flinches in spite of himself. The Magistrate of Spa taps de Monville on the chest with his index finger. "Not a word until this morning."

De Monville nods again.

"Normally this is a simple formality," continues Boniver. It is very rare for sentences not to be carried out on the initial date chosen by the Spa trial. Rare is not the right word. It's more than rare. It has never been done. It is even rarer for the Court of Justice in Liège not to reply within two days of the request.

"But, Cedric, didn't you say de Bolland had come to Franchimont?"

"Oh, yes, he came to meddle. Before he came to meddle in person, his messenger, an arrogant harquebusier from Visé, came just as we were going

## The Drop of the Hammer

to torture this Françoise Mathieu, and ordered us to stop in the name of both the Prince Bishop of Liège and the High Magistrate of Liège. Of course, we both know, the whole thing was instigated by de Bolland himself."

"Yes, I remember, Captain Dieudonné . . . . "

"I don't care if he is a Captain or not. He is an arrogant fool! And Thiry, do you know what he did? Roland de Bolland arrived at Franchimont, and started ordering everyone as if he were the Chatelain. He not only berated the jailer .. . . in front of the Sergeant not to mention the prisoner . . . . for his treatment of the witch, but broke his nose and a couple of his teeth. The man was unconscious! What do you think of that?"

"Well, I certainly . . . . "

"I knew you would agree with me." Says Boniver, interrupting de Monville once again.

"The Court of Justice of Spa met last week to discuss this problem. As I have already said, as far as Spa is concerned, Françoise Mathieu's trial is an open and shut case. Reliable witnesses have been heard and the explanation supplied by Father de Lazaar was more than sufficient. It was excellent. The Court's decision was passed based on uncontestable proof. Surely this is enough."

"Yes, I . . . . ," begins to answer de Monville, only to be interrupted by his cousin again.

"Absolutely."

"Well, I guess it's . . . ."

"Absolutely, Thiry. Spa has its hands tied. Without the return of the document duly signed by the Court of Justice of Liège the prisoner cannot be executed."

"And then today, within two hours of each other, two messages arrive at the Court of Justice of Spa. The first, surprise, surprise, is from Roland de Bolland, the High Magistrate of Liège. The letter states that insufficient proof had been provided. And, as if this is not enough, he claims the Court of Justice in Liège is unable to offer its interpretation of the case until more proof is submitted and specifically until the

Defendant's view has been heard at a retrial!"

The High Magistrate of Spa's raving continues as he once again paces the floor of his office.

"What is de Bolland talking about. Who asked for their interpretation? All they have to do is sign the document. Is that so difficult? Do you understand this, Thiry?"

"Maybe they misunderstood," volunteers the Deputy obviously trying to calm the Magistrate.

How can they misunderstand a simple procedure like this? We have been doing this for years. It is not a question of interpretation. It is a matter of officializing the sentence through a countersignature. It's the law!"

"Maybe there's a problem with the Court of Inquisition."

"No, I'm sure that is not the problem. I agree that Liège doesn't want the Inquisition to stick its nose in local affairs any more than we do. This is something else."

"You said there was a second document,

Cedric."

"Yes. The second document arrived this morning about two hours after de Boland's. It's a petition by Jules Hurlet and a couple of his relatives, on behalf of his daughter-in-law. He is asking the Court of Justice of Spa to allow Françoise to be allowed to return to her home in Creppe until the retrial. Here you read it," says Cedric handing the parchment over to his cousin as he walks out of his office slamming the door behind him.

# CHAPTER 36
## Document
## 7ᵗʰ May 1600

From: Cedric Boniver

      The High Magistrate of Spa

      Chateau de Franchimont.

To:   The Prince-Bishop of Liège

      Ferdinand of Bavaria

      and

      The High Magistrate of

      the Court of Justice of Liège,

      Roland de Bolland

      Palace of the Prince-Bishop in Liège

7ᵗʰ May in the year of our Lord One Thousand

Six Hundred

The Right Honorable High Magistrate of Spa acknowledges the Official Message sent to him informing the Court of Justice of Spa of the decision taken by the High Court of Justice of Liège concerning the accused witch Françoise Mathieu, the widow of Henry Hurlet de Creppe.

The decision communicated to the Court of Justice of Spa by Roland de Bolland, the High Magistrate of Liège, concerning Françoise Mathieu, the widow of Henry Hurlet of Creppe, accused of Witchcraft, Shapeshifting, and an attack on the person of Remacle Le Rosy, will immediately be carried out as required.

The accused person, Françoise Mathieu, will be allowed to return to the Village of Creppe, and remain with her family until the Retrial and Final Sentencing.

Signed:

Cedric Boniver

The High Magistrate of the Court of Justice of Spa

# CHAPTER 37
# 15th May 1600
# Notice

**Notice affixed upon both the Town Hall and the Parish Church walls of Spa:[30]**

The Magistrate of the Court of Justice of Spa informs the public that the Court of Spa will proceed, as per directed by the Court of Justice of Liège, to a retrial on 15 September in the year of Our Lord One Thousand Six Hundred of the case against Françoise Mathieu, widow of Henry Hurlet of Creppe, accused

---

[30] Based on the Malleus Maleficarum Part III, First Head, Questions, The Method of Initiating a Process

of witchcraft, shapeshifting and physically attacking the person of Remacle Le Rosy and initially sentenced to be garroted and burned by the Court of Justice of Spa.

Whereas we, Cedric Boniver, the Magistrate of the Court of Justice of Spa, the Honored Judges of the Court of Justice of Spa , and Father de Lazaar, the Vicar of Spa do endeavor with all our might and strive with all our heart to preserve the Christian people entrusted to us in unity and the happiness of the Catholic faith and to keep our community far removed from every plague of abominable heresy, to put down this aforementioned abomination of heresy, and especially all witches in general and in each one severally of whatever condition.

Therefore, by the authority which we exercise in this district, and in virtue of holy obedience and under pain of excommunication, we direct, command, require, and admonish that within the space of twelve days ----the first four of which shall stand for the first warning, the second four for the second, and the third four for the third warning----we give this canonical warning that if anyone knows, sees or has heard that any person connected to this retrial is reported to be a heretic or a witch or suspected especially of such practices as to cause injury to men, cattle, or the fruits of the earth, to the loss of the State., but does not reveal such matter within the term fixed, let it be known that he or she will be cut off by the sword of communication. Which sentence of excommunication we impose as from this time by this writing upon all and several who thus stubbornly would set at naught these our canonical warnings aforesaid, and our requirement of their obedience, reserving to ourselves alone the absolution of such sentence.'

## CHAPTER 38
## 15 September 1600
## Retrial   Day One

The proceedings are due to begin in two hours and already the main hall of the Chateau de Franchimont is packed with people. The initial trial had taken place in private between Cedric Boniver, the Magistrate of Spa, the three Spa judges, (Norbert Gosselin, Désiré de Soiron, Michel Dupont), and the witnesses.

Maybe it wasn't a usual procedure, but as Cedric Boniver keeps saying it was an open and shut case and of no interest to anybody.

Not so for the retrial! Everybody wants to see

what is going to happen. It has become a 'must be seen at' event. An additional attraction for the people who have started coming to Spa for the cures. Well, not just for them. Some people are first time visitors who have come to Franchimont just to be seen at the trial.

There's a great diversity among the attendance or would it be better to say spectators who have come to be entertained. The local gentry and the Bobelins are sitting on long wooden benches on either side of the hall. From where they are, they will have a clear view of the accused woman's face as well as of those of the witnesses since the bar is located right between the two sets of benches.

Here and there are scattered groups of the clergy. The largest of these groups is surrounding Father de Lazaar, the parish priest of Spa and an important witness in this trial. Quite obvious, too, among the attendance is a large number of nobles from Brussels and Antwerp who have vividly expressed their desire to attend.

The only group that understandably has a reason for attending the retrial, the simple people of Creppe and Spa, has been relegated to the back of the Hall. No benches have been set up for them. True to their reputation of being hot-tempered, a fight has already broken out among them earlier on and a man had to be carried out, clearly unconscious.

Why, in heaven's name, would all these people concern themselves with this seemingly common trial? Is it because it is a witch trial? No. Witch trials have become common place and so have executions. Is it because it is a re-trial? Certainly, that is the reason for the presence of the visiting judges, but it still doesn't explain the number of attendees. So, what is the reason? The reason is simply that the whole thing has been blown out beyond proportion and many seem to think they are going to witness a retrial quite different from what it actually is: a young peasant woman fighting for her life.

There is another member of the clergy sitting quietly in the middle of one of the benches. It is a

## The Drop of the Hammer

Franciscan monk. He is sitting quite apart from Father de Lazaar's little group. His face is concealed by his hood and is apparently totally absorbed in the simple wooden rosary he is holding in his right hand. He is generating almost as much interest as the retrial itself.

Three men, not too far from him, seem to think they are whispering among themselves. Because of the general commotion, however, their whispers are anything but confidential.

"Do you know who that monk is?"

"No, but I don't think he is just a monk?"

"What do you mean?"

"He must be a highly placed member of the clergy in the Inquisition. I saw him coming in. He doesn't walk like a lowly monk."

"Yes, I saw him coming in too. There's no doubt about it. He is an emissary of the Inquisition."

"But, why is he here?"

"I guess to be sure that it is done correctly according to the Malleus Maleficarum.

If any of the discussions had originally started as discreet, they are now all loud enough to be heard not only by the neighbor but also by everyone else. Everyone is an expert on the matter. Everyone knows someone who knows someone else who has some inside information. Everyone has an opinion about both the initial trial, this retrial and especially about the outcome which was sure to end in an execution.

". . . . this Françoise Mathieu case . . . ."

Another, older man with the slow drawl immediately designating him as coming from Verviers, says, "It is quite clear she is guilty. I say, rid us of all these vermin once and for all," fiddling with a scented handkerchief under his nose as he points to the crowd of peasants standing in the back of the Hall.

A younger man with the quicker speech of Liège agrees with him, "They smell so badly. They shouldn't be allowed to be here. It's not so much the towns people from Spa. It's those peasants from Creppe."

"Who is this star witness, we are hearing about?

Remacle de something or the other."

"I have never met him, but from what I hear he has a Chateau in the vicinity of Spa and is also the owner of a large, very large herd. A Gentleman for sure."

"And to think he was attacked viciously by this witch. They say she shapeshifted into a wild gargoyle-like animal."

"Was he badly injured?"

"Badly enough. My brother was discussing this case with the cousin of one of the judges, and he said the gentleman in question had deep cuts down his cheeks from when the thing scratched him with its talons. Not to mention, a very serious gash in the back of his head that almost cost him his life."

"Oh, the poor man! It wasn't like this when I was a child. What is the world coming to?"

The man from Verviers still fiddling with his handkerchief and glaring towards the people standing in the back says, "Respectable people are no longer safe. Either they are being attacked on the road or made to suffocate by the stench of people like those over there."

"Didn't the gentleman suspect anything?"

"Evidently not. It's his good upbringing and his kind heart that blinded him. From what I was told, he saw this woman having difficulty walking in the snow and he went to help her. Suddenly, well you know the rest of the story."

"Oh, yes."

"Hmm."

"Absolutely."

"I see."

"Unbelievable."

The two noblemen on the other side of the monk are still preoccupied with him.

"What do you expect from a person like this Mathieu woman. She killed her husband and her sister-in-law's unborn child . . . . ,of course, all this was unknown at the time."

"Is that why she is being tried again by the Court of Justice in Spa and not in the Court of the

Inquisition?"

"If you want my opinion the whole thing should be handed over to the Inquisition."

"Her place is in the Court of the Inquisition, if you ask me. By the way, I don't think we are the only ones to think like this. I have been keeping an eye on the monk."

"Yes, so have I. Definitely from the Court of the Inquisition. Don't let his simple garb fool you. If he were not someone important, he would be sitting either with the other members of the clergy or with that noisy group back there."

"I don't think this trial will be very long . . . . retrial or not."

"Neither do I"

## CHAPTER 39
## 15th September 1600

The Bailiff, who up to now had been standing at attention near the long mahogany table reserved for the Magistrates and judges moves towards the middle of the Hall with a slow measured step. Those who are closest to him and see him quieten down immediately. The others soon become quiet once the Bailiff strikes the floor three times with his staff.

"All rise, he bellows in French and Walloon. "Their excellencies, the Magistrates and the judges for this session of the Court of Justice of Spa.

Everybody's eyes immediately swing to the

## The Drop of the Hammer

main doorway from which the Magistrates and judges are expected.

Cedric Boniver enters followed by four other Magistrates, the three judges of the Court of Spa and a visiting judge from Verviers. They walk solemnly up to the ornate mahogany table and sit down. Cedric in the middle, two magistrates of lesser importance on either side of him and the Spa judges. The visiting judge sits on one of the two chairs of a smaller and less ornate table on the side. The second chair is for the advocate acting as the Accused's Procurator. A third table across from the second table is reserved for the Jury. It is much plainer both in the wood used and in its design. The procedure cannot legally start without the Procurator nor without the three-man jury the Court of Justice in Spa has placed in his hands.

Next to the simpler garments of the others, Cedric's long robe, with its full and pleated sleeves immediately denotes him as the main Magistrate. He exudes total calmness . . . . at least exteriorly if not interiorly. Interiorly, he is still fuming over what he considers an insult and a personal injury. To be forced . . . . because there is no other word to describe what has happened . . . .to conduct a retrial of a witch he has already sentenced to death is unacceptable.

For some reason it is taking the Advocate longer than expected to gather his jury and this is getting on Cedric Boniver's nerves. He is not a happy man and he is having more and more problems keeping his anger under control

The other four magistrates and the judge don't look any happier, but they are doing their very best to look busy. Boniver, on the other hand, is starting to fidget on his chair and tapping his fingers on the table impatiently. Pressing his already pinched lips closer together, he glances at the still unsigned execution documents before him.

He will never accept the idea of Liège having to give the final authorization to all the decisions made by the Spa court in matters of execution. It's called to 'Countersign', but in reality, it is simply a nice, polite way of saying "Liège decides what you can or cannot do." Up to now, it has been an irritating nuisance of no consequence. Things have changed. This retrial is dangerous as it is setting a precedent, well, not if he can help it.

This recent insurgence by the Court of Justice of Liège into the affaires of Spa and Franchimont is an insult he cannot and will not accept. It's a total disregard for his position. That's what it is. What does it make him, if he can't even sentence a witch to be garroted and burned without the authorization of Liège.? It makes him a lowly clerk with a high-sounding title. Just the idea of having Liège telling him what to do. . . .or in this case what not to do. . . . enrages him. If Roland de Bolland's intention is to make the justice in Spa look foolish he certainly is succeeding.

So, today, he is being forced to listen to a witch's version of the truth after having been sentenced. The execution is months late and she is still walking around causing problems. Boniver doesn't like lingering in general, and specifically he doesn't like being told what to do. Alright, he was ordered to have a retrial and they are going to get one. The only good thing about this situation is that at least Liège will certainly not dare intervene in the retrial itself and, for once, de Bolland has the good sense of not showing up.

The Bailiff comes up to him and whispers, "My Lord, the Procurator has arrived with the jury and is waiting in the outer room."

"Announce them, have them seated. It's about time we stated."

The Bailiff turns towards the audience and bellows, "The advocate acting as the Accused's Procurator and the jury have arrived."

Jean Dols, the advocate enters the Hall followed by the Jury: three, solemn looking, middle aged men. Although all three are members of the merchant class from Verviers, and were carefully chosen according to a strict criterion, they were only officially accepted after handing in an attestation proving their good standing in the community from the Monseigneur of the Principality of Liège.

They sit down at the third table, looking very much ill at ease and avoiding all eye contacts with the rest of the people in the room.

# CHAPTER 40
## 15th September 1600

The Magistrate of the Court of Justice of Spa nods at the Bailiff who immediately strikes the floor with his staff and bellows "Order in the Court. The session is about to begin."

Cedric Boniver stands up, "As you are all aware we have been . . . . er . . . . asked by the High Court of Liège to allow Françoise Mathieu, widow of Henry Hurlet of Creppe, to give her version of the facts relating to the case De Creppe vs. Mathieu. This is highly unprecedented. However, we are always happy to comply with requests coming from our colleagues in Liège. I will now turn the case over to Jean Dols, the prosecutor."

Jean Dols, picks up a parchment from the table, clears his throat and in a monotonous tone void of any interest whatsoever in the case begins to read:

"Your excellencies the Magistrates and honored gentlemen of the Court, the jury and members of the audience we shall begin with a review of the initial trial which took place in March of this year in the presence of his excellency Cedric Boniver, the Magistrate of the Court of Justice of Spa, and three specially chosen judges, namely Norbert Gosselin, Désiré de Soiron and Michel Dupont.

The accused, Françoise Mathieu, the widow of Henry Hurlet de Creppe was charged with hideous crimes connected to witchcraft.

The charges were brought against her by Remacle Le Rosy who on the 29 November 1599 was attacked by the said Françoise Mathieu on the road from Spa leading to Creppe. For no reason, as far as Le Rosy could see, she shapeshifted into a type of gargoyle and attacked him. Specifically, she sunk her talons into his cheeks, causing deep gashes along his cheeks and great pain. Secondly, the woman turned gargoyle hit the said Remacle Le Rosy on the head. The blow was so intense that he lost a considerable amount of blood, fell unconscious and almost lost his life.

A call for witnesses was made on 26th January 1600 by the Town Crier in Spa and the following witnesses, all proven to be God-fearing people, came forward, namely Gilson Froidville, Etienne Querlin and Catherine Ogier.

Gilson Froidville reported that Françoise Mathieu, the widow of Henry Hurlet de Creppe has the reputation of being a witch. In addition, he once came upon her near Desnié where she was gathering Lilies of the Valley and Oleander. Soon afterwards a neighbor, she was tending, suddenly died.

Etienne Querlin recalls that the day of Jehenne Anseau's execution Françoise Mathieu was crying and calling the witch a 'Poor Girl'.

Catherine Ogier saw Françoise Mathieu, a

childhood friend, give an apple to the ten-year-old daughter of Henry Badrulle and the little girl died a few days later.

The said Françoise Mathieu widow of Henry Hurlet de Creppe was then duly condemned to be garroted and burned at Oneux (Jonkeu). However, the authorization did not come from Liège as expected. Instead, a request for a retrial was requested."

Jean Dols ends his reading and turns to Cedric Boliver, who thanks him in the name of the Court of Justice of Spa for his excellent rendition of the facts. "You may sit down now, Prosecutor." Then turning to the Bailiff, Cedric Boniver says, "Bailiff, call Jules Hurlet to the bar."

"Yes, My Lord."

The bailiff moves to the center of the Hall and in a loud clear voice shouts, "Jules Hurlet, come to the bar."

Jules Hurlet, standing in the back of the Hall with the other people from Creppe steps forward. He is, as most people from Creppe, smaller than the average person and has the arched nose so prominent among the Hurlets. His drooping moustache gives him a tough look, successfully hiding a sensitivity he rarely shows and that few know. Although well in his fifties, he walks with his shoulders pulled back and his eyes still have the determined look he had as a young man.

Cedric Boniver looks at the man from head to toe for a minute without uttering a word.

"Are you Jules Hurlet?"

"Yes, My Lord."

"Am I correct, if I say that Françoise Mathieu is both your ward and your daughter-in-law?"

"Yes, my Lord. Françoise is my ward since the death of her husband, Henry, my son."

"As her guardian, I presume you will be representing her here."

"No, my Lord. I am not the person who will be representing Françoise in her defense."

The Magistrate looks up at Jules Hurlet and

with an embarrassed but far from sincere smile says, "No, of course not. How careless of me to even think that." And then adds, maybe not even realizing how insulting he is, "I am sure you prefer having someone more educated do it."

Boniver turns towards the men sitting on the benches and asks, "Who is the gentleman in charge of representing Françoise Mathieu in this affair? Please stand up and come forward."

Both the persons seated and those standing at the back are curious to see who is going to represent Françoise Mathieu. Several of the men sitting towards the front of the benches turn around to see who it might be.

No one stands up.

The Magistrate looks surprised and also a little relieved. "Am I to understand the person is not present?"

And then a soft and yet firm feminine voice says, "I am going to make my own defense, My Lord."

All eyes turn towards the young woman,

sentenced by the Court of Justice of Spa to be executed, as she leaves the group at the back of the Hall and walks head high and steadily towards Cedric Boniver and the bar. Her expressionless face and her ramrod-straight body give a clear message.

The message is "I'll be polite, but I'll not let you walk all over me. You have wrongly accused me and I'll not let you execute me. My life is mine and I am not only going to save it, but I am also going to control it."

As she passes her father-in-law, he puts out his hand and squeezed her shoulder. Françoise looks towards him and her face momentarily softens. From the way Jules looks at her, it is clear he is proud of his daughter-in-law and wants everyone to know it.

This young woman standing in court today, although accused of witchcraft and fighting for her life, shows more strength than most of the men present could and would have.

The people in the audience all begin to talk among themselves. Only the few who know her personally take pride in her strength. The majority, however, are laughing out loud and pointing at her. They see a young woman who believes she has something to say. What can she possibly have to say? Well, this is going to be good for a few laughs. How about that! A woman . . . .and an accused witch at that . . . . wanting to defend herself in court!

The High Magistrate of Spa is laughing along with the rest of the people in the Hall. It is with difficulty that he finally manages to get his laughter under control. He nods to the Bailiff who strikes the floor with his staff. Within seconds the Hall is quiet, but here and there are still quite a few smirks and sarcastic smiles.

"Girl, did I hear you say you want to give your version of the facts by yourself?"

"No, My Lord."

"Ah, that's better. Foolish young girls sometimes come up with strange things."

"My Lord, I am not a foolish young girl. I am a woman who stands wrongly accused of crimes she has not committed. It's not that I want to defend myself. Rather, it is that I am going to make my own defense."

"Are you out of your mind? You are incapable of doing something like that. You are a woman. Who ever heard of anything similar to this? Something as stupid as this? No, I don't care. The answer is no."

The Magistrate stands up as if ready to leave. He looks around and says, "I will not be party to such stupidity. A farce of justice. Everyone knows women are incapable of speaking in defense of themselves or of anyone else either in a court. At most, I would accept a reputable representative to please the Court in Liège, but not this. This is an insult to justice. If the High Court of Justice in Liège wants to accept such a farce . . . . let them. All I can say is that they are not even present during this trial and I will not have you or anybody else turn this court into a carnival."

Suddenly, the tall hooded figure of the Monk stands up. He remains planted on his two solid legs; his arms crossed for a two long minutes. It is so unexpected that everyone is silent . . . . including Cedric Boniver.

Some just stare at him. Others look from the Monk to the High Magistrate of Spa and back to the Monk. The Bailiff drops his staff.

The High Magistrate of Spa seems paralyzed in mid movement. He too is looking at the Monk. A strength, Cedric Boniver is not used to, emanates from the Monk's demeanor, the way he holds his arms crossed, the way he stares at him. This is something he is not used to. Who is this Monk? Is he from the Inquisition? What does he want?

Slowly the Monk lets his hood fall back.

The High Magistrate of Spa gasps.

Neither man says a word, but the audience feels the tension that is vibrating between the two of them. This is clearly a stand-off of some kind. Something is going on. Who is this Monk? Is he from the inquisition after all?

The Monk next takes his robe off and exposes his fine gentleman's clothes that the rough ecclesiastic robe had hidden.

Now the whole room starts murmuring. Then someone cries out what all the others were whispering, "It's de Bolland. Roland de Bolland! The High Magistrate of the Court of Justice of Liège."

Roland does not acknowledge this recognition. His eyes do not leave those of the Magistrate of Spa, as he walks out from between the benches. When he reaches the beautifully ornate mahogany table, he turns to the Bailiff and says in a low, authoritative voice, "Set a seat for me at the Magistrates' table."

The Bailiff is so beside himself that he drops his staff for the second time. He turns towards the Sergeant-at-arms and in an impatient tone says, "Well? Didn't you hear what My Lord, the High Magistrate of Liège said? What are you waiting for? Get a chair.... quickly!"

Roland walks to the back of the table where the Sergeant-at-arms has set an addition seat. It is a simple and not very comfortable seat. It is a simple, wooden chair, not an armchair.

The High Magistrate of Liège looks at the Magistrate of Spa who is still looking at him open-mouthed and says, "This chair is not comfortable. I want your armchair."

Cedric gets up. He opens his mouth to complain, but all that comes out is "I. . . .I. . . . I. . . ."

De Bolland looks at Boniver and pointing at the chair the Sergeant-at-arms has brought says, "Sit," which he promptly does.

Then the High Magistrate of the Court of Justice of Liège turns towards Françoise Mathieu, widow of Henry Hurlet of Creppe and says, "Madame, I believe the High Magistrate of Spa is ready to tell you that he is more than willing to hear your defense."

## CHAPTER 41
## 15th September 1600
## Remacle Le Rosy

The Hall is quiet, probably the quietest it has ever been in any of the many trials that have been held here over the years.

Cedric Boniver's face continually goes from tomato red to dead pale. The assisting Magistrates, the Spa judges and the judge from Verviers keep looking at each other, not quite sure of what is happening nor what is expected of them. The three-man-jury is still looking down at the table and avoiding all eye contacts. All the attendees, including the people from Spa and Creppe standing in the back of the Hall, are equally quiet.

Everyone is waiting to hear what the High Magistrate of Liège has to say. Roland does not start speaking right away. He lets the weight of the silence in the Hall stir all those faces looking towards him expectantly.

"Members of the Court of Justice of Spa, Judges, and jury as well as all of you who have come here today! I want to impress upon you that this is not a normal trial. It is a retrial. What is a retrial? It is a further trial on the same issues and with the same parties. You may wonder why a Court of Justice would want a retrial. It is used in cases of serious offences . . . . and no one doubts this particular case constitutes a serious offence. Compelling new evidence has subsequently come to light.

We have been asked by the High Magistrate of Spa to countersign the decision and sentencing reached by the Court of Justice of Spa concerning Françoise Mathieu the widow of Henry Hurlet of Creppe.

What do I mean by 'countersigning' the initial

decision and sentencing? I mean to confirm the initial decision in order for the sentencing to be carried out.

We, the High Court of Justice in Liège, have agreed not to authorize the execution because insufficient proof was presented to us. Therefore, We, the High Court of Justice in Liège, have decided unanimously to counter the sentencing as set by the Court of Justice in Spa and give the defendant a chance to reject the charges brought against her.

I will start with some general questions and then review the statements of each one of the witnesses. The prosecutor needs not intervene nor anyone else for that matter.

"What is your name and marital status?"

"I am Françoise Mathieu, the widow of Henry Hurlet of Creppe, My Lord."

"The Court of Justice of Spa has accused you of witchcraft. What do you have to say about that? Are you guilty of these charges? Are you a witch?"

"No, My Lord. I say before God that I am not guilty of the crimes they accuse me of. I am no witch.

I know nothing of witchcraft."

"And yet four people have accused you of being a witch and one of them claims you attacked him."

"My Lord, I do not know why these people have come forward to torment me, but I can prove that I have done nothing to deserve this."

"If I have the Bailiff bring Remacle Le Rosy here before you, what will you do? He is the main witness against you. You know this, don't you? Can you look at him in the eye and refute his accusation?"

"My Lord, I do know Remacle Le Rosy is the main witness against me, and I beg you to please bring him before me so that I can confront him. I want to confront Remacle Le Rosy, and I will have no problem at all looking at him straight in the eyes."

"Did you not have the opportunity to confront him during the first trial?"

"No, My Lord. I neither saw him nor any of the other witnesses during the first trial."

"And why is that?"

"The trial was conducted in private My Lord."

"What do you mean by 'in private'?"

"I mean, at the very beginning, there was me, the High Magistrate of the Court of Justice of Spa, and three judges. I was not present for the rest of the trial as I was taken away shortly afterwards."

"And where did this trial take place?"

"It took place in that horrible room where they torture people."

"I see," answers Roland turning to look at Cedric Boniver. Turning back to defendant he says, "Go on."

"Well, My Lord, I am, as you say, the defendant. Maybe it is not my role to know why things are done in a certain way. However, I overheard them talking in the room . . . ."

"Who is them?" interrupts de Bolland

"Them, My Lord, is the Magistrate of the Court of Justice of Spa and the Judges. They thought I was too stupid to understand what they were saying because I am from Creppe."

"What did they say?"

"They said, My Lord, that the trial was being conducted without the knowledge of the Chatelain."[31]

"Françoise Mathieu, are you aware of the seriousness of what you are claiming?" de Bolland asks sternly.

"Yes, My Lord, I am aware of what I am claiming. I heard them. They did not even bother to speak in a low tone so that I could not hear."

"Françoise Mathieu, are you aware that all I have to do is look at the official document to disprove you?"

"Yes, My Lord."

"And are you aware that if you are lying, this retrial will automatically be dismissed?"

Roland pushes the documents that are spread out on the table around, and finally picks one up. He takes his time to read it and then looks up at the Hall full of people. "The Chatelain of Franchimont's

---

[31] This was the case with the real Françoise during her retrial in 1616. She claimed and was able to prove that her case was conducted without the Chatelain's knowledge.

signature is missing!" Then turning towards Cedric Boniver, he asks in a harsh voice, "Would his excellency the Magistrate of the Court of Justice of Spa care to answer?"

Cedic Boniver does not bother to answer.

"I didn't think you would," the High Magistrate of Liège says dryly."

"I see. Bailiff, have Remacle Le Rosy come forward."

The Bailiff, now quite back to his usual self, bellows, "Remacle Le Rosy, come to the Bar."

All the men sitting on the benches start looking at each other. Finally, they will be able to see the gentleman in question. No one gets up. The Bailiff shouts out the name again and Remacle Le Rosy comes walking from the back of the Hall, looking half asleep and scratching his belly.

"What?" cries out the man with the Verviers accent. "That's no gentleman. He looks like a herder. I came all the way from Verviers to see a herder?"

All the other gentlemen in the Hall start talking

out loud, claiming that they had been insulted. One gentleman, got up and addressing himself to Roland le Bolland says, "My Lord, what kind of mockery is this?" adding, as he points towards Le Rosy, "We were under the impression that a gentleman had been attacked by a witch and we see this."

"Gentlemen, please calm down," says de Bolland. "I understand you. No one should be attacked by a shapeshifter; that is, if such a thing exists. That goes for a gentleman or a herder, however, we must dig deeper into this situation. Bear with me, please."

"What is your name?" he asks the herder.

"Remacle le Rosy, My Lord."

"Can you tell me what happened in the afternoon of the 29th November 1599.

"I was attacked, My Lord."

"Go on." says Roland making a circular motion with his hand.

"I was walking from Spa to Creppe, when I met Françoise Mathieu. I wanted to help her because she was having difficulty walking in the snow and she attacked me."

"Are you going to make me believe that a little woman like that could attack you, a strong herder."

"No, My Lord. First, she turned into a Gargoyle and then she attacked me. She scratched me. Deeply. You can look at my cheeks. I still have the scars," says Remacle approaching Roland de Bolland.

"Stay where you are."

"And then she . . . . I mean the Gargoyle . . . . hit me over the head and almost killed me."

"So, it's not Françoise Mathieu who attacked you but a Gargoyle?"

"Er . . . . no, yes, Françoise was the Gargoyle."

"I see. But strangely enough, I have here among my private parchments that a woman from Creppe, called Marie, hit you over the head."

"Er . . . . I . . . .er. . . ."

"Don't worry we will come back to this later." Then turning to Françoise, "Madame, do you have anything to add or ask Remacle le Rosy?"

"Yes, I do, My Lord. First of all, he is a liar. He attacked me and tried to rape me. My friend Marie who had come to meet me, saw this and hit him over the head."

"Yes, and left me for dead," interrupts Le Rosy. "Don't think I am going to forget that!"

"What?" asks the Magistrate of Liège. "I thought it was a gargoyle that hit you over the head."

"Yes, My Lord."

"Then there were two gargoyles. When you made your original complaint, you never mentioned two gargoyles. Only one."

"I felt very confused, My Lord, and in deep pain. You must understand."

"I see," answers Roland ironically. Then turning towards the defendant. "Françoise Mathieu, would you like to finally tell us what happened to you on the road to Creppe?"

"Yes, My Lord. I was walking home from my work in Spa, when I heard noises behind me. I didn't know what it was and I was afraid that hungry wolves were behind me. Then I saw it was Remacle Le Rosy. He started teasing me, telling me that I had lost something and wouldn't let me go by. I told him I hadn't lost anything. Then he started to touch me. I remember scratching him with my fingernails. I wanted to run away and he was holding me down. Remacle got very angry after I scratched him and he attacked me, and tried to rape me."

"Did someone come to help you?"

"Yes, My Lord."

"Can you tell us who came to save you. Don't be afraid. It is not a sin to come to a friend's aid. Indeed, it is a quality. The person will not be bothered by the authorities."

Really, My Lord? She will be safe, if she comes forward?"

"I give you my word, little one."

Françoise turns around to face the back of the Hall, "Marie, please come. You are safe!" And then she suddenly stops and looks at Roland. "Please forgive me, My Lord, it is not my place to call a witness."

"Did I complain, little one? Marie, whoever you are, please come forward."

A young woman comes out of the crowd at the back of the Hall and limps timidly towards the Bar where Françoise is standing. Marie keeps her eyes looking down, wanting so much to help her friend, but at the same time so afraid.

"So, you are Marie?" asks Roland.

"Yes, My Lord."

"Can you tell us what happened, Marie? Please do not be afraid. And also, please look at me when I speak to you."

Marie looks up. "Yes, My Lord. Françoise was late coming home, so I decided to go find her. I thought that maybe she had fallen and hurt herself. I was not far from the Hurlet farm when I heard screaming. I started running, but as you can see, I have a limp and did not get to her as quickly as I wanted. When I got to the road, I saw Françoise on the ground and Remacle Le Rosy trying to rape her. I took the first thing I saw . . . . a rock . . . . and hit him."

"So, that was the head wound?"

"Yes, My Lord."

"Then what did you do?"

"I took her home to the Hurlet farm, My Lord. She was hurt and not well at all."

"So, there was no second Gargoyle then?"

"No, My Lord, there were never any Gargoyles. There was just Remacle Le Rosy, a very frightened and hurt young woman, and a scared friend . . . . who did what she could."

"Thank you, Marie. Why don't you sit down on the edge of that bench? I am sure the Gentlemen won't mind making room for someone as brave as you. Gentlemen?"

The Gentlemen in question made room on one of the benches for Marie, looking quite pleased with themselves, feeling they were helping justice.

"Françoise do you have anything to add in your defence?"

Yes, My Lord, quite a lot, in fact."

"Speak."

"Firstly, My Lord, the inquest was not done in any deep zeal for justice. Secondly, Remacle Le Rosy, hated my husband, his cousin and there was also a lot of jealousy on his part. Please do not think that Henry treated him badly. The door was always open for Remacle. My husband believed in 'Family'. So, there was this jealousy on Remacle's part. Thirdly, I want it to be known that Remacle Le Rosy's son by his first marriage gave a cow to Cedric Boniver. For what reason, I ask you. And last but not least, Remacle Le Rosy made it quite clear that he wanted me to be executed. All you have to do is ask the owner of the tavern known as Storheau's Tavern."

There was silence in the Hall. For sure, everyone had many questions they wanted to ask, but before the bravery of this young woman, none dared to speak.

"Thank you, little one," said Roland de Boland. "This is enough for today. We will all meet again tomorrow."

## CHAPTER 42
## 16ᵗʰ September 1600
## Witness Two

Roland de Bolland announces to the still very packed Hall, "Today, we are going to continue by listening to the three other witnesses and to the defendant."

Cedric Boniver is still sitting next to him, not wanting to give the High Magistrate of Liège the satisfaction of seeing his chair empty, but the looks he casts towards de Bolland do not hide how he feels.

Roland de Bolland waves the Bailiff over. "Call the three other witnesses to the bar and have them appear before the Court in the order I have indicated here," he says handing a parchment to him.

"Yes, My Lord."

The Bailiff walks to the middle of the Hall, strikes his staff three times and calls out, "Catherine Ogier, Etienne Querlin, and Gilson Froiidville come to the Bar."

A bit of a commotion is heard coming from the group standing at the back of the Hall. Evidently, the three witnesses thought they had done their duty by reporting their opinions to the Sergeant-at-Arms as requested by the Town Crier, and had not counted on being called to the Bar. Nonetheless, they emerge from the group and slowly walk down to the Bar.

"The Court will start with Catherine Ogier," bellows the Bailiff.

Catherine Ogier, a plump little woman with mousey hair, steps forward, wringing her hands and looking down at her feet. Roland picks up a parchment, "What is your name?"

"Catherine Ogier, My Lord."

"I see here that you accused Françoise Mathieu, the widow of Henry Hurlet de Creppe of two separate things. Firstly, having given an apple to Henry Badrulle's ten-year-old daughter who apparently died a few days later. Is this correct?"

"Yes, My Lord."

You also claim the girl had never been ill before. Correct?"

"Yes, My Lord."

"Secondly, that your. . . . am I reading this correctly? Your cousin's next-door neighbor who told your mother who then told you . . . . does this person have a name?"

"Yes, My Lord, I suppose so, but I don't know his name. Everyone has a name."

"I see. Let's continue. This nameless person saw Françoise Mathieu, while she was gathering wood. She spoke politely to him, but had a strange look in her eyes. And you add that, by the time she had gathered all her wood, he noticed that his horse was lame and he had a hard time getting back to Creppe. Is that what you said?

"Yes, My Lord."

"Catherine Ogier are we referring to the nameless person?"

"Yes, my Lord. It's my cousin's neighbor."

"Have you ever seen or talked to this neighbor of your cousin's?"

"No, My Lord."

"I now ask the defendant, Françoise Mathieu to come forward and ask questions if she has any. Does the defendant have any questions?"

"Yes, My Lord, I do," says Françoise as she comes forward and stands next to Catherine Ogier.

"Françoise Mathieu, do you agree with what Catherine Ogier has stated and please ask any questions you might have."

"Thank you, My Lord. No, I do not agree with what Catherine Ogier has said. It is true that I gave an apple to Henry Badrulle's ten-year-old daughter who died a few days later. That is completely true. But Catherine Ogier seems to forget that I took the apple out of the basket she had just given to Agnes, Henry Badrulle's wife. She also seems to have forgotten that the little girl was complaining of a sore throat and that it was Catherine Ogier herself who said to me 'Why don't you give the girl an apple from the basket, it will soothe her throat."

Is that true Catherine Ogier?"

"Er. . . . er, I can't remember, My Lord. Maybe. Maybe not. It could be."

"I see. You don't remember," then turning to Françoise, Roland says, "Go on."

"I remember the name of the man I saw gathering wood. His name is Gustave Bontemps and he is standing in the back of the Hall with the other people from Creppe. I was polite because I am always polite. However, I was angry. He is not the one who saw me. I saw him or rather I heard him. He was beating his horse and I told him to stop. He has a reputation of beating his animals. And yes, his horse was limping badly when he left. My Lord."

"Well, that changes everything, doesn't it? Bailiff call this Gustave Bontemps to the Bar."

"Yes, My Lord. Gustave Bontemps is called to

## The Drop of the Hammer

the Bar."

A swarthy little man approaches the Bar self-importantly. "My Lord, what Françoise Mathieu says is true. I am, how can I say it, a little heavy handed. But I want the court to know that I made no official complaint against Françoise Mathieu and until this moment, I did not know that Catherine Ogier had involved me. Françoise Mathieu should have minded her own business, but I have nothing against her."

"Well, then Gustave Bontemps, can you explain how the story that. . . . let me see if I have this right. You told your next door neighbour who is the cousin of Catherine Ogier, who also told her mother . . . . correct me if I am wrong, but the story has changed completely!"

"No, no, My Lord. You have it right. I told my neighbor what had happened, but. . . .please, believe me, My Lord. . . . I have no idea how the story changed."

"And, you agree that your horse was lame because you beat it and not because of Françoise

Mathieu?"

"Yes, My Lord."

"Bailiff, return both Catherine Ogier and Gustave Bontemps to the back of the Hall." As the Bailiff takes them away, Roland de Bolland turns towards Cedric Boniver and just looks at him . . . . long and hard. The Magistrate of Spa returns his look arrogantly. Not a single word is said between them, but both men know what the other is thinking.

## CHAPTER 43
## 16th September 1600
## Witnesses Three and Four

Roland looks at the two other witnesses and asks, "Which one of you is Etienne Querlain?"

"I am, My Lord," answers the taller of the two, a man about forty years old.

"Ah, yes, I see here that you accused the defendant of crying when she saw Jehenne Anseau being first strangled and then burned. According to your statement she said 'Poor Girl'."

"Yes, My Lord."

"Do you still agree with your complaint?"

"Of course, My Lord."

"Does that mean you enjoyed seeing Jehenne Anseau being strangled and burned."

"My Lord, I did my duty. We were asked to attend and I attended."

"But did you enjoy seeing Jehenne being strangled and burned?"

"I…I…I don't know what to say, My Lord."

"It's a very easy question. The answer is either yes, you enjoyed it or no, you didn't enjoy it. So, tell me, did you enjoy it?"

"No, My Lord, I did not enjoy it."

"Why not?"

"My Lord, I beg you, don't ask me. You know the answer."

"No, I don't know the answer. That's why I am asking you why you did not enjoy it?"

"My Lord, I have already told you that I did not enjoy it."

"Why?"

"I don't know, My Lord, if you have ever seen it done. It is horrible. I saw the executioner strangling

Jehenne Anseau, and it felt as if I were being strangled myself. I could no longer breathe. She was struggling. I saw life being sucked out of her. My Lord, please don't make me go on," says Etienne Quirlin as he breaks down and sobs loudly.

"Thank you for your sincerity, Etienne Quirlin."

"Bailiff, take him back, and if he prefers to leave the Hall, let him," says Roland softly. And in a sad voice he addresses both the Court and the Audience. "I wish to address the members of the Court of Justice of Franchimont and Spa, the Magistrates, the judges, the Prosecutor as well as the gentlemen who have come to hear this trial and the people of Spa and Creppe standing in the back. If a man of around forty breaks down like this as he remembers and talks about the execution of Jehenne Anseau, how can you accuse a young woman of crying and saying 'Poor Girl'?"

The Hall is quiet. Here and there, someone is blowing his nose. Then a heavy silence settles upon the whole Hall and for several minutes no one moves, no one speaks, everyone is lost in his or her own private thoughts. Even Cedric Boniver seems lost in his thoughts.

It is finally Roland de Bolland who breaks the silence, "Lets listen to the last witness. Will the third witness step forward. What is your name?

"Gilson Froidville, My Lord."

"Ah, yes," answers Roland looking at a parchment he is holding in his hands. "You claim that Françoise Mathieu, the Widow of Henry Hurlet de Creppe is a witch and has been one for at least six years."

"Yes, My Lord."

"How do you know this?"

"My Lord, I can't explain how I know this. I just know it."

"Am I to understand, you know it because you experienced this knowledge through the intervention of the Holy Ghost?"

"No, My Lord."

"Oh. But you know it."

"Yes, My Lord."

"You went to the Sergeant-at-arms after the announcement made by the Town Crier and claimed you knew this young woman was a witch. You must have based it on something valid or as I have already mentioned maybe it is the Holy Ghost who whispered it in your ear?"

"No, My Lord."

"Good, that's settled then", Now, tell me on what you based the claim you made."

"Well, for one, on all the herbs I saw her picking."

"What kind of herbs?"

"Poisonous herbs, my Lord."

"Did you not claim she was picking Oleander Leaves and Lilies of the Valley?"[32]

"Yes, my Lord."

"And are Oleander leaves and Lilies of the

---

[32] Both Oleander leaves and Lilies of the Valley are poisonous and if eaten can cause irregular heartbeats

Valley poisonous?"

"Yes, My Lord."

"How do you know?"

"Well, My Lord, I have been told."

"By whom?"

"By my wife, My Lord."

"Françoise Mathieu, were you gathering poisonous herbs, the day Gilson saw you. . . . and specifically, were you gathering Oleander leaves and Lilies of the Valley?"

"No, My Lord."

"But you were gathering plants of some sort, am I correct?"

"Yes, My Lord."

"Will you whisper to the Bailiff the names of the plants you were picking? Bailiff, go to the Defendant and do not repeat what she says to you until I ask you to."

"Yes, My Lord." The Bailiff, walks up to Françoise and she whispers something to him. He nods and returns to his place.

# The Drop of the Hammer

"Gilson Froidville, can you describe the plants Françoise Mathieu was picking."

"Easily, My Lord."

"Good. I am listening."

"Well, one had leaves that were dark on the upper side and whitish underneath. It had creamy white flowers and a very strong sweet smell. She was gathering a lot of those."

"Was that the Oleander or the Lilies of the Valley?" asks Roland seriously.

"The Oleander, My Lord."

"What was the other?"

"The Lilies of the Valley. The other one was a pretty plant with white flowers and a very yellow middle, My Lord."

"I see, you seem to have looked at them closely."

At this point, the sound of a woman laughing in the back comes pealing through the Hall. The Bailiff immediately steps forward and bellows in his usual loud voice, "Silence, in the back. Respect the

Court of Justice otherwise you will be put out." The laughter immediately ends.

"Just a minute, Bailiff, ask the woman who was laughing to come forward to the Bar."

The Bailiff who has no idea who the woman is that he has to call, looks a little lost. "But My Lord, I don't know who it is."

"That's easy, Bailiff, just ask for the woman who laughed to come forward."

"Yes, My Lord." Says the Bailiff, then he turns, strikes the floor three times with his staff and bellows, "The woman who laughed is requested at the bar."

A woman of about thirty comes out of the group at the back of the Hall, glances at the Bailiff insolently and mumbles to him as she passes by "Can't even laugh anymore."

She walks up to the Bar and arms akimbo looks at the High Magistrate of Liège.

"What is your name?"

"Bella Beaulieu."

"And what do you do?"

"I serve, clean and do other things at Storheau's Tavern when it is very busy and also when it is not so busy."

The Bailiff intervenes before Roland de Bolland can continue. "Call the High Magistrate of Liège 'My Lord' when you address him."

Bela rolls her eyes at the Bailiff, turns to Roland de Bolland, winks at him and says "Sorry, My Lord. Please forgive me."

"I see. May I ask you why you laughed?" Asks Roland smiling.

"Well . . . . er, My Lord, the man doesn't know anything about plants and he is testifying against that young woman over there. And because of that they want to sentence her to be garrotted and burned." Bella stops talking and bites her lower lip. "Am I going to get into trouble because I laughed, My Lord?"

"No, Bella, you are not going to get into trouble because you laughed. However, I think maybe if I knew why, it might help the case."

"Oh! Well, My Lord, I laughed because that idiot, you know the last witness there," she says pointing at Gilson Froidville, "he can't tell the difference between Oleander, Lilies of the Valley, Mead Wort, and Chamomile." Bella turns towards Froidville and sticks her tongue out at him.

Roland unsuccessfully tries to suppress a smile. "Go on."

"He described Mead wort and Chamomile. And the idiot thinks he described Oleander and Lilies of the Valley," and then looking at the Bailiff she adds "My Lord. And. . . . and. . . . and. . . . ."

"Go on," says Roland softly.

"Well, you see. . . . er . . . . sorry. . . . My Lord. I'm just a serving girl in a tavern. And maybe I shouldn't be saying this, but I don't see anything wrong with this young woman. This is not the way I see it."

"How do you see it, Bella?"

"My Lord, as I said, I am just a serving girl in a tavern. I do what serving girls in a tavern do." At this several of the men standing in the back of the Hall start laughing and a couple let out loud wolf whistles.

The Bailiff begins to strike the floor with his staff, bellowing, "Order in the court! Order in the court!"

Bella doesn't move but she looks down at the floor.

"Bella?" says the High Magistrate of Liège softly.

Bella looks up with tears in her yes. "I'm sorry, My Lord. This is not my place. May I go back?"

"On the contrary, Bella. I think you are exactly where you should be. The court would like to hear what you have to say."

"My Lord, I don't know this young woman and I don't even know how to sign my name. I may just be a tavern serving girl, but I do know one thing, My Lord. All I heard, was jealousy and meanness. I don't know if there are witches or not. I never met one. But you don't sentence someone to be executed simply out of jealousy and meanness."

"Thank you, Bella. You may go back. Bailiff can you tell us what Françoise Mathieu told you?"

"Yes, My Lord, she said Mead Wort and Chamomile"

The court room is silent for what seems a long time.

Finally, Roland de Bolland, the High Magistrate of Liège, stands up. "We could bring in more witnesses to show that Françoise Mathieu, the widow of Henry Hurlet de Creppe is innocent of the crime of witchcraft. However, I don't see any reason for calling them, as there are no longer any witnesses against her. As far as I am concerned, Françoise Mathieu is a free woman. There are no valid complaints left against her and the Court of Spa should reverse the original sentence of execution." He then turns towards the Magistrate of Spa, who is still looking down at the table. "Does the Magistrate of the Court of Justice of Spa agree?"

Cedric Boniver looks up, nods and in a low voice, says "I agree. There is no case. Françoise

## The Drop of the Hammer

Mathieu is a free woman."

And pandemonium breaks out!

## CHAPTER 44
## 18ᵗʰ September 1600
## Two days after the retrial

Pierre Colson, the Town Crier is standing in front of the Perron. As usual, he is glaring at the people to make them be quiet.

On a normal day, Colson has to quieten them down because they are busy gossiping about all kinds of things which the Town Crier feels are of no importance. Today is different. They are talking about what he is going to announce: the sentencing or rather the reversal of the Order of Execution for Françoise Mathieu, the widow of Henry Hurlet de Creppe.

All kinds of rumors are flying about and no one

knows exactly what is happening. Most of the people of Spa know her or have heard of her. The majority of those who are today congratulating each other that justice has done a good job are the same ones who had originally clamored for her execution.

The Bobelins are only concerned because. . . . well, frankly, when you come to Spa for the waters there is not much going on other than the water. This story will give them something interesting to talk about over supper tonight and when they return to their normal life in Liège, Brussels or anywhere else they come from.

Pierre Colson clears his voice, and then bellows "Hear ye! Hear ye! The Governor of Franchimont, the High Court of Justice in Liège and the High Court of Justice in Spa, have unanimously agreed to reverse the sentencing of Françoise Mathieu, the widow of Henry Hurlet de Creppe due to new evidence which has been examined.

Let it be known that Françoise Mathieu is now a free woman………!"

## Chapter 45
## 5th June 1601
## Liège

## The Palace of the Prince-Bishops

Roland de Bolland's footsteps echo in the halls of the Palace of the Prince-Bishops. He reaches the heavy wooden door leading out to the second inner courtyard and brusquely pushes it open. [33]

---

[33] The Prince Bishops' Palace (also referred to as the Episcopal Palace) where Roland de Bolland has his office still exists today. It is a magnificent building reconstructed by Erard de la Marck after the fire of 1505. It took years to rebuild. The courtyard and peristyle were finished by 1525, the main façade in 1734 and finally the West wing in 1849. At the time of our story, it was the residence and power center of the Prince Bishops. Today it houses the provincial

# The Drop of the Hammer

On the opposite side of the courtyard is a young page of about fourteen trying to juggle pebbles . . . . unsuccessful, but trying hard. His attention is so fixed on what he is doing that he neither hears the door opening nor hears the High Magistrate walking towards him.

When Roland sees what the boy is doing, a wave of uncontrollable irritation washes over him. His cold steel blue eyes narrow. "There you are Thibault! What do you think you are doing, young man? You are here to work, not to play," barks the High Magistrate of Liège. "Drop those pebbles instantly."

Thibault doesn't have to be told twice. He drops the pebbles and, staring at the ground, turns towards de Bolland towering above him.

As usual, he is speechless before the big man. Roland de Bolland is big in size, but also in importance. He can't remember a single day when the

---

government on the one side and the Court of Justice on the other.

magistrate has not seemed ready to fly into an uncontrollable rage over. . . . over. . . . well, over nothing at all. Nothing he does is ever good. It's always the same thing.

"What were you doing?"

The young boy bites his lower lip and then mumbles "juggling pebbles."

"Speak up," yells Roland, "and stop mumbling."

"Juggling pebbles, My Lord," he answers still keeping his eyes down.

"I see. And is there something interesting on the ground? Huh? If there is, tell me!"

The page shakes his head, no.

"Well, then look at me in the eyes when I talk to you," says Roland, his voice loud and harsh.

Thibault quickly looks up and when his eyes meet Roland's, he starts trembling.

Roland feels a new wave of irritation wash over him. "Pick up the files that are on the table near my office door and take them to be archived. And then get out of my sight. When you are done, wait for me in the hall outside my office and don't come near me until I call you."

The Page's eyes widen, and without a word runs off to do what the Magistrate has told him to do.

As soon as the boy is out of sight, shame and embarrassment overwhelm Roland. The boy hasn't done anything wrong, and he tries hard. He used to do the same thing when he was his age. Thibault doesn't deserve this treatment.

It is with intense heaviness and sadness that the High Magistrate of Liège returns to his office. The interior is cold, but he is sweating. As the man slowly climbs the stairs, he stops short. Was that a movement over there to the right coming towards the staircase? No. There is no one. He could have sworn that a young woman with soft brown eyes was walking towards him, her hands stretched out to caress his face.

Roland's heart starts beating rapidly. Françoise! Beads of cold sweat tickle down his face.

Françoise!

He quickly runs the last few steps hoping against hope that maybe he was right after all. Françoise!

He reaches the top step. Françoise!

There to the right where he was sure he had seen her. . . . is a statue. The statue of justice. He walks by it every day.

Roland sits down on the long wooden bench along the opposite wall and covers his face with his hands. He slowly breathes in and out to calm himself. The wild, irregular beat of his heart is gradually getting back to normal. What is left is pure despair.

He gets up and sluggishly walks down the corridor and back to his office. Once in, he removes his doublet, throws it onto a chair, and walks to the window. The warm sun pours into the office through the little panes creating a pattern on the parquet. The office is stifling and oppressive. He opens the window and a soft breeze brings in the sweet smell of linden calming his troubled mind.

# The Drop of the Hammer

After a while, he decides to go back to his desk. Roland picks up a document, tries to read it, but he is unable to concentrate. "What's the use?" he mumbles as he drops it to the floor.

He can't work. He can't think. He can't do anything, and this has been going on for months.

His lips are dry and his throat is parched. He gets up, walks to the small inlaid table below the Gobelin wall tapestry. Roland puts out his hand to pick up the carafe full of wine. Undecided, he pulls his hand back. Then deciding that he wants the wine after all, he fills the glass to the brim and takes it back to his desk where he drinks it down in one gulp. The big man leans back in his armchair and closes his eyes.

Eight months! Eight months have gone by since the reversal of the execution order. Eight long months. Not one day has he been free of this restlessness that fills his soul. Every little thing irritates him. He can't even have a normal conversation with his colleague without being irritated, and turning the conversation into an argument. He doesn't even want to begin to think what he puts Thibaut through every day.

He constantly thinks about the Hurlet trial during the day and his nights are one long nightmare full of executions and torture. Last night was the worst. He woke up screaming Françoise's name. Three times he fell asleep and three times he woke up in a cold sweat. Finally, he had willed himself to stay awake. . . .not daring to fall back into a nightmare again.

It's not reasonable and he knows it. The problem is that he can't help himself.

Françoise lives in his mind and in his heart. He sees her everywhere.

Françoise smiling and he wants to kiss her.

Françoise crying and he wants to press her to his heart.

Françoise defiant and he wants to cheer her on.

For the first time in his career, he is unable to let go of a trial. Usually, within two hours of the termination he is able to mentally file it and forget it.

# The Drop of the Hammer

This time it is different.

Today, like every single day since the end of the trial, Françoise materializes in front of him.

His thinking is interrupted by a timid knock at the door. He picks up a parchment making believe he is reading it.

"Yes, Thibault come in," he barks out. "I thought I had told you not to disturb me. You'll have to learn to follow orders in the future! Come in! I hope you have taken the files down to Archives. There are some more on the chair near the door. Take them down to the Archives, too. Don't lose any of them. They're ready. Take them!"

The door opens. Roland can hear the page entering softly and silently.

Without even looking up at Thibault, Roland gets up and walks to the window. He realizes that the page is just standing there. "Thibault, take the files down, now!"

"It's not Thibault," answers a soft voice. "It's me. It's Françoise.

## CHAPTER 46
## 5th June 1601
## Françoise

The sound of Françoise's voice jolts him straight and paralyzes him. It can't be. It's his imagination playing up again. He desperately wants to turn around, and at the same time he doesn't want to end the moment. Roland is certain it is his mind playing tricks on him, but, if he could retain this particular moment for the rest of his life, how wonderful it would feel.

"It's me, Françoise," repeats the soft voice he has been yearning to hear for so many months.

He needs to know, if it is his mind playing tricks on him or if she is really there, standing behind him.

Roland brusquely turns around and as he does so, he overturned the small table on which the carafe and the glasses rest. They slide onto the floor with a crash, breaking into an uncountable number of pieces. He tries to catch the carafe, but only manages to cut the palm of his hand on the broken glass.

Françoise is standing there a few feet into the room, a little hesitant, but nevertheless determined to stay.

Roland stares at her. He registers every movement, article, expression and color. Her white cap has little blue flowers embroidered on the rim. The same little flowers adorned the ribbon tied under her chin. The blue of her partlet and gown complement each other. Francoise is the most beautiful woman in the world. Please don't let this be a dream, the big man prays.

Speechless he looks at Françoise standing near the door. He wants to say something. He knows he should say something and he wants to say something.

Roland opens his mouth but no sound comes out.

He neither trusts his eyes nor his mind. Has Françoise really come to his office? Has he lost his mind?

Roland stands there, breathless, unable to move Again, he prays silently, "Please God, please. Let me hear her voice again. Let it really be Françoise and not a trick of my mind."

"I had to come", says Françoise. Her eyes do not leave his for a second. "I could no longer stay away." Françoise looks up at him.

The sound of Françoise's voice frees Roland. He moves from the window and slowly crosses the room. Francoise lifts her face up to his.

Roland raises his hand and caresses her cheek. "You should not be here, Françoise," he says.

"I had to. I cannot stand it any longer. You are my first thought, when I wake in the morning, and my last as I lay down to sleep. A hundred times a day your face. . . . "

He raises his finger to her lips. "I know. I

know. A hundred times a day your face appears to me and I hear your voice calling me. I know."

"You too?"

Roland nods. "How did you get here Françoise?"

"I came with the Misson brothers. They brought some goods to sell at the market. I have to meet them at the close of the market. They said they would wait for me in front of the Cathedral.

Françoise's eyes fall upon Roland's hand. "You are hurt! You're bleeding. Let me take care of that." She walks to the center of the office with a determined air. Arms akimbo, Françoise turns on her heels as she inspects the room.

When she sees the little pewter bowl and pitcher in a corner, she gives out a little cry and looks towards Roland triumphantly.

"Go sit at your desk. I'll soon take care of your hand. Move the documents you prepared for Thibault so I can put the bowl there."

Roland does as he is told. He picks up the

documents from the desk and drops them on the floor. He leans back in his chair and watches Françoise as she busies herself with the bowl, the water and the small towel. It feels good to be in her care.

A smile tugs at the corner of his mouth. He tries to hide it, but instead his face breaks into a wide grin.

Françoise looks up at him with that questioning look she sometimes has. "Why are you grinning like that? Did I say something funny?" she asks.

Roland shakes his head. "No, nothing funny at all. I simply remember another day, another cut, another hand needing care."

Françoise looks up at him and nods. "Yes, I too remember it well." She smiles at him. Then looking around the office, "Hmm, are you going to tell me you have no geniever for me to clean the cut?".

He looks towards the cabinet behind his desk and points with his chin.

# The Drop of the Hammer

The young woman follows his gaze. She walks to the cabinet, opens the door. A jug of geniever stands alone on a bottom shelf. She looks towards Roland and back at the bottle. As she stoops down to get it, she says, "I like it when you do that."

"Do what, Françoise? You like it when I let you tend my cuts", he asks jokingly. "When I look at you?" "When I want you," he adds mentally.

"I like it when you look at me like that", she says softly.

"How do I look at you?" Roland asks.

She stands up and walks to the desk. Françoise sets the jug on the desk and gently raises her hand up to Roland's face. "I like it when you lift an eyebrow and give me that questioning look."

A feeling of total contentment overwhelms the big man. His hand goes up to hers. Without taking his eyes away from her face, he slowly brings her hand to his lips and kisses it. Her brown eyes lock into his and she smiles.

A knock at the door interrupts them.

## CHAPTER 47
## 5th June 1601
## Françoise and Roland

A young, timid voice says, "Sir, it's Thibault. You said you had other documents that need to be taken to the archives, but you never called me. I waited in the hall just like you told me."

Roland does not take his eyes off Françoise's face as he answers the young page. "That's alright, Thibault. They aren't ready yet. I'll have them ready for you tomorrow. I have work to do. Can you see that I am not disturbed?"

"Yes, sir", answers the young man clearly surprised in the High Magistrate's change of tone.

"Er. . . . Sir?"

"Yes, Thibault. What do you want?"

"If you don't need me, may I go to the kitchens?"

Roland laughs as he answers. "Whatever you want."

Françoise smiles as she bents over his hand. She cleans the cut first with clear water and then, holding his hand over the bowl, she pours some geniever over the cut.

Roland looks up at Françoise's white linen cap which he was certain she has embroidered herself. His mouth goes dry. He imagines himself removing it and letting her long hair fall onto her shoulders. He wants so much to feel the softness of her hair as he slips his fingers through it.

"There", she says as she straightens up. "It should be alright. It's not as deep as it looks. Does it hurt?" she asks.

Roland shakes his head.

The young woman picks up the bowl and starts

moving away. Roland grabs her hand and stops her.

Roland, I need to put all this away," she says, using his first name as if she had always used it. She points at the jug, bowl, and towel.

He takes them out of her hands and sets them on the floor. "It can wait." He gets up from his armchair and gently draws her closer.

He raises his hands up to her cap and slowly tugs on the ribbons. He feels a shudder run through the young woman, but she does not pull back. The cap comes off and falls to the floor. Gently, as if he were tending a young, wounded animal, his hands seek the two combs holding her bun together. He takes them out slowly and her tresses fall heavily onto her shoulders. He gasps.

Suddenly he sees a scared look cross her face and he abruptly steps back, his palms out and his two arms up in the air.

"It's alright, Françoise, it's alright. I don't want to scare you."

Françoise bites her lower lip and turns her back

to him. She keeps her face down and he can see her entire body trembling.

"I promise, I won't touch you if you don't want me to. Please don't be afraid of me," he pleads. "I couldn't bear it." As he says these last words he moves to stand before her.

"Look at me, Françoise. I'm not going to touch you. Just look at me. I won't hurt you. I promise." He stoops down to cox her into looking at him.

Françoise looks up into his face. She smiles sadly at him and some color comes back into her cheeks. "There you did it again. That funny smile."

Serious again she sighs. "Roland, please don't think. . . . I don't want you to think that I. . . . Roland, I'm not scared of you. I could never be scared of you. I want to hold you in my arms. I. . . . I. . . . .I want to feel your hands on me but. . . . " She breaks off her sentence.

"But what?" he asks urging her to continue.

Roland sees the sadness in her eyes and thinks he has never seen such beautiful eyes.

"Roland, I am just a peasant girl from Creppe. I know how to sign my name but otherwise I can't read or write. My hands are rough from the chores I do. These clothes I wear are my very best, but. . . . they look like rags next to those worn by the ladies you are used to. I spent weeks doing this embroidery just for you," she says pointing at her bonnet. "I don't know what to do. We have no future together but I need you as I have never needed anything or anyone before." Françoise stops speaking and seeks out his eyes.

Roland feels his heart break as he listens to her. He walks back to his armchair and sits down.

"Is that what is bothering you? You think I am comparing you to, what you like to call, the women I am used to?"

Françoise nods and looks down.

"Françoise, I cannot compare you to anyone I have ever known because no other person has ever taken up the room you take in my mind or in my heart. I can't even sleep or work properly any more. Your face appears before me a hundred times a day and if I hear someone speaking at a distance, I think it is you. And do you think I care about the roughness of your hands or the fact your cap is made of linen instead of silk? Is that it? Yes, I know we have no future together. However, I believe, no, I know, we are no longer the same since we entered each other's lives. And you, Françoise Mathieu of Creppe will always be part of me until I die."

Francoise doesn't move a muscle, but tears begin to roll down her cheeks.

Roland gets up and walks up to her. He puts his hands on her shoulders and then brings them up to either side of her face. He gently tilts her face up to his. He slips his fingers through her long hair and he hears her breathing quicken.

The big man lowers his lips to hers and kisses her lightly. Then he kisses her again, this time letting all his penned-up passion pour out. Françoise clutches at his shirt as she returns his kiss. He can feel her passion matching his as she puts her arms around his neck and freely returns his passionate caresses

His hands come down to her breasts and he delights in the feel of them as they push against him. He kisses her lightly on the forehead and then pushes her slightly away. Françoise looks up into his face. He sees surprise, but also passion and love in hers. Not leaving her eyes for a second, he brings his hands down to the front of her platelet and undoes the eyelets.

Françoise raises her hands to help him and he says "No. I know how to do this. Let me. Please." Françoise smiles and lets her arms drop along her body.

Roland caresses her cheek with his own and says in his raspy voice, "I don't want you to undress for me. I will undress you."

Françoise looks down at his strong hands as he deals with the eyelets. She thinks how these beautiful hands handle parchment all day long, but can also wield a sword with force.

Roland undresses her slowly. Each eyelet

seemed to take an eternity. The slower he goes the more she feels her body tremble and the more she desires him.

Suddenly everything around her turns gray as she becomes dizzy and her knees buckle.

Roland's strong hands slide to her sides and help her stay on her feet. "Steady, girl, steady", he whispers to her in his raspy voice. "Take a deep breath. Another one." When she seems steady on her feet, he asks "Are you alright, now?"

Françoise nods, too choked up to say anything.

He removes the platelet and drops it onto the armchair. He starts unlacing the open-fronted gown she is wearing beneath it. Slowly he pulls it over her head.

Françoise now stands before him in her loose kirtle. Roland chuckles, "Why do women wear so many layers?"

Françoise opens her mouth to answer, but he silences her with a finger against her lips. Smiling he bents down to her ear and whispers, "I'm not complaining, you know. I love it."

Françoise smiles back at him.

He brushes his lips against hers and whispers, "Françoise Mathieu of Creppe. Thank you for coming into my life."

## CHAPTER 48
## 5 June 1601

Hours later, curled up in Roland's arms and wrapped in his cloak, she is sleeping peacefully. He looks at her face and knows she will soon walk out of his life. But he loves her like he has never loved anyone else.

"Françoise" He calls softly. It's time for you to get up or the Misson brothers will return to Creppe without you.

Françoise's eyes flutter open and she smiles. She puts out her hand to caress his cheek and gets up.

Roland goes back to his armchair and watches

her as she gets dressed.

"Françoise, I can't let you out of my life. Not now. Not ever."

She comes over to him where he is sitting, and as he had once done before when she was a prisoner and he the High Magistrate, she leans over him, her two arms leaning on either side of him. "Roland, we need to be happy with what we have. The High Magistrate of Liège cannot have in his life an illiterate peasant girl from Creppe . . . . especially one who was once accused of being a witch."

"Françoise, the sentence was overturned. You are a free woman."

She smiles and tenderly kisses him. "That does not count in the life of a High Magistrate nor in the world you live in."

# The Drop of the Hammer

Françoise slowly goes back to getting dressed and soon she is ready to leave.

Roland comes up to her and they hug tightly.

Françoise smiles at him and without a word she leaves his office. Her steps echo as she goes down the stairs. He hears the big wooden door creak open and then slamming closed.

The High Magistrate of the Court of Justice of Liège walks to the open window. The sweet smell of the Linden trees outside comes in with the breeze.

He looks down and there she is. Françoise walks a short distance then stops. She looks up to his window and stands there motionless.

She smiles.

He smiles back.

Then Françoise turns towards the Cathedral.

# ANNEX

# ANNEX

## I.

### Jehenne, daughter of Henry Jehan Anseau

of Spa

English translation :

*Creppe Sur La Voie du Temps Passé*

P. Gendarme and J.Lohest

Page 139

Based on Albin Body's *Spa, Histoire et Biblographie*

## II.

### The real Le Rosy vs. the real Françoise

English translation :

Pierre DEN DOOVEN

*Sorcellerie Dans Le Ban De Spa*

Source:

*Creppe Sur La Voie du Temps Passé*

Pages 139 – 141

And

http://users.skynet.be/maevrard/sorcelleriespa.html

Note that the inquest deals with both Françoise, the widow of Henry Hurlet of Creppe and Catherine, the wife of Antoine le Parmentier

### III.

**What are the "fees, costs, expenses and damages" referred to in the trials.**

Source: Walthère JAMAR,

*Chevron dans le passe*

http://users.skynet.be/maevrard/sorcelleriespa.html

Act recorded in Chevron, on 23rd April 1605.

### IV

**The Mob**

English translation of:

Pierre DEN DOOVEN

*La Chapel du Chevalier Maudit*

(The Chapel of the Cursed Horseman)

pp.88-89

# I

# Jehenne, daughter of Henry Jehan Anseau of Spa

On the 3rd February 1582, Jehenne, the daughter of Henry Jehan Anseau of Spa was denounced. The first to come forward as a witness against her was Abbot Leonard. According to his deposition, Jehenne was a known witch, and pregnant women were afraid of her. He also claimed that she could transform herself into a "neur tchè" ( a black cat), did not go to church and, more importantly, several members of her family had already been burned at the stake as witches.

The second witness was Mathieu, the son of Mathi from Creppe. He declared that she had sat at a table with a child and that later on the child had died. In addition, he confirmed that Jehenne's grandmother, father, an uncle and two other relatives had already been burned as witches.

More witnesses stepped forward, each one

confirming her guilt and especially her family. The unfortunate woman was garroted before having her body delivered to the flames.

## II.
## The real Le Rosy vs. the real Françoise

Following an inquest ordered by the Chatelain of Franchimont at the beginning of 1610[34], two women were accused of being witches on the 3rd March of the same year at the request of Henry Maljean, representing the Chatelain of Franchimont.

The first was Catherine, the wife of Antoine le Parmentier and the second was Françoise, the widow of Grand Henry. Both women were from Creppe. As usual, an appeal was made for witnesses and the first one to give evidence was Remacle le Rosy of Creppe.

This man declared that Catherine, was a Vaudoise[35] and had been one for several years. He

---

[34] A.E.L. Justice de Spa n° 203.
[35] The word Vaudoise used here as a synonym for 'witch', goes back to the 12th century: Pierre Valdo founded a group in the region of

# The Drop of the Hammer

also added that he believed she had killed his first wife. In addition to this, she had also caused the death of livestock. As for Françoise, the widow of Grand Henry, he claimed she poisoned her husband and even worse than this she caused the death of a child in her daughter-in-law's womb.

He was followed on the 4th March by other witnesses.

Gilson Froidvlle, of Spa, declared that the two accused women, have been witches for the last six years and are still witches. The previous summer, he had gone to Desnié with his dogs. They ran off the path and started barking. Gilson immediately went to see what was happening and he saw Grand Henry's widow. He asked her if she had come to gather firewood and she answered him rudely. Maybe she was gathering poisonous plants.

Even worse than this, in the village of Creppe[36], a certain individual, Antoine le Parmentier .

---

Lyon. They were condemned as heretics by the Church
[36] A village near Spa.

. . . it is not stated whether he is the husband of Catherine or not, but there are strong presumptions that he might be . . . . has a certain reputation.

The witness described him as follows: "He is short and has a black beard with some white parts, who walks with his head down looking at the ground. It was said several times that he is a witch." Nonetheless, the Antoine le Parmentier in question was not inconvenienced over this.

The next witness, focused on the women. Her name is Catherine, the wife of Ogier Nicolet of Creppe and is around 40 years old. However, her statements were said with hesitation.

She had heard that the daughter-in-law of Grand Henri's wife, had had a still born child and that it was her mother-in-law's fault. In addition, the latter had given an apple to the daughter of the late Henry Badrulle of Spa. She ate it and soon after she died.

Etienne Quelin of Spa, went into the forest with his wagon full of wood and, unfortunately, he met Catherine le Parmentier. The horse suddenly

# The Drop of the Hammer

became ill and had a hard time getting back to Spa.

The next witness, Jehenne, wife of Jehan Gillet Toussain confirms the story about the apple and states that the daughter of the late Henry Baddrulle was older than thirteen when she fell ill. The girl died soon afterwards.

Maroie, the wife of Jehan Andrien of Spa, also stepped up as a witness.

The inquest continued until the 5th of March, but it doesn't give us any information other than what we have already summerized above. It is a fact, however, that all these stories were rather trivial[37].

On the same day, that is to say on the 5th of March 1610, Henry Maljean declared, in the name of the Chatelain of Franchimont, that he had no other witnesses to call except perhaps one or two if necessary.

The Court of Justice of Spa, announced that since this was a criminal matter, the Aldermen of

---

[37] All these witnesses were from Creppe. It seems that the greater part of Creppe joined force against these two unfortunate women.

Liège would be contacted for their advice and counter-signature.

For some reason, it was only on the 24th of July of the same year, that the Alderman [of Spa], Toussaint le Cerf, was sent with the inquest, depositions and evidence.

The Aldermen of Liège quickly reacted:

"To the Court of Justice of Spa,

"On this day, the 29th of July one thousand six hundred and ten having gone over the inquests brought to us by your messenger concerning the crime of witchcraft and others, by those mentioned, having seen the evidence presented in the inquests in question on Catherine, wife of Antoine le Parmentier and Françoise, widow of Grand Henry, we charge that they be cleared of the reputation of being witches ... By the ordnance of the High Justice of Liège."

And so, the Aldermen of Liège judged that the charges made against these two unfortunate persons were not serious enough to have them burned at the stake. As the reader can easily see, it was all a lot of baseless gossip which is "the daily bread in our villages."

On the 7th August, the Justice of Spa informed the two accused women of the decision. Both worked at eliminating the testimonies that had been made against them.

Françoise, the wife of Grand Henry of Creppe, moved heaven and earth, and by the end of August 1610, she presented her defense at the Court of Justice of Spa.

In the archives this file is entitled 'Purgation [clearing] of the charges made by Françoise the widow of Grand Henry of Creppe against the Officer of Franchimont and all alleged interested persons.'

First of all, she objected to the alleged inquest and proposed to prove her good reputation. She married Grand Henry and from this marriage several children were born who 'have a good name, reputation and conversation, although they are laborers and earn their living by the sweat of their brows.'

She also stated that the inquest put forth by Henry Majean was not due to any zeal for justice, but rather for specific reasons and even carried out without the knowledge of the Chatelain.

That the author or rather the instigator of the inquest in question, Remacle le Rosier, deeply hated her and her family. She also added a very serious accusation, saying that the son of Remacle had given a cow to Henry Maljean. What was the intention behind this?

We can easily guess.

She then mentioned the following fact: on Palm Monday in Spa, while in the house of Godfrin Xhrouet, Remacle le Rosier had scandalously insulted her and her son, declaring also that he intended to see three women from Creppe, accused of witchcraft and burned.

In order to carry out his project, he contacted Bertholet so that the latter would 'cover him in writing' [a written alibi]. Françoise was in possession of this element and it was presented to the Court of

Justice of Spa

Therefore, his deposition, as well as those of his wife and son, had to be, beyond all doubt, rejected as well as all the other testimonies. They were based only on 'hearsay without even mentioning their origin' concerning her so-called reputation founded on careless talk attributed to her daughter-in-law. In fact, all that was needed was to have her appear before the court and it would immediately become clear that the real instigator was Remacle Rosier.

In conclusion, she demanded to have him appear before the Court of Justice of Spa, so as to be sentenced to 'pay all fees, expenses, and damages.'

On the 4th of October of the same year, she addressed the Court of Justice of Spa, through Bertrand Thonon, a lawsuit against Remacle Henry Henrar, called le Rosier of Creppe in order to prove that he was a cruel enemy---'even criminal'-of the plaintiff and her son.

After reminding the court of the comments made by the latter in the house of Godfrin Xhrouet around the beginning of Lent, already mentioned above, she said that the son of Remacle Storheau could be interrogated concerning what was said by Remacle le Rosier in a public tavern run by a certain Gilson Froidville. This confirmed the first case. As for the rest, she was willing to leave it up to the discretion of the judge[38].

The case dragged on and on to the 23rd of February 1612, when the Aldermen of Liège sent the following judgement:

"Having seen the documents brought to us by your messenger concerning the acquittal, between, on the one hand, the Officer of Franchimont and, on the other, Françoise, the widow of Grand Henry of Creppe. She is acquitted but will nevertheless be condemned to pay all expenses.[39] By ordinance of the High Justice of Liege

Catherine, the wife of Antoine le Parmentier,

---

[38] A.E.L. Justice de Spa N° 203, passim. Concerning the Henrards of Spa.
[39] Idem

followed the same procedures. By a decree dated 23rd February 1615, she was acquitted by the Aldermen of Liège of all charges of witchcraft. She was, however, ordered to pay all the expenses.

## III.

### What are the "fees, costs, expenses and damage" referred to in the trials.

During the Burning Times, as it is still the case today, trials cost money. The tiniest and sometimes most insignificant things done, said, sent, carried, fed etc. had to be paid . . . . and they added up! The following, will give you a good idea of the fees involved. From an Act recorded in Chevron, on 23$^{rd}$ April 1605.

To Lymael : 35 florins, 2 patars brabant.

The guards: 24 patars.

Feeding costs and candles: 5 patars.

Feeding costs of the executed prisoner during

her stay in prison: 6 patars.

Night guards: 2 rixdallers.

Expenses relative to Seigneur Potestat's horse during the trial period: 1 florin brabant.

Wood and fagots: 15 patars.

Court fees: 17 florins brabant.

Executioner's fees: 14 florins

Sergeant's fees: 1 florin brabant.

Clerk's fees: 1 florin brabant.

Messenger who had to go get the Executioner in Raier: 3 patars Brabant. The executioner was busy doing another execution in Saint-Nicolas-le-Liège

## IV. The Mob

### La Chapelle du Chevalier Maudit    pp. 88-89

The old woman, bent under the weight of a bundle of dead wood, was arrested by two men-at-arms as she was leaving the Staneux woods and brought to the Chateau. She was locked up in a filthy

## The Drop of the Hammer

cell, while upstairs in the great hall, the Chatelain, Henri de Gronsveld dressed in his purple knee breeches and doublet is entertaining his guests.

Three days go by during which the villagers become more and more excited Every evening the mob gathers at the foot of the ramparts clamoring for the old witch's body.

The Court of Justice met on the 5th day and before the unconscious old woman, the Lieutenant governor who is replacing the bedridden Chatelain violently demands the death penalty.

It was accorded.

Outside, the mob welcomed the news with joy and a sigh of relief.

It was on the day of St. Michael, the 9th day of May that an armed cohort, pikes on their shoulders and dressed in the green and gold doublet of his Most Serene Highness, exited the main door of the Chateau of Franchimont.

In their midst, walked painfully the old woman. All you could see was her little bird of prey head that seemed to be carried along by the pikes.

Behind them, a chubby faced priest, routinely reciting the beads of his rosary followed the mob of Bertrands, Bonivers, Grégoires, Jacobs, Henrottes, their wooden shoes noisily striking the gravel.

(.........)

The long procession went down the hill, past the chapel, turned towards the hamlet of Marché followed the winding Hoegne Valley to Theux.

Once there the mob spread out slowly, sweaty, breathless under the scorching sun.

The villagers were leaning out of their windows in the hope of catching sight of the victim. And once they did, they poured a barrage of insults on her.

"Old witch."

"Devil's devotee"

"Satan's daughter"

"Foul witch"

They stopped in front of the mayor's house. The armed cohort stepped back, and as the mob laughed and jeered at her, a basket full of muck was

# The Drop of the Hammer

thrown in the old woman's face.

And so, it went on, all the way from the Brouxherie, to the cemetery, to the place called the Ley. It was an endless series of mockery, jokes, songs, and jeering of all sorts. When the church bells sounded three o'clock, the procession----much bigger now that the curious had joined in---- reached the Gibet (gallows) Hill.

Once up the hill, the mob stopped and formed a semi-circle in front of a pole raised in the middle of the level ground, next to a stack of twigs.

The priest went towards the old woman raising his long black crucifix above her as he gave her an absolution. He then held it out to her, but she pushed it away laughing sarcastically.

The mob began to shout and murmur.

The Chatelain's representative gestured impatiently.

The executioner approaches, placed a cord round her neck, and hoisted her up the pole. For a short moment, her long body shook like a rag, stiffened and then slowly stirred under the impulse of a strong westerly wind.

Guillaume Despré insulted her and shook his fist at her.

A few minutes later, the mob, after having made certain she was dead, started to shout with joy.

Two men held up the body as the executioner, astride the pole, untied her.

Then they threw her body onto the pile of fagots as if it were a despicable object and an aide clutching a flaming torch set it afire.

# ABOUT THE AUTHOR

Mary De Gruttola is an American writer and author of *My Darling Ron* and *The Drop of the Hammer*

Although her novels are fiction, they are deeply rooted in true events ------whether they took place in the 1600s in what is now Belgium or in present day Brooklyn

Born in a military family, Mary soon caught the travelling bug which stayed with her long after she no longer had a military dependent ID card. The latest count of different addresses where she lived more than 6 months is 40.

It is from all this travelling that she draws her inspiration.

Mary graduated from Brooklyn College with a BA in teaching (major) and languages (minor), before going on to Boston University Brussels to obtain a Master in International Relations. She speaks five languages

She now lives in Malta whose straight-line distance is 113 miles (182 kms) from Sicily and 223 miles (359 kms) from Africa.